the Wednesday Daughters

Center Point
Large Print

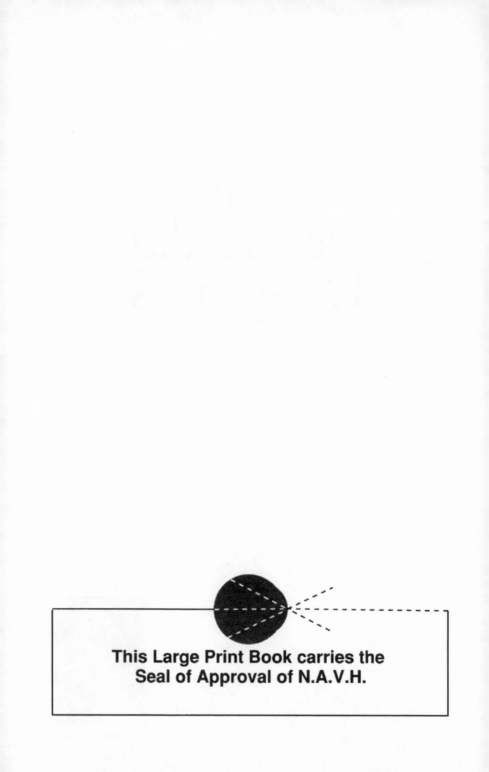

**This Large Print Book carries the
Seal of Approval of N.A.V.H.**

the
Wednesday Daughters

meg waite clayton

CENTER POINT LARGE PRINT
THORNDIKE, MAINE

The Wednesday Daughters is a work of fiction. All incidents and dialogue, and all characters with the exception of some well-known historical and public figures, are products of the author's imagination and are not to be construed as real. Where real-life historical or public figures appear, the situations, incidents, and dialogues concerning those persons are entirely fictional and are not intended to depict actual events or to change the entirely fictional nature of the work. In all other respects, any resemblance to persons living or dead is entirely coincidental.

The text of this Large Print edition is unabridged.
In other aspects, this book may vary
from the original edition.
Printed in the United States of America
on permanent paper.
Set in 16-point Times New Roman type.

ISBN: 978-1-61173-794-3

Library of Congress Cataloging-in-Publication Data

Clayton, Meg Waite.
  The Wednesday daughters / Meg Waite Clayton. — Center Point Large print edition.
    pages ; cm.
  ISBN 978-1-61173-794-3 (library binding : alk. paper)
  1. Family secrets—Fiction. 2. Female friendship—Fiction.
  3. Palo Alto (Calif.)—Fiction. 4. Domestic fiction. 5. Large type books. I. Title.
  PS3603.L45W423 2013b
  813'.6—dc23

                                                    2013016364

For Mac
my Lake District cottage companion

and in memory of
Aunt Margaret and Father Pat

I will share this room with you
And you can have this heart to break.
—*Billy Joel, "And So It Goes"*

the Wednesday Daughters

1

Autumn is far away the best time at the Lakes.
—Beatrix Potter, in a September 1903 letter to her
then publisher and eventual fiancé, Norman Warne

WE WEDNESDAY DAUGHTERS WEREN'T BORN
on Wednesdays, and we aren't blood relations. We
don't gather to write at picnic tables like our
mothers did. We're just daughters of friends
who've called themselves "Wednesday Sisters"
since before I was born, daughters who became
friends ourselves the way girls who grow up
together sometimes do, whether they have much
in common or not. Perhaps that *is* a lot to have in
common, though: a shared childhood, friends
who've known you since before you knew
yourself.

We're all old enough now to understand what
Aunt Kath forever tells us—that life and living
aren't the same—and our moms long ago moved
on (more or less) from mothering us to other
passions: Aunt Linda's cancer-survivor runs,
Mom's infertility support group, the novels
Frankie and Brett still write. But they've brought
us together for holiday dinners and barbecues so
often over the years that at some point we started

gathering ourselves, our childhood bonds deepening despite, say, the dozen years that separate Anna Page and me. It's that combination of our mothers' friendships and our own that sent three of us together to the English Lakes—the fall of 2011, it was—and allowed us to share the comfort we found there in one exquisite wooden puzzle box. We are, in the Wednesday Circle, our mothers' daughters: Kath's Anna Page, Linda's Julie, and me, Ally's Hope. And this is our story, which is, I suppose, a love story. Or two. Or, actually, probably four.

"You'll want to be hearing the quiet of the evening coming up," the boatman suggested as he led us to a rowboat rather than a motorized launch. "Your head's a marly if you'll have an engine spoilin' this." Such funny phrases, I thought as he loaded our suitcases and set off across Lake Windermere. Like so many of the expressions Mom brought home from her stays here: "queue" and "toff" and "fancy," "single-track" instead of "one-lane" to describe the winding roads. But as the daylight softened from blue to salmon to steel with each hushed push of the wood oars, I *could* hear the quiet. Even with the squabble of geese down the shoreline, the occasional gunshot clap of a car passing over a trestle echoing off the hills, I could hear the quiet of our little boat slipping as surely forward as time itself.

12

It was mid-October, the air fresh with the smell of lake water and field grass and forest, the promise of frost. On the hillside we'd left behind, the maze of stone walls dwindled. The black-faced sheep we'd seen out the train window faded to nothing as lights blinked on in the shops trailing down from the station to hug up together at Bowness, the boats in the harbor bare-masted as full sails were exchanged for fireside seats in restaurants and pubs and homes. Ahead, two white swans dug at the lake grasses. The thick woods on the shore beyond them took shape as individual trees. A stone chimney poked above the treetops upslope, collecting more stone around it: other chimneys, a square tower, various slants of roof that were all of a same.

"*That's* your mama's little writing cottage, Hope?" Anna Page asked, fingering her hair, which was wavy-dark and wild in the still of the approaching evening.

The boatman—Robbie, he'd said his name was—glanced over his shoulder, his hands on the rough oars not young, but steady and surprisingly well kempt. "That's the one to gawk at, the big house," he said, his voice Irish rather than English; perhaps that was the hint of not quite belonging I sensed in him. He raised the oars and pointed to the right of a lone wooden pier and a dilapidated boathouse. "There's a cottage there through the scrub, see?"

A glimpse of cornflower blue took shape through the tangle of branches—a door overhung with vines on a cottage I'd seen only in photographs: a simple rectangle of gray stone; low walls around a patio; a last straggle of geraniums in a window box. I trailed a hand over the boat's edge, the echo wake of my fingers folding into that of the drifting boat as I imagined Mom writing at a wrought-iron table on the patio, her feet up on a second chair. When it was colder, she would have moved inside, written at a desk beside a wood fire, or at a table piled with books and papers, pens and paper clips and Post-it notes, empty teacups scattered as if to catch drops from a leaking ceiling in a life that held little rain—except maybe the disapproval of Ama, my dad's mom, who spent a lifetime trying to make a proper Indian wife of her Caucasian daughter-in-law.

"That's the pier Mom uses, then, I guess," I said. "She keeps a bicycle and a small boat here, so she doesn't need a car."

Kept a bicycle. Didn't need. Mom didn't need anything in this world anymore except for me to pack up what was left of her life in England, the way I'd not yet managed to pack up her pajamas and teapots and hairbrushes at home, her puzzle box collection, her manuscript drafts of the children's books she'd spent her life writing but had never seen in print.

"Aunt Ally said there's a ghost who walks those hills?" Anna Page said to Robbie.

Robbie answered softly, " 'That old Crier of Claife on Furness Fell, / as long as ivy evergreens shall twine, / May sally forth at will from his ravine, / And rouse the boatman with his human yell.' "

Julie blinked back the same surprise I felt at the fact of this boatman spouting poetry—a poem he'd have memorized to amuse the folks he took on tours of the lake, but still. "A ghost," she said, and I remembered Aunt Frankie joking about a ghost friend of Mom's who played piano at an old mansion in the park at home. I imagined Mom insisting that the ghost of the grizzled old character who'd ferried her across this English lake could have been enlisted to take us.

Anna Page leaned close to Robbie and whispered in his ear, the sprinkle of grays at her part line a bit tacky—although that was just *me* being tacky; Anna Page had no marriage to end first, and never had. She could have as many doors as she wanted. She could paint them any color she chose. Which she did; even at fifty-one, Anna Page took in men as often as I took in the Sunday paper, and took what she wanted from them, and set them out with the recycling bin, or that was the way it sometimes seemed. Julie could have as many doors or men or anything else as she wanted by then, too, with her divorce from Noah filed. I was the only one of us with a marriage left, or with what passed for one.

"They say he killed someone," Robbie said to Anna Page or to Julie, I wasn't sure which, but it was Anna Page's laughter that warmed the evening in response.

"Lordy, did Ma pay him to say that?" she said to Julie and me. Then she delivered, in a near-perfect mimic of her mother's Southern accent, the Gatsby line our moms all whipped out at the slightest provocation: " 'You look at him sometimes when he thinks nobody's looking at him. I'll bet he killed a man!' "

I heard Mom's voice wrapped around the words, Mom's laughter.

"Not a bloke but a lady," Robbie insisted as he set his weight to the oars again. "His British wife."

"His British wife," Anna Page repeated, charming him with the hint of tease that worked so well with men.

"He had two, didn'e," Robbie said. "One wife in India and a proper British wife as well." He laughed uncomfortably, glancing my way as if his words might offend me when they wouldn't offend Julie or Anna Page. He thought I was Indian. People who aren't Indian always do.

"Two wives," he repeated more gently, staring shoreward with eyes as deep as the lake in a face that had seen as much weather, eyes that just might understand how two loves could be held in a single heart. "Or that's the blather here," he said.

He dipped one oar and raised the other to ease us toward the pier, where he hopped out and secured the boat to a mossy post, the swan pair watching suspiciously from a jetty of flat rocks on the other side of the boathouse, where the original pier must have been. "They say old man Wyndham who killed his British wife is the Crier of Claife, the ghost who calls across to the ferrymen at Nab. The only one who ever went to him, though . . . that poor bloke wouldn't speak of what he'd seen, and still he died the next day."

An awful animal sound broke the silence then: the bay of a wolf or a coyote, perhaps, deep and primitive. It had gotten dark so quickly.

" 'Course, another story has a monk taking a Bible across the lake on Christmas Day," Robbie said, "plying the ghost 'with candle, book, and bell' and confining him to the quarry and woods 'until men should walk dryshod across the lake.' "

"Couldn't just exorcise him altogether, I guess," Anna Page said.

Robbie met her amused gaze and held it. "Ah, but that'd spoil the gallery, wouldn't it? How's a body to boast he's been trailed at dusk by a hooded figure in a wood that can claim no ghost?"

The gentle lap of lake, the *cheep-cheep* and *tit-tit-tit* of evening birds, added to the quiet as I removed the iron key and pushed open Mom's blue cottage door. Inside, it was chilly and dim, the air fusty with the odor of the books in the glass-fronted cabinet left too long unopened, their pages unturned. A deep claw-footed slipper tub sat not in the bathroom but on a rectangle of limestone set into the wide-plank floor between the fireplace and the end of a double bed. How often had I barged in on Mom's bubble baths as a child, the smell of vanilla candles mixing with that of vanilla bubbles as she laid a wet washcloth over her breasts?

Julie put an arm over my shoulders, and Anna Page draped one around my waist from the other side, sandwiching me in their warmth. "Damn, this makes Barton Cottage seem grand," Julie said as they tilted their heads down toward mine: dark, dark, blond.

"Duck, duck, goose," they used to call out when we were younger, although they were too old for the game by the time they played it with me, and they always let me win.

Anna Page supposed it wouldn't take long to clean out the place, while Julie crossed the room and clicked the lamp switch beside the bed, to no effect.

"'It's a sign,'" Anna Page said—one of my mother's favorite expressions delivered in her best imitation of Mom's shy wisp of a voice.

"A sign we should have taken *your* mom up on

that offer of a few nights at her swanky London flat, Ape, rather than having her join us here next week?" Julie said.

"Lord, Ma thinks we're still sixteen and can't survive without a dang chaperone," Anna Page replied, as if her mother were in England solely to vex her, rather than, say, to visit one of her authors who was a favorite for the Pulitzer Prize.

Julie's ring-laden fingers followed the cord to the plug, and a small click sounded as the light popped on, illuminating a pitched ceiling that gave the room the illusion of space. "How funny: there's an on-off switch on the outlet," she said. She squashed a spider with a swift pinch of finger and thumb before I could stop her, before I could begin to say the lines Mom used to quote from *The Tale of Mrs. Tittlemouse* as she corralled spiders and put them out: *Go away, you bold bad spider! Leaving ends of cobwebs all over my nice clean house.* Except she would misquote it, she would say "bad bold spider," and even as a toddler, I would set her straight.

A door in the far corner of the single room opened to a hand sink with no mirror in a bathroom so narrow you had to leave the door open to wash your hands. Another led down a stairway to a small kitchen in which we found Mom's bicycle taking up most of the space. It all seemed so empty: the double bed, the tiny love seat, the slipper tub.

As Anna Page spotted a radiator and went to turn it on, Julie said she imagined there would be small plates of crumbs resting on the pages of open books here, like in Mom's dining room at home.

"And manuscripts covered with red ink," Anna Page said.

"I imagined the tub would be in the bathroom," I said.

Anna Page didn't think the radiator was working, so Julie went to have a look (as if there might be some other way to turn the single knob, and she'd do it better than Anna Page).

Two quick raps on the door startled us, and a man burst in without waiting for an answer, all broad chest and broad jaw and thick silvering hair. He was older than we were but younger than our mothers, with a dark, solid face that might know every Lake District scandal in history but would take them to his grave.

"Allison, you didn't call!" he said. "You'll freeze without—" His dark eyes registered a hint of ire behind silver wire-rims as he muttered something that might have been apology or cuss. He turned the hard black door handle and back-stepped over the threshold, nearly knocking his head against the low doorframe. Behind him, a huge dog—black and white, with a lion head and long hair—sat unmoving on the stone path. "I beg your pardon," he said in that imperious tone older men deliver so well, not begging anything, "but do you belong here?"

Julie eyed the trace of mud his hiking boots left on my mother's cottage floor as she might eye a library patron requesting "the Count of Monte Crisco" or "Tequila Mockingbird," or wanting to do "an interplanetary loan." "I beg *your* pardon," she demanded, "but do *you?*"

"The gate is marked 'private,' " he said. "You're quite off the public bridleway."

Anna Page, with a quick flip of her hair that as much as said he was her type—a bit arrogant and in need of being taken down a peg—said, "Your ma's neighbors sure are friendly here, aren't they, Hope?"

He turned to study me, the imperiousness softening. "You're Allison's daughter? You're Asha?" He stepped forward again, not quite convinced, as, behind him, the dog settled back. "And one of you is—No, neither of you is Santosh, are you? You're Asha's friends, then, here with her on holiday at her mum's cottage?"

On holiday. We didn't deny it. It wasn't entirely untrue. Tucked into Anna Page's bag was a booklet for easy walks in Grasmere and Ambleside and, unbeknownst to Julie, two of Alfred Wainwright's volumes of more ambitious hikes. Julie, who isn't much for bugs or dirt, had brought a collection of Wordsworth poems for this land of Dove Cottage and "a host, of golden daffodils,"

21

and she'd arranged "cookery lessons" at a place called Lucy's that offered "Proper Puds and Sweet Solutions," "Afternoon Tea and Temptations," and "Cakes Fit for a Queen."

"I meant to see if your mum wouldn't have a bit of help setting a fire in the grate, and perhaps a tipple after her journey," he said with a quick flash of teeth not battered into picket-fence submission, an expression I supposed could pass for a smile. He glanced around the cottage, doing the arithmetic on bodies and beds. "But I don't suppose she'll be joining you, then, will she?"

Anna Page slipped her clean, careful fingers—surgeon's fingers—through mine. "Mrs. Tantry died a few weeks ago," she said.

He wrapped a hand around the edge of the still-open door as Anna Page's fingers tightened on mine. Anna Page loved my mom as much as I did, and she loved her better.

"Allison?" the man said. "But Allison isn't—"

"Are you okay?" Anna Page asked, letting go of my hand and moving toward him. "Do you need help?"

The dog seemed to surge forward without coming any closer, his tail lowered and still.

"I . . . Forgive me, I . . ." He turned abruptly to leave, then turned back to me, blinking as if I were just coming into focus. "You'll have the desk, of course, Asha. And the pictures. Yes, you must have the pictures," he said, and he stepped out the door, latching it behind him, leaving us alone again in the glow of the single bulb.

Aunt Ally had a lover, too? Anna Page almost blurted the words out as the blue door closed, or that's the way she tells it now, anyway. As with much of this story, what I know of the rest of that evening—what happened after I was asleep, for example—I know from the rehashing afterward. We Wednesday Daughters, like our mothers, love to tell stories on ourselves. Aunt Kath tells her own version of that evening, by the way, in which we arrive at the cottage "looking like something the pooch found under the porch"—never mind that she didn't join us until six days later and has no idea what she's talking about. She doesn't know Julie's part of this story, for example; we've never told Julie's part of this story to any of the Wednesday Sisters, and I'm sure we never will.

Anna Page opened a gray-blue metal chest beside the fireplace: newspapers, an ash brush, a scoop of some sort, a box of Cook's matches. I examined a photo of the grandparents I'd never met, and another of Sammy and me the morning I started kindergarten, my chubby hand grasping a Snow White lunch box that had been Anna Page's. Julie found a small watercolor inside the glass-fronted bookcase, which she declared must be "that Beatrix Potter duck." She handed me the little painting as Anna Page began piling large and irregular-shaped coals from a bin beside the fireplace onto the grate.

"Don't start that thing, Anna Page!" Julie warned. "We'll die of carbon monoxide poisoning." Then to me, "What is it, Hope?"

Anna Page, too, was studying me then, their faces as expectant as when they'd stood at either end of a twirling rope, urging me to jump in.

" 'Where do you go every afternoon by yourself, Jemima Puddle-Duck?' " I said, although the purple-velvet-vested character in the painting—one I knew so well without ever having seen her—wasn't Jemima. I gathered the best I could of a smile. "It's a *goose*."

"You silly goose, Jules!" Anna Page said. "Don't you know a duck from a goose?"

Julie gave her a look. "One quacks and the other honks," she said. "But painted ones don't do either."

"Dang, she's getting sassy," Anna Page said.

The long matches I found wouldn't stay lit, and the shorter ones succeeded only in searing the edges of the paper. I pulled some fire starters from the metal bin—the slimy white slabs filling the room with eau de gasoline when freed from the plastic wrap—and broke off three perforated rectangles; if I wanted to burn down *my* mother's cottage, I would damn well do it. Four more blackened-but-not-burning-edge attempts later, Anna Page grabbed the matches and tossed a lit one directly onto a starter. It burst into flames that shot up the chimney, surely threatening the trees outside.

"Shit!" Julie shouted, and she began to laugh unabashedly, and we were all laughing then, as the ash from the burning paper fell through the grate and smoke poured everywhere, the kindling popping sparks to the edge of the hearth as the fire made a whipping sound, like a strong wind. Even with the screen replaced, sparks and ashes splashed forward from the grate and slipped out under the screen.

"It's a scene from one of Mom's books," I said, staring into the mess of ash and singed paper bits. "The watercolor. It's Gabriella Goose from 'The Tale of Gabby Goose.'"

Julie brushed a few fallen coal bits back behind the screen with the metal scoop.

"I didn't know your mom painted," Anna Page said, her low voice almost lost in the sound of the fire.

I stared at the funny way the coal burned—not evenly on the surface the way barbecue charcoal does, but becoming craggy, riddled with holes. I wanted to put Anna Page out the way Mom put out the spiders. I wanted to tell her she didn't know anything about my mother, and her mother didn't, either, Aunt Kath who went off to an office every day, leaving Mom to help Anna Page with term-paper footnotes and sanitary pads and boyfriends, to give her love-life advice that I, years later, would remember rather than hear firsthand.

"I should have saved her," Anna Page said. "If only . . ."

If only Dad had been alive to call for help. If only I'd stopped by for coffee on the way to work, as I had so many mornings after he'd died. If only Mom had been Anna Page's patient or even mentioned to her the "bit of toothache" she mentioned to me. Toothache. Indigestion. The little flip-flop of her heart that sometimes made her stop and touch her chest. All signs Anna Page would have recognized as a heart going bad. How hard had Mom's heart tried to keep going before she died?

I was in my pajamas and drifting off to sleep under my mother's batik bedspread, the lights on and Anna Page whispering to Julie that she was going outside in search of cellphone reception, when Julie backed up against the book cabinet and something clicked. "Oh!" she said as the face of the center drawer opened forward.

"It's a desk?" she whispered uncertainly, pulling on the edge of wood and sliding it out. "It is. A hidden little drawer-desk."

I fought against the drowsiness of the pill Anna Page had given me. The drawer face was lying flat, on hinges, revealing wood-divided cubbies holding pens and paper clips, a stapler, a tidy stack of black moleskine notebooks like the ones in which I used to write. Julie was about to open the top journal, but Anna Page took it from her and set it in my hands. I opened it and blinked against the jumble of letters and numbers on the first page:

7.0.1999, ehqrs mhfgs zs sgd bnsszfd.

Gibberish. My mind going, or my mother's having gone, or both.

"I didn't, either, Anna Page," I mumbled, pressing my mouth to the journal, inhaling the scent of leather and ink and paper as I gave in to the sleeping-pill heaviness. "I didn't know Mom could paint."

2

From the Journals of Ally Tantry

19.8.2008, Keswick, in the English Lake District. Beatrix and I have arrived at a shabby little bed & breakfast which has to commend it not much more than location: from here we can take the Keswick Launch across Derwentwater and walk to Lingholm and Fawe Park——which Bea assures me still looks the way it did when she painted it for Mr. McGregor's garden. We're having tea on the patio under an umbrella, in plastic chairs at the lake's edge. I've slipped my shoes and socks off and stuck a quick toe in the water. Bea has untied the old-fashioned lace-up-forever things she wears (she refuses to trade them in for today's practical flats, much less sneakers, which they call trainers here), but she's quite shocked at my suggestion that she roll down her stockings in public. No amount of trying to persuade her to trade her full-length skirts for slacks works, either.

——But you're dead, Bea, I remind her. How can it possibly matter? You've been dead for years.

——Would you have me give up my cane, too, Allison? she insists. And what about my sheep?

Beatrix is mad for sheep, I'm afraid. Really, you will want to avoid the topic. "Our Water Lily was quite famous," she'll tell you without a hint of modesty, the beginning of a monologue about the salvers and teapots and tankards her ewes won. There will be photographs: Bea so stooped over a cane that you can't imagine she could get anywhere at all, but there she is in the middle of a pasture with a motley-looking sheep. And she sketches them. Do not——I warn you, do not!——express any interest in seeing her drawings of the sheep.

She chooses a second scone and stares across the lake to mountains that belong on a child's model train set, or a grown man's one.

——Most people, after one success, she says, are so cringingly afraid of doing less well that they rub all the edge off their subsequent work.

She looks like Kath as she says this——her expression like Kath's when I'd mentioned to the Wednesday sisters that I might come here to research a Beatrix Potter biography I might write. "Isn't your mama from those parts?" Kath had asked, and the others had been suspicious, too, Frankie and Linda pointing out that I'd have to stick to the truth, and Brett saying, "No telling it slant," quoting Emily Dickinson the way she is forever quoting people more clever than us. "I'm 'potty for Potter,'" I'd insisted, echoing the improbable pitch I came upon in a tourist brochure at the Manchester train station on my first trip to England, with Jim on a business trip. The brochure (offering three days and two nights at a house that once belonged to Potter and was now an inn) beckoned improbably: "Are you potty for Potter?"

Bea offers me the last scone before taking it herself.

——Yes, Allison, she says. Potty for Potter. So it does seem you are. But if we can't be a little crazy when we're writing in our journals, where can we be?

And she's off on a tear about "Mr. Warne" (as she calls him) agreeing to publish **Peter Rabbit** the summer she stayed here, in 1901. The book started as the most charming picture-letter written to her former governess's five-year-old son when Bea herself was twenty-five, the strong forward slant of her cursive intermixed with sketches of an expressive black-ink bunny face. She'd given up on finding a commercial publisher and self-published the book with black-and-white sketches before Warne became interested.

He was the one who insisted on the watercolors——Peter's blue coat.

I suppose I like to imagine Bea wrote her stories the way I wrote mine: for children she longed to have but couldn't, with the superstition that writing the stories might somehow break the curse of childlessness. It was different for her, of course. I married young but miscarried so many times that I'd begun to despair of ever bringing a child to term. Bea was forty-seven before she married, too late for children, the way I worry it will be too late for Hope.

3

"A minnow! a minnow! I have him by the nose!"
——from **The Tale of Mr. Jeremy Fisher**
by Beatrix Potter

ANNA PAGE NUDGED JULIE'S THIN SHOULDER and whispered that she was going down to sit by the lake. Julie, fast asleep on the love seat in Mom's cottage, didn't stir.

Anna Page nudged her again. "I wanted to let you know where I was, just in case."

"In the lake," Julie mumbled.

"*By* the lake," Anna Page said.

Julie opened her eyes and peered at Anna Page from under eyebrows that are straight across and not insubstantial, not overthinned or overarched or over-anythinged, and yet with the slightest narrowing can bring even the most ardent teenagers flirting in the library stacks to a hush. She's all long straight arms and nose and neck, long straight fingers abundant with rings that ought to be too much but aren't, with only an occasional earring tangled in the sheet of her impeccably highlighted hair out of place. Always silver earrings, which she wears in such abundance that it stops people, as if they can accept a librarian who doesn't wear glasses, but one with multiple ear piercings is more than they can take.

"Fine, I'm awake now," she whispered to Anna Page. "I'll come with you."

"You were sleeping. Stay here with Hope and sleep."

"You can't go out by yourself, Ape." Julie hauled herself up, the jet lag creasing her face. "What if that creepy neighbor with the dog is out there somewhere? What if the murderer-husband that Robbie the boat rower described is on the loose?"

Anna Page said Julie had read *Jane Eyre* too many times, and Julie countered that Anna Page hadn't read it enough. "Rochester didn't kill his wife. She jumped from the roof."

"You'd jump, too, if someone kept you locked up," Anna Page responded, knowing Rochester's wife was crazy but ignoring the inconvenient detail. Vexing Julie has always been the easiest way to get her to insist on doing what she thinks you don't want her to do. And even Julie will tell you she was plenty vexed with Anna Page as she followed her out the door, as Anna Page meant her to all along.

Outside, the darkness under the tree canopy was almost total, the frightening thrum of insects making Julie's skin creepy with the thought of being swarmed with disgusting flying things. If she wanted to kill someone, this was where she would come, she said—not that she expected Anna Page to admit this was a stupid idea; Anna Page isn't much for admitting stupidity.

Anna Page, without breaking stride or turning, asked, "Did you ever imagine Aunt Ally might have a lover?" And when Julie didn't answer, "And why does it make me feel better that my daddy wasn't the only one?"

Julie had felt odd enough being out at night with Anna Page even before the conversation turned to the other Kath—a heart surgeon at Stanford like Anna Page and her dad, with whom Anna Page's father had lived for decades without ever divorcing her mom. It was as if Anna Page were on a midnight walk not with her but with her sister, with Jamie arisen from the dead. God knew the three of them had been out at night together often enough as kids, Anna Page tossing rocks at their bedroom window and Julie and Jamie climbing out into the night to go wherever she wanted to go. But that was decades past, and Jamie was dead. Jamie had been dead a few days short of a year, leaving Isaac without a wife and Oliver without a mother, Anna Page without a best friend, Julie without a sister and with all her guilt.

"I'm pretty sure Aunt Ally and that guy with the dog were just friends," Julie answered finally, as if friendship were something less than love, as if Jamie must have cared more for Julie than for Anna Page just because they'd shared the same bedroom, the same faces and hair and hands, thigh muscles, elbows. The same tastes for Brussels sprouts. Red shoes. Men who told goofy jokes, or at least appreciated theirs.

"You'd look great as a D-cup." That was the way her twin sister, Jamie, had received Julie's declaration that she was going to have a prophylactic mastectomy—with no more fanfare than if she were changing her hair color or deciding on a pair of boots. It was a Tuesday. They were sitting at a table at Osteria, waiting for their mother. Outside the window, a clump of bicyclers stopped for a red light, Palo Alto sweat-for-lunch types.

"Remember when we used to stuff Kleenex in our bras?" Jamie had said. "The first time Isaac saw me topless, he said, 'Wait, where's the beef?' "

"He did not!"

" 'I ordered the Quarter Pounder, not the kid's burger!' That's what he said, I swear."

Jamie was already dying by then. You couldn't take anything she said seriously. She was already dying and she had accepted that, and she was doing her best to help the rest of us accept it, for the sake of her husband, Isaac, and their five-year-old son, Oliver.

"If you're going to do it, you may as well get something out of it. At least a C." That's what Jamie said.

What Julie's husband, Noah, had said was, "But you tested negative for the gene." As if there were only one BRCA entry into the breast cancer world, as if the fact that her genes were identical to her sister's and Jamie was Stage IV, metastatic at presentation, meant nothing. It was in Jamie's brain before they knew it was anywhere. In her brain that was exactly the same as Julie's brain, except not.

"I'd have to buy a whole new bra wardrobe if I went to a D," Julie said. "Underwire? Don't you need underwire if you're a D?"

"So you've scheduled it." Jamie slid a finger under the edge of her wig and scratched. She'd have gone bald if it wouldn't have been too scary for Oliver, all that naked skull. "If you're telling me about it, then you've scheduled it. You won't let me talk you out of it."

"Would you try?"

"Pffft. I'm not exactly the poster child for keeping them, Jules."

Outside, the light changed, and the pack of bicyclists pushed on again.

"Thursday," Julie said. This was Tuesday.

"Recover quickly," Jamie said. "I need you on deck for Isaac and Oliver." And before Julie could object that Jamie wasn't going anywhere, Jamie said, "Don't get them set too high, Jules. They always look fake when they're set too high. Remember when Rachel had hers done, how ridiculous she looked? If you show up Friday with your breasts on your shoulders, I'm sending you back for a redo."

The three of them—Julie, Jamie, and their mother—had lunch together at Osteria twice each year, on Aunt Linda's birthday and on Julie and Jamie's "shared" birthday, although in fact they didn't share a birthday, they were identical twins born in different years, Jamie a few minutes before midnight, on December 31, 1963, and Julie a half hour later, on January 1, 1964. They'd always had birthday celebrations together, though, because if you had two different parties with all the same friends (and they always shared friends), the second party would be a letdown, Julie's would be a dull echo of Jamie's, which would always come first.

These celebrations were supposed to be festive,

but Julie never felt festive eating at restaurants; she couldn't shake the memory of that breakfast at the Plaza Hotel when she was a kid. "Mommy has to go to the hospital early tomorrow morning for an operation," their mother had told them after they'd finished their strawberries and whipped cream, if not their waffles. She might look kind of weird after the surgery if she needed a mastectomy, she'd told them. Then she'd begun telling them how they made her the happiest mommy in the world. "No matter what happens, I want you to remember that," she'd said, "even when you're a hundred and two." They'd all giggled, and Julie had said even when she was a hundred and ninety-two, and Jamie, not to be outdone, had said, "When I'm two thousand!"

Julie fingered the row of silver earrings on her left lobe. "Remember the two-headed snake we saw that afternoon in New York, James, after the strawberry waffles?" she asked. "If I could have, I would have set it loose on you."

"Eeeeeewwww," Jamie said, the same way they'd said it when they were kids together, wondering if there were some connection between the weird-looking snake and their mother's warning about how she might look after her surgery.

Julie turned from their mother chatting with the restaurant owner—her face so like their faces—to her sister's mirror of her. It would turn out to be the last birthday lunch they might ever be mistaken for each other. By the New Year, when their own not-quite-shared birthdays came, Jamie would be gone.

"I used to wish you dead sometimes," she said to Jamie. "Not really, you know, but . . . I used to wish there wasn't anyone like me, that I was just myself and there was no matching you."

She was looking for absolution, she knew that. For Jamie to forgive her for stretching yarn across their shared room when she was nine, forbidding Jamie to step on her half. For hiding Jamie's envelope from Yale, the school they both wanted to go to, but Julie had so longed to have that moment of pride to herself. Julie chose Yale to get far away from everyone, including Jamie; Jamie chose Yale because Julie was going, because Jamie never had been able to imagine the two of them apart. And there Julie was, facing a future without Jamie, regretting that she'd ever thought she wanted what she could no longer bear. Looking for absolution for all the meanness she'd inflicted over all the years of sharing rooms and lives and looks, all the small ones and the one big one, too. She hadn't told Jamie about that, and she didn't suppose Isaac had, either, but the truth was, she was afraid to know.

Across the room, their mother set a hand on the restaurant owner's arm and said some last thing, then turned toward them, all her accumulated years showing in the set of her shoulders, the frown she was trying to work back into a smile.

"Jamie, I—"

Jamie leaned across the table and set a hand on Julie's, stopping her.

"Definitely nothing less than a D-cup, Jules," she said. "A D-cup in expensive hand-tatted lace. Wouldn't that be fun?"

Julie had stuck with the same B-cup she and Jamie had shared since puberty, though, the same ratty bra wardrobe. It would be too odd to look in the mirror every day at a different body, to have that reminder that she'd chosen different breasts, and why. Julie has scars, yes, much like Jamie's. But they tuck underneath, where she doesn't see them unless she looks.

Ahead, on the pier, a shadowed figure: a coyote or a cougar? Did they have cougars in England? Julie didn't know.

When the shadow emerged as human—someone sitting on the pier—Anna Page called out in a hushed voice, "Robbie?"

They weren't teenagers anymore, but Julie was overrun with the awkward irritation she'd always felt on those nights when Anna Page dragged Jamie and her out to meet boys, even when the boy Anna Page had arranged for Julie to meet was cute. Robbie was already turning to see them, though, and waving, leaving her no choice but to stomp on this little tryst.

She probably had coal dust on her face, she thought; it had been far too cold for the tiny shower in the tiny bathroom, and she wasn't about to bathe in the tub by the fire. She should have known Anna Page was planning a midnight rendezvous: she had left a ring of gray around the slipper tub.

Anna Page's hand on Julie's back urged her forward, as it had so often when they were teenagers out meeting boys. In retrospect, Julie would see this for what it was, Anna Page Woodhouse in action, trying like Jane Austen's Emma to make matches while steadfastly avoiding commitment herself. (Anna Page's efforts to find the right someone for this friend or that worked out just often enough—with Jamie and Isaac, for example, or with Kevin and me—that she took to thinking herself a yenta, which Jamie was forever reminding her meant "matchmaker" only on Broadway; everywhere else, it meant "gossip" or "shrew.") That night, though, Julie was too wrapped up in her own awkward emotions to do anything but try for humor. "And I was thinking it was past everyone's bedtime," she said.

"Aye, but I'm seventeen and insane, aren't I?" Robbie answered, the phrase annoyingly familiar. Some rock song, Julie imagined. Some TV show.

"Seventeen?" Anna Page teased. "I wouldn't have guessed."

Robbie laughed softly. "Sorry!" he said brightly, as if it were the most delightful thing in the world to apologize. "I don't mean to misrepresent. Maybe I'm fifty-seven and insane."

Maybe I'm forty-seven and insane, that's what Julie thought, although she'd turned forty-eight that year, on her first not-quite-the-same birthday without Jamie, the first age Jamie would never turn. New Year's Day and the library closed, but she'd slipped out of bed after Noah was asleep, and biked there. She'd left the lights off as she collected the jumble of books by the return slot and scanned them in, organized them by call number on a cart and tucked them back where they could be found. She'd searched fourteen long rows of books before coming upon a copy of Brenda Rickman Vantrease's *The Heretic's Wife* under R instead of V. That order restored, she sat on the floor, leaning back against the three copies of *Middlemarch* she couldn't persuade anyone to read, turning the smooth, soothing pages of the publishers' catalogs and imagining from the artwork and the descriptions which books Jamie would have chosen to read.

"There's a grand bit of sequin tonight on the Big Dipper's handle," Robbie said. "A super-nova—something you see once in a blue moon." The three of them climbed into his boat, and he rowed them to the center of the lake, where he dug around in a pack tucked into the bow and pulled out a small telescope. He helped Anna Page position it, touching her shoulder and her arm and her hand.

"I see it!" she said delightedly before giving Julie a turn.

"And yet what you're seeing isn't there anymore," Robbie said. "If you were sitting in the Pinwheel Galaxy, there's not a bit of that supernova left. The brilliant flash, she'd be the remnant of the star's death."

Julie lowered the telescope to see Robbie staring off at the dark shore, a single light visible in what must be the tower of the big house, Julie supposed.

"The Crier of Claife, he'd be out wandering on such a fine night, wouldn't 'e," Robbie said.

"A fair-weather ghost who kills his wives?" Julie said.

Robbie smiled, his face light in the darkness. "But it was only the one wife he killed, wasn't it? The English one."

Something in his voice left Julie wondering how his lips would taste, which she supposed was one part his knowledge of the night sky and one part her suspicion that Anna Page meant to be kissing him in that boat, or perhaps screwing him. The fact that Julie was approaching fifty and she still wanted men to choose her over Anna Page was a sad comment on their friendship, but there it was.

"You're from Ireland, Robbie?" Julie said. "And you came to England when you bought the boat business?"

"Ah." Robbie stared up at the sky for such a long time that Julie expected him to start talking about the stars again.

Robbie Smythe. The name seemed familiar, but surely that was the thinking of it again, or the commonness of the name.

"Well, I'd been here before, on holliers, hadn't I. The land of Wordsworth and all tha'. I di' not buy the boats until after the old man died, though. He'll be haunting the boathouse, with a mick having his business now." He laughed half-heartedly.

"Why did you leave Ireland?" Julie asked.

He looked away, in Anna Page's direction. She'd been the one he had arranged to rendezvous with, of course. Julie never quite understood why men were so often drawn to Anna Page. Julie was as attractive in a blonder, good-girl way, and men weren't forever falling all over her.

"I suppose I've come on an errand for my wife," Robbie said uncertainly.

Julie, with a pointed glance at Anna Page, said, "You're married."

"I lost Cornelia a decade ago, and our daughter as well."

"I . . . I'm so sorry," Julie stammered, mortified

at the hint of triumph that had been in her voice.

Toward the shore, a gentle splash sounded. "That'll be the Crier in for a swim," Robbie said, although it was only the flap of wings on water, a swan foraging for a midnight snack.

"So you're here on . . . like a dying request?" Julie said.

"I suppose it's what I imagine her dying request would have been."

"And you've just come on this errand for her now?"

The three of them stared up at the sparkle of star that they couldn't see without the telescope, that wasn't really there.

"I've put it off, haven't I?" he admitted finally. "But it's an old broom knows the dirty corners best." He dipped a hand in the lake and let it dangle there. "It's a . . . a friend of hers I've come here to meet."

As Robbie set his hands on the oars again, Julie imagined him carrying a lantern, wearing a hooded robe and walking through the forest, searching for the bones of his dead wife and child, as Isaac might go out in search of Jamie if he didn't have Oliver.

"That thing you said earlier," she said. "Seventeen and insane?"

Robbie studied her, his eyes the blue of the lake in the evening as the sun set. "It's from *Fahrenheit 451*, idn' it?"

Anna Page said, "Kurt Vonnegut."

A hint of a smile touched Robbie's eyes, but he didn't correct her. " 'When people ask your age . . . always say seventeen and insane,' " he said. "Isn't this a nice time of night to row? I like to smell things and look at things, and sometimes stay up all night, rowing, and watch the sun rise."

He leaned in to the oars then, headed back toward the shore. And because he didn't correct Anna Page, Julie didn't, either, tempting as it was. But she did think *Ray Bradbury*. With perhaps a few edits compliments of Robbie Smythe thrown in for good measure. Even the firemen in Bradbury's dystopian novel didn't use water, and if there was a boat to row anywhere on the pages of *Fahrenheit 451*, Julie didn't remember it.

4

From the Journals of Ally Tantry

13.2.2009, Hill Top Farm, Near Sawrey. On the way to Beatrix's house today, she pointed out little things that, if you've read her books and know they're there, you recognize: the Tower Bank Arms from The Tale of Jemima Puddle-Duck; the cottage that was Ginger and Pickle's store and the charcoal burners' hut from that book; the hole where Benjamin hid before rescuing the Flopsy Bunnies, up on Oatmeal Crag; and the beehive set in the garden wall that appears in The Tale of Jemima Puddle-Duck, when poor Jemima despairs of having her eggs forever found and carried off. Bea pointed out that she included the gate in Jemima, too, as well as the front door, which she also drew in The Tale of the Pie and the Patty-Pan. I didn't tell her that we'd rarely read that one.

Bea and Norman——not Mr. Warne this morning but Norman——had dreamed of living together on a farm up here, but Bea didn't buy Hill Top until the winter after he died, when she was thirty-nine. She spent her grief learning the boundary fences and property lines, and commissioning work to be done. When she returned the next spring, it looked quite ugly, she told me. The winding road with its charming tumbledown wall covered with polypody was straight and white and bare; soil was piled in heaps everywhere; and most of the work had been improperly done.

I wonder how much of the change in her perception of the farm was due to the improvements she commissioned and how much to the stark reality of arriving alone and unmarried to a life she meant to share with a man who was dead.

——I could not even be seen to mourn Norman's death, as I'd ceded to my parents' demand to keep our engagement secret, she said. When I became engaged to Mr. Heelis years later, my father and I about came to fisticuffs, much like Tommy Brock and Mr. Todd.

In case you don't know, Tommy is the badger in Mr.

Todd's book, and Mr. Todd is himself a fox, and Bea's family was of the class who prefer their daughters remain spinsters rather than "marry down" to earned, rather than inherited, wealth.

——My parents used the law as an excuse for their opposition to me marrying Jim, I told her. He was from India and it was illegal in Maryland for whites to marry nonwhites.

It's one of the things Bea and I have in common: sour-faced mothers who would have us remain spinsters rather than marry men we loved. That and the shared name in our family trees.

——I can't figure out how to tell Jim I went to Manchester when he was in his meetings in London that time he and I came to England together, I said. And I can't exactly tell him about the marriage license I found there without telling him I went.

Mother's maiden name——Caroline Anne Crompton ——listed as the bride for a groom who was not my father. Crompton, which was Bea's paternal grandmother's name, although the two are separated by generations.

I'd found the address given for my mother on the license, but it was a gas station, and the boy pumping gas had gawked at me as if I were batty. "A house, miss?" he'd said. "There's been only this petrol station as long as I've known."

I've never told Jim about that and I've never told him about the two days I spent wandering around the narrow roads on my first trip to the Lakes, either. It all seems so silly, trying to find some connection to my mother's past here. But where else can I look with the trail in Manchester gone cold? Never mind that my search for the groom's address the first time I came to the Lakes turned up nothing more than a one-track road through maybe four houses, none big enough to warrant a name.

——Jim grieves for the way my parents cast me out when we married, I said to Bea. He feels angry at them, and he feels responsible for the pain they caused by abandoning me.

——Of course he does, Bea said.

——Even though it was their fault, not his, I said.

——I know, dear, she said.

——It feels a little like betrayal, to bring my parents back into our lives. What point is there to it, with them both so long dead? It feels a little like betrayal even to talk to the Wednesday Sisters about it behind Jim's back.

——And so you haven't, Bea said.

I thought I might tell the Wednesday Sisters about the marriage license the first time I said I was coming to the Lake District, but how could I say it without sounding nutty? I wanted to travel thousands of miles and spend thousands of dollars to get to the English Lake District because my mother who'd disowned me might once have been engaged to a butler or a cook or a stable boy from a house near Windermere? And before I could explain myself, Frankie had said, "Ally is sixty-five years old, Linda, and she's never

47

even slept in a room by herself except in her own bed when Jim is away on business. Can't you see she might **want** to go alone?" So there I was, handing over my ticket to Hill Top Farm. Just Bea and me and the ghosts of our mothers. Bea isn't Frankie. She isn't Linda or Brett or Kath. But I can talk to her about my mother without betraying Jim.

——Those are your shoes, Bea? I said, noticing a pair of gardening clogs tucked under a chair by the fireplace.

She looked from the shoes under the chair to the lace-ups on her feet today.

——Have you ever seen such a place for hide-and-seek, and funny cupboards and closets? she asked (refusing to engage about the shoes). But oh, how the people here laughed at my purchase of Hill Top, she said. Of course, the rats **had** opened up a hostel here, every rodent from every corner of the Lake District making a point of stopping in.

She pointed to the places in the floorboards that were repaired with cement, where the rats had chewed the wood through——rats she dispatched without possibility of heirs, I'm sorry to report. Never mind the cute little critters in her books; our Bea is a practical gal.

The low-ceilinged farmhouse is quite modest for a woman who grew up in wealth, who made a fortune as a writer and left fourteen farms and four thousand acres of land to the National Trust——together with her flocks of Herdwicks, she is quick to remind me.

Upstairs, she directed me to a letter she'd gotten even after she was quite famous, from a magazine editor who did take one story but rejected the others, one on the excuse that it was "not altogether happy." Not altogether happy——an apt description of Bea's reaction to seeing her little books set about beside the real-life inspirations: the stairways, the grates, the clocks, the ceramic ham in the dollhouse, which Tom Thumb shattered in his attempt to have it for dinner.

——Heavens to Betsy, that's all you wanted to show me, Bea? A rejection letter?

——It is.

——If there is no end of failure, I said, then perhaps there might be no end of success, too, if you just go on about putting words to paper?

——If there is no end of failure, Allison, Bea said, success must be the act of putting words to paper as best we can.

We've left Hill Top now and settled in at a tea shop in Buckle Yeat cottage, the backdrop for the puddle ducks' excursion up the road in **The Tale of Tom Kitten**. Bea's gaze is fixed on Esthwaite Water while I'm trying to commit the details of Hill Top to my journal.

——You must keep writing, Allison, Bea says (as if I'm not doing so when she says it). There is something delicious about writing the first words of a story. You never quite know where they'll take you.

——Did you actually say that, Bea? I thought that was a line in a movie.

——But it's quite a fine line, isn't it? Although I do think I'm less prim than I was portrayed there, don't you?

——Less prim? Or less thin?

I eye the second scone she's selected.

——You're in your sunset, Allison, she says, and you've never published——

——I never **wanted** to publish my children's stories. I only wrote them for Hope and Sammy.

——So you say.

She takes her time about having a bite of the scone.

——You must keep writing, Allison, she repeats. Whatever it is you write. You ought to find a place here in the Lake District, like my Hill Top. Use this excuse of writing about me if you wish. A woman does need her own space, doesn't she?

——Beatrix Woolf, I say.

I tell her that tomorrow we'll take the launch across to Wray Castle, the first place Bea stayed in the Lake District, in July 1882, when she was sixteen and Annie Carter Moore was still her governess, not yet the mother of the children to whom Bea wrote picture-letters she would turn into books.

——We'll take our journals along, Bea says. Perhaps sketch pads. You can start painting where I started, and I'll encourage you as Mr. Rawnsley encouraged me. Wouldn't that be fine?

——It would be chilly, painting outside in February, and I don't sketch any better than I paint, which I don't, I told her. Then I asked if Rawnsley was the model for

Mr. McGregor. People seem to think he probably was.

——Mr. Rawnsley always was digging around in the dirt, although not so much garden dirt as anywhere-else dirt. But you write fiction, Allison. What do you think?

——I've only ever written geese and alligators and penguins, I say.

——As have I, she says. It's so much easier to tuck a bit of oneself into a puddle duck, isn't it? Nobody thinks to look for you there. Often you don't think to look yourself.

5

"Who in the world is this?" inquired Johnny Town-mouse. But after the first exclamation of surprise he instantly recovered his manners.
——from **The Tale of Johnny Town-Mouse** by Beatrix Potter

JULIE WOKE TO SUNLIGHT EDGING THE WINDOW shades and an insistent knocking at the cottage door. She bolted up from her bed on the love seat and fumbled with the key. The lock was an old-fashioned fire hazard requiring the key to get out as well as to get in, but she'd locked it again when she and Anna Page returned from stargazing with Robbie. "The danger of a wife-murdering ghost who can't get past a lock," Anna Page had joked, "is far worse than that of being trapped inside trying to work the dang key as the cottage burns down?" But Julie hadn't relented.

She cracked the door open and peeked out at the neighbor with the frightening dog. Fresh clothes but with dark circles under his eyes, behind his glasses. He had three shoe boxes in his arms. In the van, the dog looked up and kept looking.

Anna Page, in the bed, said grumpily, "It's freezing in here! Close the dang door!"

I heard them from the cottage kitchen, where I sat with my coat on against the cold, looking through Mom's three moleskine journals, the pages and pages of letters that made no words.

"Haven't you a fire?" the man asked Julie. "Good God, let me set one in the grate for you."

Julie stepped aside to let him in—never mind that Anna Page wore only an oversize man's oxford-cloth shirt she'd kept when she'd abandoned its original owner. The neighbor muttered something about ashes, and before I realized it he was clomping down the stairs, looking startled to find me sitting at Mom's kitchen table. I closed the journal before he could see it and said good morning, and he retrieved a big metal drawer from the space under the stairs. I headed back up with him, and in no time he had a fire blazing in the main room, with the ashes falling neatly into the added ash drawer. No smoke pouring everywhere. Not so much as a spot of coal on his khaki trousers or his fleece.

Julie pulled the lid off one of the shoe boxes he'd set on the love seat. Gray hiking boots.

"I thought those . . . I meant to . . ." The neighbor turned to me. "I made such a dog's breakfast of things last night. I only . . . it was such a shock about your mum."

"These are my size," Julie said, although they were an eight, and Julie wore the same 7½ she and Jamie had worn in high school. Size 8 was Jamie's size, their feet having ceased being identical when Jamie was pregnant with Oliver. Oliver, who'd tossed a single tulip on his mother's coffin—yellow, her favorite, and Julie's, too—the poor little guy saying, "Bye-bye, Mommy," and waving his empty fingers that were his mother's and hers as well.

"Your size, brilliant," the neighbor said. "I have other colors, but I prefer the gray."

He disappeared into the van, calling back that he hadn't brought quite as many sizes of hiking clothes; he was a fair guess at clothing sizes, but feet didn't always match the rest. He emerged with several plastic store bags as big and full as the bags we'd loaded with Jamie's sheer night-gowns and slippers and moisturizer, crystal perfume bottles, unused tampons, blue eye shadow none of us had worn since junior high—Jamie's things that, when faced with the jumbled

Goodwill bins and the blank white donation forms requiring us to itemize every size-8 shoe, every B-cup bra, we'd loaded back into Anna Page's pickup and taken to a self-storage place across 101, where they still are.

Mom's neighbor set the bags on the love seat and began extracting microfiber tops and wool socks and jackets, as sure of his choices for us as Kevin might have been. The man owned a chain of hiking stores all over Britain, he explained. "I thought I might take you on a hike to one of your mum's favorite places, Asha. All of you, of course."

Your mum. Your mum. Your mum. Each utterance of the word a blow. Your mum who was off her rocker, wasn't she? The journals full of nonwords Exhibit A for the case.

Anna Page, not at all self-conscious of the fact that she was wearing only the oversize shirt, got the neighbor out the door, and Julie turned the key again, muttering that the guy might seem more presumptuous than creepy if it weren't for that awful dog.

"Mom would have loved the dog," I said.

We can't help how we look on the outside, she liked to say.

Anna Page was already stripping off her shirt and pulling clothes from the love seat, holding a yellow and gray jacket to my face, then putting it in my hands. "Do we go on this hike, Hope?" she asked. "Or do we beg off?" She extracted a microfiber shirt and examined the tag. "Hmm . . . which one of us do you suppose he thinks is extra large?"

Another knock sounded, and Anna Page, naked, ducked into the tiny bathroom as Julie opened the door.

"I hate to be a bother, but there are mackintoshes in the bags."

Julie and I gazed upward: perhaps the clearest blue sky we'd ever seen.

"Things are very changeable here," the neighbor said.

"I'm sorry," Julie said, "but I don't believe we even know who you are."

He seemed a bit affronted. "I live up the hill. My family have been here since . . . well, practically since the Romans left the Lakes."

"And you have a name, presumably?"

"Of course. Yes, I'm Graham. And this is Napoleon. He doesn't make you nervy, does he? I can leave him back if he makes you nervy. I'll come for you in an hour, then. Or you can give us a bell from the pier when you're ready."

"A bell?"

"I'm afraid the only mobile reception in this part of the woods is at the pier's tip end."

Julie was in the bathroom and Anna Page down at the pier calling the hospital to check on her patients when I retrieved my mother's puzzle box. Intricate and seamless, the inlaid wood in the top panel forms a woman in a sky-blue kimono, her lips pressed to the forehead of a dark-haired baby above whose head is looped the palest halo of gold. I sat on Mom's bed with the slipper tub between me and the fireplace, and I touched a finger to the halo of this box that, from the outside, appears to have no way in, no hinges or doors, no openings, no way to access whatever treasure it might enclose.

Some of the puzzle boxes Mom collected in the years after her mother died were as small as matchboxes, some big enough to hold loaves of bread. One took 324 steps to open, its outside simplicity masking a complicated mechanism inside that left room for only the smallest of treasures. But this Madonna and child was her first. Her grandfather had brought it from England when she was a girl, and her sister had found it in the attic of their childhood home after their mother died, after the funeral my mother didn't attend.

What kinds of treasures belonged in a puzzle box? "Anything you like, anything of infinite value, any secret you want to keep just for yourself," Mom told me with an air of delighted secrecy the night her sister returned the box to her. I was not yet school-aged, and it was dark and late, and the smell of wood fire and hot chocolate, together with the fact that Mom was letting me stay up way past my bedtime, was treasure enough. After my aunt left, Mom put the box in my hands and set my index finger on the baby's halo. "To open it," she said, "you trace your finger from here around the edge to the third flower, see? Then you slide the flower down."

When I asked how she knew, she looked at me with her big brown eyes, and she blinked and blinked. "Some things in life, Hope, you just have to know," she said. "Someone tells you and you remember it, and you tell it to someone else. Sometimes you tell it directly, and sometimes you tell it through stories. It's one of the ways we show our love."

After Mom had walked me through all the steps to open the box that night, she let me slide aside the top panel with the mother and baby to reveal the secret inside.

"It's empty, Mommy!" I said. "Where is the treasure?"

She took it from me and touched a fingertip to the smooth, empty wood, and she sniffed the way I wasn't supposed to sniff; I was supposed to get a tissue. She pulled me to her, tucked my head under her chin. It frightened me a little, the silence with only the burning wood and the chocolate and the vanilla smell of my mother, the shuddering of her chest against my ear, the kisses she placed atop my head once, and again.

"I don't know where the treasure is, Hope," she said finally. "I'm sorry. I don't know."

Sitting in her cottage, my fingers worked the puzzlebox by memory. I moved one piece, adjusted another to engage a third, slid the first piece back in the other direction before adjusting a piece on the adjacent side, all the while trying not to think of the non-word gibberish in her journals.

When I finally slid the Madonna and child aside, I dipped my fingers into my mother's ashes. Not ashes, really. Only the dry bone fragments left after the rest of Mom was vaporized, dry bone crushed by machine into a fine sand. ("Lordy, dying isn't as glamorous as they make it sound in Sunday school," Aunt Kath had said about that.) I tucked a bit of Mom into my coat pocket before Julie came out of the bathroom or Anna Page returned, or I lost my nerve. Move slip slide engage, through the steps to close the box again. I worked the delicate wood quickly, to keep my treasure safe.

The lake was lapping clear and fresh as we hiked along the colored-leaf path to a signpost: Public Bridleway, Hawkshead 3m. Graham led us around a gate of sorts—a single wooden beam stretched between two posts, with a latch at one end and a hinge at the other to allow vehicles to pass. The steep uphill path beyond the gate was paved with slates so poorly set they made the going more difficult. He'd left Napoleon at home, which was a bit of a relief.

"Mind your steps," he advised, catching Anna Page's arm as she slipped a bit on the stones. "Public works, these paths are."

Mind your steps. Is that how my father would have said it? He hadn't been gone six months, and already it was so hard to recall his voice. But he'd have said "Careful here" or "Watch it, it's slick." Unlike so many Indians of his generation, he must have learned English from an American.

"A snake!" Julie called out, stopping dead in her tracks. "Was that a snake?"

Graham pointed to a red squirrel, which shot off in a jagged path and bolted up a tree. "Only the adders are poisonous, in any event," he said, "and their venom won't likely kill an adult. Some say if you come upon one coiled on the bridleway, you might step across him without any bother; they're rather timid and will play quite dead and let you carry on."

"You recommend this?" Anna Page said. To which Graham conceded that he did suggest giving them wide berth.

He went on at length about the forest wildlife: golden eagles, although you didn't see them often, and red and roe deer, and rabbits. "There used to be boar and wildcats, but the biggest danger now is the weather, do let me impress that upon you. It changes precipitously."

We were high enough to have a view of the lake and the clouds over the far hills, the bracken on the nearer fells heading toward brown, although the ferns in the forest were still a firm green. When Julie said she'd left her lungs at the bottom of the hill, we paused to catch our breath, Graham taking no break from his lecture on hiking partners, maps and weather gear, and emergency kits. I slipped a bit of Mom surreptitiously into my palm, to let her have one last look at the lace veil of trees, the fall colors, the stone walls marching up the fells to their peaks, fencing in nothing at all. Who in the world had gone to the trouble to build them?

"Look," Anna Page said.

A broad rainbow arced fatly over the bracken-brown hills to the north.

"Each color is as wide as a whole rainbow," I said.

"It's a snowbow," Graham said. "It's snowing over the border, in Scotland. It's not yet November, but it's been snowing there since the sixth."

"There isn't such a thing as a snowbow," Julie said. "Rainbows come from sunlight refracting in the smooth surface of raindrops, which snow-flakes don't have." Something she learned from a children's book. When library patrons need answers, she often directs them to children's books, with their simple explanations, their easy diagrams.

I tucked my mother's ashes back into my pocket, remembering the snow falling in Kevin's tiny hometown in Minnesota the day we married, in April, Kevin uncomfortable in a stiff Ken-doll tuxedo, me dragging the weight of my train behind me like the expectations of marriage to come. "It's a sign," Ama had said when the fat white flakes began to fall. She never said what it was a sign of, though, or I wasn't listening when she did.

The four of us continued up the path, through a stretch of ugly cleared forest, a minefield of stumps that looked like the end of the world. Anna Page slipped again on the stones, and Graham caught her arm, saying, "Do mind!" He called back to Julie and me, "Mind, there's a step-down," pointing to a funny slanted step where a break in the stone wall would allow rainwater to funnel off the path.

"Careful here," my father would have said— about the step and about Graham as well.

A fair hike later, we looked from a sheep field down into a valley and pond backstopped by a woods and a mountain range. The fields were more of what we'd been hiking through—the same tufty grass, inelegant and wild and muddy, with the occasional cow paddy ("Mind your steps!"), the occasional bright red farmer's marking on an otherwise lovely white sheep. It was the colors and shapes that made the view so striking, I decided as I surreptitiously held a bit of Mom out toward it all: the gentle gray of the clouds stacked behind the mountaintops echoed in the maze of stone walls; the arc of the pond's shore feathered with reeds; the leafless Abbott and Costello trees in the foreground, one round and branchy, the other tall and sparse.

Anna Page pointed out a waning moon showing as a filmy white crescent in the daylight, where it didn't belong. I wouldn't have said I was annoyed at her for pointing it out, and yet I felt so irritated all of a sudden, at Anna Page and at Julie and at this man who was all "mind your steps," and always so politely when what he was saying was mind the cow dung on the path, the goose poop on the rocks. The crescent moon—which would grow slimmer the next day and the next, and would disappear entirely on no-moon day at the beginning of Diwali the following week—wasn't there in the painting in my mother's cottage, but this was the place that was depicted, the home of Gabby Goose. Why did that feel so like a betrayal, that Mom chose to give the goose I always thought belonged to me a home here, in this place I didn't know?

"This is Moss Eccles Tarn," Graham said. "It's part of Beatrix Potter's estate. That lane across the water leads down to Near Sawrey and Hill Top Farm."

"Summer evenings, she and her husband rowed

here in a flat-bottomed boat," I said, remembering my mother talking about Potter sketching and her husband fishing while I, already weary of her obsession, half listened. Then she'd died and I was left with only a few fuzzy memories of what she'd told me and the nonsense in her journals. It was spooky every time I opened them: Mom's handwriting, *ehqrs mhfgs zs sgd bnsszfd*. Three journals written over several years. 1997. 1998. 1999.

"This was your mum's favorite place, Asha," Graham said, looking away.

"Her favorite place was Point Lobos," I said. "And that dramatic stone arch at Pfeiffer Beach." Knowing as I said it that those were *my* favorite places, seawater filling the air with sound and splash and turmoil. Mom would have loved this quiet path through these quiet woods to this quiet valley with its smooth pond, its quiet calm.

It was that calm of hers that so frustrated me, the sense that all the world's problems could be solved if everyone just took a few deep breaths. Even in the last conversation I had with her, when I was working up the nerve to tell her my marriage was ending, her response had been "Asha, Asha. Do take a deep breath." As if a deep breath would bridge all the gap between Kevin and me, the arguments over so many stupid things: when to replace the garbage disposal or stop for gas, where the spare key was supposed to be and who hadn't put it back, how to do so many tasks the doing of which didn't even matter, loading the dishwasher or parking the car, cutting the roses, covering the grill. Arguments that always boiled down to who was being selfish and who wasn't—the who being me and the selfish being yes because I wasn't getting any younger. Layers of bickering painted over the ground of our childlessness.

"Mom talked about a waterfall here," I said.

"A waterfall?" Graham asked. "Perhaps you mean the small dam there?"

"Her favorite place here had a waterfall, a big one," I insisted, although I couldn't actually say she'd talked about one place more than any other. So much about her world here surprised me: the blue door and the coal fire, the slipper tub, the tiny bathroom and the towel warmer your knees bumped against when you used the toilet. "There was a flood here," I said, grabbing at a memory. "One of the first times she came here, before Thanksgiving a couple years ago." *I just about lost one of my shoes among the cabbages, Hope,* she'd said, the quote we called on from *Peter Rabbit* to convey fright, because Peter was "most dreadfully frightened" when Mr. McGregor spotted him and sent him fleeing through the garden, losing his shoes. "And the waterfall usually ran several paths," I said, "but there was so much rain that it all joined together in a big rush."

"She told me that, too," Anna Page said. Then to Graham, "Aunt Ally thought Hope and I both would have loved to see the power of the falls."

"You'll mean Stock Ghyll Force, out beyond Ambleside," Graham said. "John Ruskin called it 'the loveliest rock-scenery, chased with silver waterfalls, that I have ever set foot or heart upon.'" Then to me, "We ought not to have ventured out in all that weather, your mum and me, and yet it was irresistible." He and Anna Page both taking this single memory I'd been able to call up about my mother's time here, and wresting it from me.

6

From the Journals of Ally Tantry

12.5.2009, Ambleside, on Lake Windermere. We spent a bleak afternoon yesterday at the Armitt Library, Bea a bit put out by anything that distracted me from her mushroom drawings. I do want to know all about her, but I was more interested in what the archivist told me about Ainsley's End, where Mother's fiancé had lived. It is across the lake after all, not far from Beatrix Potter's tarn. So this morning I shared with Bea my idea that we might find someone to rent us a boat to take up to her pond. I didn't mention Ainsley's End or my mother and the fiancé.

——Moss Eccles Tarn? Bea asked. But you needn't rent a boat. Mr. Heelis and I keep one there.

That was years ago, I explained to her, but Bea is quite stubborn when she gets an idea in her head.

——I prefer to have my own boat, I said, trying another tack.

——You might have said so, she responded snippily. Then you ought to talk to the gentleman in Bowness who straps a boat to his motorcar and takes it across on the ferry, and all the distance up the hill. There isn't a soul in Hawkshead will do that for you.

——Heavens to Betsy, Bea, why didn't you say so earlier?

——You were standing right beside me when that archivist mentioned him. You simply didn't register it. You were too busy getting all wrought up about Ainsley's End being across the lake even though you couldn't find it.

——I wasn't getting "all wrought up."

——You must pay more attention, Allison. There isn't a thing I know that you don't know as well.

As we crossed the lake with the grizzled old boatman, Bea talked about the many times she'd taken this same ferry across from Near Sawrey to Lindeth Howe.

——My brother, Bertram, used to say Mother was the sort to push you around in a perambulator until you got out and said you would rather walk, Bea said. But Mother never sent a perambulator for me, much less the motorcar. She forever left me to hike the whole long

66

uphill on some excuse, generally having to do with the car having just been varnished.

Like with her sheep, you don't want to get Bea started on her mother, but there was so much sadness in her squishy face that I let it go.

——The squishiness, that's in **your** face, Allison, when the subject of our mothers comes up, she said.

I set my face to something less squishy and settled into a conversation with the boatman. Oh, how he could talk, that way people have of talking up here, as if every sentence ought to be structured as a question, and with the most delightful expressions. "Yan, tan, tethera," he taught me. "One, two, three." It's the way shepherds counted sheep not that long ago, a last remnant of ancient Cumbrian language. I learned all about fell racing and hound trailing, too, and about Wordsworth and his sister wandering upon a nearby field of daffodils that inspired his iconic poem. The boatman also had stories about Bea, who denied the truth of every one of them, and about Donald Campbell setting the water speed record here on Lake Windermere only to crash his boat and die on the dining room table at a nearby estate.

——At Ainsley's End? I asked.

——At Belle Grange, miss. 'Course, Ainsley's End has a story of its own, some says. That's the place what was once belonging to the Crier of Claife, who wanders the woods that side with his lantern. A haint.

I studied the submerged cable on which the car

ferry is pulled across the lake, trying to mask my disappointment. Just an old ghost story.

——Some says he's a-looking for his wife, for she did disappear. Some says she disappeared of his hand and he be checking each night that her bones isn't coming up to trouble him. I likes that one: the haint not wanting to be spooked his own self.

He laughed warmly, and I laughed with him, because I could tell he wanted company.

——The hills? I asked, hoping at least to get some better idea where Ainsley's End might be.

He pointed uplake to a small pier jutting into the water.

——Them chimneys above the wee pier, they be the Ainsley's End chimneys, where the beauty what was Mrs. Wyndham used to warm her hands.

I started at the sound of the name. Wyndham. The groom's name on my mother's marriage license.

——Mrs. Martin Wyndham?

——Rich as Croesus, was old man Wyndham, but crazy from the Indian war. Lots was crazy from the war, though, that war and ever' t'other. Cain't blame a man for that.

7

"How do you do, Mr. Jackson?
Deary me, you have got very wet!"
"Thank you, thank you, thank you,
Mrs. Tittlemouse! I'll sit awhile and dry
myself," said Mr. Jackson.
He sat and smiled, and the water dripped
off his coat tails. Mrs. Tittlemouse
went round with a mop.
——from **The Tale of Mrs. Tittlemouse**
by Beatrix Potter

"HEAVENS TO BETSY!" ANNA PAGE SAID IN A voice that mimicked my mom's as we ducked out of the thunder-and-lightning downpour into a house back near the cottage. Inside, our rain gear poured slippery pools all over an old stone kitchen floor. I sank my fingers into my mother's ashes in my pocket—if any of Mom was lost in the dash through the rain, I couldn't tell—wondering if that tarn was where she meant me to leave her. I had the idea she wanted her ashes spread wherever Beatrix Potter's were, but where was that? One source said they were scattered on the banks of Esthwaite Water, where she and her husband often walked when they were courting. Another said the secret of where she rested had died with the farmhand tasked with reuniting the couple after Heelis died.

Graham hung our jackets from pegs in a low-ceilinged kitchen and turned on an electric kettle. He poked the fire back to life in a fireplace with a cast-iron insert like the one in the cottage and a geometric tile surround. "The house is a bit of a sprawl, but I'm happy to give you a show-around," he said as we crowded up to the warmth. "We're at the end of the line—quite literally—and the power does blinker out in weather, so I can't promise the old place won't go dim. But travelers to the Lakes always do seem enamored of the old homes here: Hutton-in-the-Forest, Sizergh Castle, Levens Hall. Abbot Hall as well, although that's now an art gallery."

As he and Julie chatted about some of the writers' homes in the area—John Ruskin's Brantwood, Wordsworth's Dove Cottage and Rydal Mount—I wondered at his comparing this shabby kitchen to a castle.

He scalded the teapot before filling it with leaves and steaming water, the way Mom always did. "Would you care to see the library?" he asked Julie. "We could perhaps tell ghost stories there, or in the Prospect. I'll have Mrs. Anders bring the tea." He opened a door at the far end of the kitchen, into a cabineted and countered hallway—the butler's pantry—opening into a high-ceilinged

70

formal dining room that seated thirty, with fireplaces at either end, crystal chandeliers, and views out to a rose garden put to bed for the winter, a geometric herb garden, stone walls and paths and steps and a large fountain. He toed a floor button at the end of the table, then escorted us through sitting rooms of various sizes, from intimate to grand. We were in the library—two stories of floor-to-ceiling books—when a stern gray-haired woman came to ask where he wanted the tea served. "In the Prospect, please, Mrs. Anders," he told her. "And you might towel the mackintoshes as well."

I'd lost count of the rooms by the time we'd finished the tour, in a bathroom bigger than Mom's entire cottage, with a slipper tub and a fireplace and wide-plank floors that Graham was delighted to point out had been patched with squares of leather and nails a century ago. We hadn't even seen the bedrooms, most of which were closed up; Graham didn't like having underfoot the kind of staff necessary to keep the whole house open. "Mrs. Anders arranges help from the village when it's needed," he said, leaving me to think of those English novels Aunt Kath was forever urging us to read, in which the downstairs servant classes seemed forever to be leading more proper lives than the aristocracy.

The tea was waiting for us when we arrived in the Prospect, an upstairs sitting room that was all fireplaces and wood paneling and huge arched windows, a downlake view stretching to my mother's cottage while, uplake, high square towers and round turrets loomed in bleak gray stone adorned with medieval crosses and buttresses.

"That's Wray Castle, which isn't a real castle, of course," Graham explained. "It was built in 1840 by a Liverpool surgeon in want of squandering his wife's gin fortune. She never did set foot in the thing. It says something, doesn't it, that the sorry old beast is too tacky for a liquor heiress?" He turned to me and said, "That's where your mum was the day I first met her. She shared tea with me after the skies opened up, as you are now."

Julie said, "And the guy who lives there, he's the one people say is the Crier of Claife?"

Graham stared out at the faux castle. "I'm afraid you're mistaken," he said. "Wray Castle is quite empty, and it has been for years."

Graham's house was originally a "traditional firehouse-type plan"—a single rectangular room with a fireplace—according to a National Trust history he showed us. Roofs had been raised, rooms and floors and whole wings added over almost four centuries, the kitchen built in a separate building "so that if the thing caught fire, only the kitchen staff would perish." Graham and Julie and I sat in an alcove with a love seat and two chairs centered on a fireplace, a needlepointed screen and two family crests over its mantel, while

Anna Page wandered the room like a Jane Austen character taking a turn around. No pianoforte, although there was a table in one corner where you could play whist if you knew how to do such a thing.

A second fireplace—one big enough to dance in—anchored the room, and portraits hung everywhere: a lady with thin eyelids and a double chin in an oval frame, an older gent with a goofy abundance of curls, two siblings who seemed to have inherited the same unfortunate hair. The ceiling beams bowed, leaving me wondering what was overhead.

Anna Page fingered her hair—still wet around her face, despite her jacket hood—as she studied a collection of silver trinkets. Then (was she doing this?) she picked something up and stuck it in a pocket of her pants. It was such a smooth move that I wasn't quite sure I'd seen it. It seemed so improbable.

"Your family has lived here for generations, Graham?" Julie asked. "And your offices are here in the Lake District?"

"The corporate offices are not," Graham said, "but the chap who runs the show hasn't much need for me to be around."

"I see," Julie said, her tone thick with admonition: if he had nothing better to do with his time, surely there was a library nearby where he might volunteer to shelve books.

Across the room, Anna Page picked up another something and studied it, but this time she set it back down and came to join us. She stood by the chair closest to the "fine marble fireplace with hob grate" listed with the bell pulls and cornice as having been added in an 1830s remodel. "We have our first cooking lesson tomorrow," she said.

" 'Cookery' lesson," Julie corrected. "And it's not until Saturday, Anna Page."

Anna Page touched her pocket where I thought I'd seen her tuck the trinket, as if she were the thieving upstairs or downstairs scoundrel who would, in the end, receive her just deserts. She settled into the chair by the fire and asked where Napoleon was.

"Napoleon doesn't come above the main floor," Graham said, "and he sleeps in his cage."

It was less comforting than he meant it to be.

"And your ghosts, where do you keep them?" Anna Page asked. "You did promise ghosts."

"Ghost stories, I believe was the offer. Muncaster Castle claims to have several: An eleven-year-old girl who died of screaming fits in the Tapestry Room. A jester. A carpenter who had the misfortune of falling for the daughter of the house. A servant girl who fancied a handsome young footman."

Muncaster. Wasn't that where my grandmother was from? Mom's mother, whom I never met.

"That was Mary Bragg," Graham said. "The stories about her agree only on the idea that she was found drowned. The version I favor has an older servant fancying the same footman, and paying two others to cosh poor Mary on the head as she walked the road to the back gates. The body was hidden in a boggy field, then dumped in the river below the castle, but she kept reappearing."

"I find it hard to believe a woman would be so set on a footman that she'd have her competition snuffed," Anna Page said.

"I find it hard to imagine a corpse that surfaces so determinedly wouldn't find justice," Graham replied with unexpected humor. "A white-clothed lady now haunts the roads around the castle, though, or so they say at Muncaster—which does, I'm sorry to report, charge admission for their tour, not that that would have anything to do with claiming to have so many ghosts."

"And the carpenter?" Anna Page asked.

"He had his head cut off and is said to be looking for it still, isn't he?"

"Or for his long-lost love?" Anna Page suggested with the faintest lift of brow. "When it comes down to it, aren't all tragic stories about love?"

When we left Graham's not much later—armed with an invitation to return for dinner the following evening—we looked back through the high stone posts to leaded-glass windows, a square tower that was five stories high surrounded by slate roofs, copper-blue gutters and gardens and winding paths. Each section of the mansion was a slightly different hue, although the patterns and sizes of the stones were indistinguishable. A keystone over the windows to the left of the door read "1629 RWK." The top of a downspout on the wing to the right read "MW 1765," and one with a golden angel read "MW 1752."

"If the castle is abandoned," Julie said, "that has to be the big house."

"Good Lord, Jules," Anna Page replied, "you didn't buy Robbie's nonsense about local gentry killing their wives, did you? Tell me you believe that stuff about the ghost of the girl who died in fits, too. Tell me you believe some poor carpenter is out looking for his dang head!"

My mom would have, though. Mom would have believed in all those ghosts.

"I'm afraid my mom may have gone batty before she died," I said, although I didn't manage to get the words out until we'd stepped through the blue door back into my mother's tiny cottage. Before I could change my mind, I retrieved the journal I'd been worrying over all day and showed them:

7.0.1999, ehqrs mhfgs zs sgd bnsszfd. adz hr lzjhmh gdqrdke bnlenqszakd hm sgd

rkhoodq sta, mdudq lhme sgzs sgdqd hr
tmozbjhmf sn ad cnmd.

——xntc ad lnqd bnlenqszakd hm sgd ahf
gntrd, rgd rzxr....

Julie took the journal and flipped forward a
page, and another and another. "Was your mom
coming here in 1999?"

"Is that a date? July zero?" Anna Page asked.
"And anyway, the fact that the journal is here now
doesn't mean she wrote it here. Are they all like
this?" She took another journal from the desk and
opened it. She didn't say anything.

"Maybe it's a cipher?" Julie suggested. "Like
those puzzles we used to do as kids?"

"It appears to be some kind of list," Anna Page
said with a cautionary glance at Julie that had
me wondering which would be crazier: Mom
writing lists of gibberish or taking the time to
transpose every single letter she wrote into a
different one.

"But why would Mom bring her old journals
here? And where are the newer ones?"

Julie said, "Aunt Frankie burned them. They
have a deal with each other that they'll burn their
journals after they die, before even our dads can
see them." She'd overheard her mom asking Aunt
Frankie if they should talk to Sam and me first,
but Aunt Frankie had already done it. " 'If you
don't burn mine if I go first, Linda,' Aunt Frankie

77

said, 'I'm coming back to haunt you.' And they had a laugh about there being no decent place for a ghost to settle in the neighborhood anymore, with that old mansion that used to be in the park torn down."

"That mansion was torn down the day you came home from the hospital, Hope," Anna Page said. "Remember that, Jules? Would you ever have guessed back then that—"

She stopped abruptly and suggested she would make us some pasta for dinner; she'd seen a bag of penne and some olive oil in the cupboard.

"What?" I said, because if Anna Page is offering to cook, something is up.

Anna Page said if we didn't want pasta, she could find something else.

"Anna Page thinks your mother was having an affair," Julie said.

"Julie!" Anna Page said. "Not in *1999*, for God's sake."

She opened the bin by the fireplace and began building a coal fire. Julie opened the drawer of the cabinet that hid Mom's desk, peered into the small rectangular emptiness, and closed it again, wood exhaling against wood accompanied by the almost musical note of the brass handle rattling its backplate.

"It doesn't make your ma a different person, Hope," Anna Page said.

Julie unwrapped a single fire starter and set it in

the grate, then picked up the long-handled coal tongs and waited while Anna Page laid the paper and kindling.

"I used to think it made my daddy one thing and my ma another," Anna Page said, "but they're just who they are."

"My mother wasn't like that," I said.

"Like what?" Anna Page said. "Do you want him to be some—"

"He's not *anything,* Anna Page," I said. "The fact that you want to screw him the way you want to screw every man you meet doesn't make him anything to Mom!"

I turned my back to the shock in Anna Page's face—shock overlaid with a patina of hurt. I rooted in the chest for matches, stirring the guilt of her hurt into a pot of my own, letting it all stew together without apology. It wasn't her fault that Mom had this other life here, that there was this man who knew her so well, whom I knew not at all. It wasn't her fault that her mother never published "The Tale of Gabby Goose" or any of the other stories Mom had written for Sammy and me, or that she was so hot for this Beatrix Potter book Mom had been working on, which had nothing to do with us. Even at the funeral, Aunt Kath was talking about that miserable Potter book, asking if Mom ever talked to me about what she'd written.

Julie said, "Shit, Ape, can't you ever let things

go?" She thrust the coal tongs out, and when Anna Page put her hand up to block them, Julia thrust the scalloped, coal-dirty ends closer to her face, backing her up against the slipper tub until Anna Page called out, "Uncle! Aunt! Grandmother! Second cousin thrice removed!"

A smile tickled Julie's lips, and her eyes edged toward crescents, but she didn't relent with the tongs.

"Don't," Anna Page insisted.

Julie edged the tongs right to Anna Page's nose, leaving her no choice but to grab the scalloped ends with her bare hands, nicely blackening her fingers.

"Don't!" she repeated emphatically. "Really, Jamie, don't!"

Julie blinked, holding the tongs tightly, her gray eyes filling with the same pain we'd seen so much of this first year without Jamie. In the silence, I remembered Anna Page, not long after Jamie died, saying to me, "Julie's death would have left so much less devastation. Not even a husband now that she and Noah have split, not a best friend that I know of, unless it was Jamie, who was my best friend even if she was her sister's, too." We were all in the raw-loss stage of grief back then; she hadn't meant what she'd said. I'd swallowed the hurt, thinking, *If Julie has a best friend, it's me; if I have a best friend, it's Jules.*

Anna Page eased the tongs from Julie's hands

lest she drop them, saying, "I'm sorry, I'm so sorry, Julie. It's just . . ."

It was just that Jamie had died a year ago. First Jamie, then Dad, then Mom, all in a single brutal year.

I joined them by the cold cast-iron fireplace, and I handed Anna Page the matches. She took one, and lit it, and set it to the paper, held it there until the paper caught. We stood together, the three of us watching as the flame crept toward the white block of fire starter, which caught and flared up into a surge of petroleum warmth.

8

I remember I used to half believe and wholly play with fairies when I was a child. What heaven can be more real than to retain the spirit-world of childhood, tempered and balanced by knowledge and common-sense.
——Beatrix Potter, in a November 17, 1896, journal entry

I DON'T KNOW IF I THOUGHT OF MYSELF AS different from other children before I started school. I was always the youngest of the Wednesday Children until my brother, Sam, was born, there was that; but if they'd ever been uncomfortable with my mixed heritage, they'd adjusted by the time I might have realized. If they said anything at all about my appearance, it was to tell me I was beautiful: Aunt Kath and Aunt Frankie especially. Aunt Linda was always scolding them, saying they should praise my genius rather than my beauty, although how a four-year-old is supposed to be a genius unless she's Mozart, I'm not sure. The first time I remember feeling different was at my little Palo Alto grammar school, which nowadays has lots of Asian kids, although fewer mixed-race kids than you might think. It had been Anna Page's school, and Julie's and Jamie's, and Maggie's and Lacy's and Sarah's and all the Wednesday Sons' as well. I'd watched them go off every year without me, and when my turn for kindergarten came, I'd picked my favorite outfit to wear, the butter-yellow flowered gingham jumper in the photo on Mom's night table, and armed myself with the Snow White lunch box that I didn't need.

I had recess at a different time than the bigger kids, and I didn't know anyone on the swings or the monkey bars, playing tag out on the field or on the foursquare courts. I knew how to play hopscotch—Anna Page had taught me, and her sister, Lacy, told me I could just line up for a turn—so I stood behind a girl with a long blond braid that reminded me of Julie and Jamie, and made me feel less alone.

The girl who'd been on the hopscotch court finished and hurried around to line up again. "Hey," she said. "I go behind Meg!"

The girl with the braid turned and peered at me with an odd expression in her gray eyes, not unlike Julie and Jamie's eyes. "What are you?" she asked.

At first I thought she must be talking to the other girl, and even after I understood the question was for me, I didn't understand it. Did they play hopscotch differently at school? Did you have to pretend you were a cat or a dog, or be on one team or another, or pretend you were a fairy princess, like on Halloween?

"I'm Hope," I said.

"But what *are* you?" she demanded.

By then, the other girls in the hopscotch line were watching us.

"I'm in Mrs. Kennedy's class?" I said uncertainly.

"I had Mrs. Kennedy last year," another girl said. "She's nice."

"But I mean, what are you?" the girl with the braid repeated. "Where are you from?"

I knew this one. My address! I'd practiced my address and phone number; if I ever got lost, I was to tell a policeman I was Hope Tantry and give them my address and phone number, and they would help me get home.

"I'm Hope Tantry, and I live at 1180 Channing in Palo Alto, California," I said. I was going to do my phone number, too, but with all those girls staring at me, I couldn't remember it.

"Where before that?" the girl insisted.

"She's black, Meg," the girl behind me said.

I said, "I am?"

"No, she's not," Meg said.

One of the teachers came over to see what was going on. Not Mrs. Kennedy but someone else who said, "Girls, this is Hope Tantry. She's Indian."

I was going to say "I am?" again, but then I remembered Ama, who lived in India. And before I could say anything, the girl with the blond braid—Meg—was popping her hand back and forth on her lips and making a warpath sound. She started prancing around me, her braid stretching up and down her back as she bobbed her warpath head, the other girls joining her even as the teacher insisted, "Girls! Girls!" This was years before Disney made any kind of Indian girl a hero, or made us anything at all.

It's such a small thing when you have it: a sense of belonging. You don't realize it's there until it's gone.

By the time I went off to Smith—a school I chose not only for its academics but also because a women-only college would save me the humiliation of being a wallflower even in classrooms—I'd been asked so many times "What are you?" and "Where are you from?" by people who expected to hear "Mumbai" or "Delhi" that I'd developed a push-button response: "I was born at Stanford Hospital in Palo Alto, California, where I grew up. My dad is from India, but he came to the University of Michigan for law school in the 1960s and has lived here ever since. My mom is a Caucasian who grew up in Maryland. They're both American. And so am I."

Sometimes I want to answer those questions with another question: How much time do you have? Sometimes I want to say, *My race doesn't tell anything more about me than yours does about you.* Sometimes I want to say, *Oh, I just check all the boxes so I'm sure I get it right.* But once you lose patience for the questions, you lose patience for the answers. I went through a period in college answering, "I'm a border rat. What the fuck are you?" It always shocked people to hear the F-word coming out of "such a sweet little mouth" even at Smith, but they never did ask anything more.

You don't make friends that way, though, so I learned eventually to stick to the script. It's the details that convince people, or at least keep them from asking more. If I said my dad was Indian, for example, people might see me as growing up on some Cherokee reservation with fancy casinos and crummy schools. I say "from India" so they can at least conjure up the proper stereotype: crowded slums and saris, henna-painted skin.

The funny thing is, I don't exactly feel Indian even if I do look it, even if I've felt pulled in that direction. Not by my dad so much as by my Ama. She's dead now, and I didn't ever see her often, but I wrote to her in India at least once a week all my childhood, and you can say things in a letter that it's hard to say aloud. Ama had expectations for me as well, though—ones that were as hard to get my head around: that I should wear a sari and garlands and circle a holy fire seven times at my Minnesota wedding; that Julie, my maid of honor, should carry around a tree for Kevin and me; that Sammy, like all good brothers, should have taken us to visit Ama the day after our wedding rather than driving us to the airport for our honeymoon flight. Dad said I could ignore all of it, that Ama was just being Ama, trying to manipulate me into marrying a nice Indian boy. But I don't know. When Kevin and I had our horoscopes done—"Why not, if your Ama wants us to?" Kevin had said—they matched.

The first time I met Kevin, eighteen months before we married, he didn't seem fazed by my mixed race. I was at a tailgate party at Anna Page's insistence. Never mind that I hadn't gone to Stanford and didn't care for football, never mind that I'd begun to think of myself as a professional woman who, like her, didn't want to marry; I still found it hard to defy her. She said

Kevin didn't seem all that great on paper but he was the nicest, most charming guy she'd met since Isaac, and he was funny. He taught fifth grade—she'd met him when he brought a class on a field trip—and he reminded her of my dad. No, not Indian. Red hair and freckles. His kids called him "General Opie," although they were far too young to have seen *The Andy Griffith Show*. "You can't *not* fall for a guy who is that wonderful with kids," she said.

By the time the others began unpocketing game tickets, Kevin had me laughing so hard that I had the hiccups. He suggested a ride on his bicycle handlebars might scare them out of me. It was starting to rain, a few drops that maybe would continue or maybe wouldn't, but he smiled his Opie smile and said, "I don't mind a little rain. Do you?" He buckled his helmet under my chin, made a tiny paper airplane of his game ticket, and serenaded me with "Raindrops keep falling on my head" as we wobbled off.

While we biked through the Stanford math and science buildings, he taught me silly lyrics about geometry to the tune of the song "867-5309/ Jenny," substituting 3.14159, the numbers that started pi. We circled Lake Lagunita, no lake at all that time of year, and cut through the New Guinea sculpture garden, the setting of the first short story he'd ever published. "On Friday nights when the artists were creating the sculptures, they played native reed pipes and did face and bark painting," he said. "It was spooky-amazing. The story wrote itself." He'd published only two stories in small literary magazines even he hadn't heard of before he started looking for places to submit his work, but he called his writing "my work." The work he did to support himself—what anyone else would call his work—was teaching, but he was so easy about it all, as if the writing was the accomplishment, as if the publishing was a different, less important thing.

I told him my mother had written for decades and hadn't published a word. I didn't say anything about writing myself. I'd stopped writing altogether not long after I started practicing law.

"Rodin took twenty years to finish *Gates of Hell*—not that I'm comparing my genius to his," he said a little later as we wandered on foot through the statues in the Rodin sculpture garden, all those hard, dark bronze surfaces shaped into heartbreak, dampened in the light rain. He reached out and touched my hair then, for the first time, I would have told you, but he later confessed that as we'd biked, he'd leaned forward into the wildness of my windblown hair below his bike helmet on my head, basking in the brush of it against his cheeks, and eyes, and lips. "My favorite Rodin is *The Kiss*," he said, moving his hand to my hip like the male lover in the statue, "although the figures don't actually kiss. Their kiss is interrupted. Their lips don't touch." He smiled and leaned forward as if to kiss me, but he didn't. Teasing me. I leaned forward and kissed him. He tasted faintly of the coffee we'd had at the tailgate party, with Anna Page.

He took me to Palo Alto Bicycles that afternoon, where he proceeded to question every detail of every derailleur and brake, while my main concern was whether each bike came in red. He chose reflectors and lights, then asked the clerk how much it all came to. As I pulled out my credit card, saying under my breath from habit, " 'What is seven pounds of butter at 1/3, and a stick of sealing wax and four matches?' "—how many times had Mom and I quoted that Beatrix Potter line as we paid for groceries and clothes and books?—he pushed aside my card and handed the clerk his.

" 'Now the meaning of "credit" is this,' " he said. " 'When a customer buys a bar of soap, instead of paying for it, she says she will pay another time.' " He bowed low, the way Pickles does in *The Tale of Ginger and Pickles*. "Fifth-grade economics. The kids are skeptical about reading something they think of as a baby book, but . . ."

"The policeman with bead eyes and his helmet sewed on with stiches—'Bite him, Pickles! He's only a German doll!' " I said, resisting the urge to correct his inexact quote from the book.

"God, how they laugh!"

"But you can't go buying bicycles for women you've only just met," I protested.

He smiled his strawberry-blond smile and said, "You have no idea of the things I can do."

"I'm quite sure my mother would disapprove of me accepting a bicycle from a boy I hardly know," I insisted.

"I'm a *boy* now, am I?" he replied.

It wasn't until we'd been dating for months that I worked up the nerve to ask if he'd slept with Anna Page. "You don't want me to be the kind of 'boy' who kisses and tells, now, do you?" he teased, which made me laugh and left me wondering enough to put the question to Anna Page. "What else am I to do with my castoffs but throw them to friends?" she answered in a tone that left me thinking she was joking but not entirely sure and no longer wanting to know. It was ridiculous. I hadn't wondered if she'd slept with Isaac before she'd introduced him to Jamie. Even if she had, it wouldn't have meant anything; Anna Page never did seem to mean anything when it came to men. And by then, Kevin and I were deep into a whirlwind romance, already headed for that Minnesota altar even if we hadn't admitted it to each other yet.

That had been my choice, the Minnesota wedding, with only the Wednesday Gang and our families, and a few of his family's friends in Kevin's tiny hometown, where if you weren't a blond or a redhead, you were from someplace else. That was what Kevin's father had said the first time I met his parents, as his mom was getting over the shock of having a daughter-in-law-to-be who was half Indian.

I know a lot more about being mixed now. I know that when I was born, the U.S. census didn't allow for the possibility of me. Neither Dad nor I fell into any of the recognized racial groups. We were both "other," he Indian and me a half. In earlier census years, some category of mixed race was recognized. You could be all black, or you could be mulatto, or for a brief period, you could be a quadroon (one fourth black), or an octoroon (one eighth). I might have been considered mulatto. My children, if I ever had children with Kevin, might have been quadroons. The first time there was even an identifiable place for us on the census was in the year 2000, when I was nearly thirty. For the first thirty years of my life, whatever I was hadn't been worth bothering to list.

9

8.11.2009, Ambleside. We were stomping around Wray Castle again today, walking along the lake, when it began to pour, and a man took pity on us and asked us in for tea. Now he's invited me to dinner, and I've accepted. What a silly old fool I am.

Well, if I can't admit this in my journal, then what good is a journal? Today was the third time we took the launch to Wray Castle and walked the path along the lake, past the stone entry posts with the bold "No Motor Vehicles Beyond This Point" sign, the fine print of which allows "except for Ainsley's End." The house rather looms as you approach it, but I linger on the public bridleway below it, as if I half expect to see my mother's face in the high tower window—never mind that she's been dead for decades.

Today we worked up the nerve to mount the stone steps and duck into the portico on the excuse of the rain. That set off a frightening dog inside, bringing the dog's only slightly less frightening owner to the door. He insisted on making tea, and we sat in a room with inviting pink couches and green chairs, a warm fireplace, the rain safely beyond the hexagonal leaded glass. There was the most delightful cabinet there, with a hidden desk that pulls out where the center drawer ought to be——a desk, he told me, where Bea is believed to have written some of her books. Bea raised an eyebrow at this, but I ignored her and told him anyone might write anything at such a charming desk.

He asked me if I wrote, and with the question, something soft showed in him, or the suggestion there might be something soft underneath his proper British façade. He seemed almost to hope I did write, and yet I couldn't somehow tell him I wrote children's books, so I told him what I tell everyone, that I mean to write something about Bea.

——I have a New York publisher who's interested in it, I told him.

It isn't exactly untrue; Kath thinks her house might publish it if it offers "some fresh angle on Potter." I don't know why I didn't just tell him I'm trying to find out about my mother——to say straight out that I believe my mother may once have been engaged to someone who lived in his house. But he's even younger than I am; he started Oxford after I left Michigan. He wouldn't have been born when Father brought my British war-bride mother to the States. And he's Graham Wyndham V, which makes the Martin on the marriage license an uncle at best. He'd think me an absolute fool to imagine he might know anything about a woman his uncle didn't marry years before he was born.

——You might have asked him about your mother

at the start, Allison, Bea says. For all you know, he might have old man Wyndham locked in his tower.

Heavens to Betsy, you could imagine Graham being a lock-them-in-the-tower type, couldn't you? Although one imagines the person locked up there would be some woman. What is it about handsome men that makes them seem so untrustworthy? Or is that just me?

10

It is very odd to see an owl with hands, but how could he play on the guitar without them?
——Beatrix Potter, in a March 6, 1897, letter to her cousin Molly Gaddum

THE LIGHT WAS REDDENING, THE QUIET OF THE evening coming up as Anna Page set off toward the woods that second evening, alone. She did remember Graham's lecture about weather and maps and emergency kits, but the sky was clear, and she needed a moment to herself. She wouldn't get lost walking along the dry stone wall. "Dry" because the stone was stacked without any binding. "Some are old, but most date only from the enclosure movement starting after the medieval period," Graham had said, as if that weren't old.

Old is relative, she thought as she passed

through the break in the wall she'd missed earlier, the path to Graham's estate. She stuck a hand in her pocket and wrapped her fingers around the puzzle box she'd nicked from his silver collection. *Old is relative.* She was decades older than her daddy had been when he'd introduced her to the other Kath, who had seemed so old.

She must have been eleven or twelve then—that Saturday they'd stopped at the hospital to check on his patients on their way to the Stanford-Cal football game, just Anna Page and her daddy. Except they bumped into another doctor on the way out of the hospital—Dr. Johnson, her father said, but he called her Catherine. Then Anna Page's father was telling Catherine she should sit with them, they had four tickets and were only using two. It hadn't struck Anna Page as odd that they had four tickets—her sister and brother usually got to come to the games—but she did have some inkling that something wasn't right. Perhaps she had some idea, too, that her father wasn't living at home by then, that despite his sitting with them at the dinner table as often as any busy heart surgeon might, and reading the newspaper every Sunday morning at the breakfast table, he had not slept in her mother's bed for over a year.

When Catherine said she bet Anna Page would be an even better surgeon than her daddy when she grew up, Anna Page insisted she meant to be a stewardess so she could go everywhere. Catherine smiled indulgently. "You're not going to spend your life pouring Scotch for old fools like your father, now, are you?" she said. "If you want to go wherever *you* want to go, Anna Page, you go to medical school."

Anna Page looked right at Catherine the way she always has been able to look right at a person. "You best be like the old lady who fell off the wagon," she said in her best imitation of her mother's accent, which she could deliver even then, " 'cause you don't know a dang thing about my daddy or me."

"Anna Page! You apologize to Dr. Johnson right this minute," her father said. Then to Catherine— to the other Kath—"I don't know what's gotten into her."

Catherine touched his arm and said, "She's fine. She's lovely, Lee." She laughed and said, "She's just like you."

Anna Page's daddy turned to watch the kickoff, and Anna Page never did apologize. To this day, she can't say what bothered her more: that her daddy had insisted she do so, or that when Catherine waved him off, he let it go.

"Next time," her daddy said, "I'm going to bring Little Lee and Lacy and leave you two behind. Lordy, you'll be conspiring together against me before I know it, my two sassy girls." Leaving Anna Page wanting to say, *She's not your girl,*

Daddy. I'm your only girl. That was what her daddy used to call her before her sister was born: his only girl. She couldn't do anything about her sister except eventually stop speaking to her (although it was Lacy who'd stopped speaking to Anna Page, and Lacy can start an argument in an empty house). But on that afternoon when she met this Dr. Johnson who would turn out to be the other Kath, she was not about to conspire with her, or even be polite. "I'm going to be a stewardess," she insisted, "and go anywhere I want."

Now her office is like her father's but more chaotic: dog-eared and torn medical journals crowd the bookshelves and desk, the visitors' chairs, spilling onto the floor as she makes room for people to sit. It's part of her armor against the many times she was assumed to be a nurse, or squeamish, or lacking in dedication. She was asked once during an interview for a pediatric transplant fellowship how she would operate when she was pregnant, and although she meant to remain childless, she answered, "My reach to the operating table will still be shorter than yours must be to accommodate that gut, sir." Anna Page's armor doesn't always protect her, but she never does take it off.

"I love surgery for the same reason I loved to row in college, for the excuse to avoid the dreaded early-morning trifecta of coffee, croissants, and conversation," she likes to say to the Wednesday

Daughters, if not to our moms. She does engage in the morning—it's hard to imagine a more intense engagement than having someone's heart literally in your hands. But it's always someone else's heart she's holding, someone else she means to save.

You can't say that to Anna Page, though. It only gets you a tirade about how half of all marriages end in expensive legal fees and devastated children, in women who give up their dreams for the sake of families only to realize their hands are empty, all the hearts they've been tending are racing away. Or it gets you a lecture on how exciting it is to hold an actual heart in your hands, to feel it firm and soft at the same time. "Even Catherine says I'm as good as Daddy technically, and better in other ways," she will tell you if you give her the opening to brag. Which is, I suppose, how Anna Page ended up being a heart surgeon. For all the protesting she did as a girl about meaning to be something else, for the number of majors she went through on her way to chemistry, she always was good at the sciences, and good with people as well. That's the best part of her, the Anna Page behind the façade of not appearing to care who secretly weeps alone at home after her long days in the OR, even when her patients have survived.

Or maybe that's not it at all. Maybe Anna Page is more like me than I imagine. Her favorite place always has been right at her daddy's side despite the fact that she doesn't always know it, or admit it, or want it to be. And Uncle Lee is proud of Anna Page, never mind that he doesn't tell her he is. It's a complicated thing for a man like him to see anyone surpass him at the only thing he's ever really loved. It's complicated, too, for a daughter like Anna Page, who thinks being good at something and loving it are the same thing, who has seen how bad her father is at loving and how good he is at surgery, and decided that's a better choice than being like her mother: steadfast at loving but with nobody's heart left to hold.

That night in the Claife Heights woods, Anna Page, pausing to consider the way she ought to go, stared up at a fat old tree, one half of its split trunk shooting straight overhead where it might fall of its own weight and block the path, the other angling away, then bending straight upward, the arched wood contorted and unnatural. The light was lower than she'd realized.

She turned to retrace her steps, thinking how old she'd thought Catherine was and yet how young even her parents had been when her daddy took up with the other Kath. Why had her mother spent all those years holding on to something that never was? Was that motherhood? Sacrificing your own happiness for the illusion of a normal home?

The stone wall she'd followed uphill was nowhere in sight, and the path before her forked where she could see it wouldn't have seemed to from the other direction. She'd have had to look back to the left to see the merging path. Or to the right? One of those funny path drains slanted away at her feet beyond the split on one side. She'd stepped over a drain, but was it here? She took the other path, then looked back at the tree with the funny curving split, trying to remember whether this was the angle from which she'd first seen it.

She started paying attention then. The light was fading fast, the air thick with the smell of dead leaves and moss and wood. The quiet of her feet on the soggy leaves and the slippery stone met the occasional scamper of a red squirrel, or a deer, perhaps. Wild boar used to inhabit these woods, Graham had said, but no longer did. Of course, cougars didn't patrol the streets of Palo Alto, and yet one ended up in a tree on Walnut Drive. The poor creature hadn't done a thing to anyone, but he'd been shot dead.

Anna Page came to another fork, both paths leading downhill, which should be toward the lake. She took the wider one, thinking surely the path she'd come up hadn't narrowed as much as the other. When she came to a third fork, both paths heading uphill, she knew she'd taken the wrong turn at the funny tree. And it was getting dark so quickly.

She was making her way on the slippery rock

path, reconsidering this direction, when she heard something. Where her footfalls would have landed, she could just make out a long stretch of what might be wavy gray-red diamond. She backed away slowly, trying to calm the rush of blood through her pulmonary artery, where she might bleed to death in a very few heartbeats were it ever compromised. When she thought she was far enough, she turned to run, only to see a shadow of a figure ahead.

11

From the Journals of Ally Tantry

10.11.2009, Thwaite Howe Inn, Ambleside. **Bea is right! I don't exactly draw at her level, but I can draw. Graham has converted an old greenhouse on his estate into a studio, where Bea says even her old eyes might paint again. She insists she won't, that she only finished as many books as she did because the Warnes needed her to. She hadn't published a book in four years when Harold Warne was caught passing bad money——twenty thousand pounds!——all to save a fishing business which nearly took the publishing house down with it.**

——Poor Fruing was walking with Harold in Covent Garden when the police came right up to them and

arrested Harold, she says. Harold was sentenced to eighteen months of hard labor at Wormwood Scrubs, and Fruing was left to try to save the business, with me as its biggest creditor.

I glance up to see a sail snapping on Lake Windermere, a thing I might draw someday.

——He wanted to save the family reputation, but one can't hold very well to one's reputation with a forger in the family, Bea says. It made me cranky to have to produce books under those conditions, yet I couldn't let the firm go under, I couldn't let that be the legacy of my Mr. Norman Warne's life. I was so very fond, too, of his mother and Millie. But Fruing would have me writing those d ... d little books when I am dead and buried.

——But you are dead and buried, Bea, I remind her.

——I am utterly tired of them, and my eyes are wearing out, she says.

It occurs to me for the first time that even the animal characters in her books don't have idyllic lives. Ginger and Pickles close their store for want of profits. Peter ends up sick and in bed, having narrowly escaped becoming rabbit pie. Poor Jemima never does hatch her eggs.

——Remind me what a "thwaite" is, I say. And a "howe."

——A thwaite, dear Allison, is a clearing——land cleared for planting. And a howe is a valley. Her tone a bit miffed. She does prefer to be the center of attention.

——So this inn at the edge of the lake where there is no valley is named "Clearing in the Valley Inn"?

——Do I look like I am the owner and could change that?

——I thought you owned everything here, Bea.

——Yes, well, don't remind anyone of that, or they will call the whole Lake District "Potter's Corner" simply to attract you tacky Americans.

I do take umbrage at being called tacky.

——You aren't as tacky as most Americans, Bea concedes. And there was that lovely Marian Perry who came to visit me from ... was it Boston? But you do vote.

As a young woman, Bea had presented a scientific paper on her beloved mushrooms that, although dismissed at the time, turned out to be important. She wrote books so she could be financially independent, and became famous in her own right as a result. After she'd made a success with writing, she went on to be the queen of Lake District sheep. And yet there is no convincing her on the value of suffrage. It's such an incongruity. Perhaps defying her family and her rank in society with her writing left her feeling the need to conform in other ways. Perhaps falling in love with men who were considered beneath her left her wanting to give them some authority over her that would save them from feeling inferior.

——Is that why you never wanted to publish your children's books, Allison?

——Is what why I never wanted to publish?

——Because you didn't want Jim to feel inferior.

——Of course not! Whatever gave you that idea? Jim isn't inferior to me.

——Nor was Mr. Heelis to me, Allison. Nor Kevin to your Hope, even though her salary is quadruple his. But the truth and what people think is truth don't always match.

When I stop to think about it, I remember when the Wednesday Sisters first learned Jim was Indian. "But you're such a pretty girl," Kath had said, as if nobody in her right mind would marry a man of color if she had any choice. I remember the first time I took Hope to the park, that nasty woman assuming Hope wasn't my natural child because of her skin color, asking why I hadn't adopted a baby who was white.

——Bea, do you think Hope would be happier if she married someone who was mixed? I ask.

——What do you think, Allison?

——I think Kevin adores her.

——But doesn't Jim adore you? And yet your heart goes all slippy-sloppy when Mr. Wyndham takes your hand to show you that you can draw.

——It wasn't like that, I protest.

——Wasn't it? Then do tell me, what was it like?

The water is utterly still, the quiet disconcerting.

——I don't know, I say.

——But you do, Allison. Look more closely. It isn't adoration that you need, is it? And Hope is very like you.

Later: I'm comfortably settled in bed at this charming inn when Bea says,

——When my mother refused to capitalize my allowance, I used to rant about what a fool she was letting all her money go to the supertax or the death duty when she might allow it to come to me. But I didn't need money. I don't suppose one ever becomes emotionally free of one's parents, does one?

——I don't know, I say.

——My brother might never have told our parents he'd married Mary Scott if I hadn't met Mr. Heelis. It emerged in a burst of frustration when they tried to enlist him to persuade me that marrying a country solicitor was beneath me. I imagine Bertram felt the guilt of not having supported me when I was engaged to Mr. Warne, because he chose that moment to tell them he'd been secretly married for eleven years.

——Eleven years!

——Even then he claimed his wife was a farmer's daughter, which was no great claim in their opinion but was less horrifying than the truth. She was the daughter of a wine merchant!

I listen to the lake lap at the boats and the shore in the darkness beyond the window, thinking of my sister. She moved to California after college because I was there, yet she never broke ties with Mother and Father. Perhaps she'd urged them to reconsider, to see me again, or perhaps she hadn't. If she did, it had no effect.

——I do think the opposition only made Mr. Heelis and me fonder of each other, Bea says. We were married in a quiet little ceremony at St. Mary Abbots——too fancy for us, but at least it was done and we could collect our new bull and go home.

I click on the bedside light, a sadness creeping in at the memory of Jim and me saying our vows in front of a justice of the peace, without a single friend standing by. Why hadn't we included friends?

——Your new bull, Bea? I ask.

——A lovely white bull we collected at the Windermere train station, on our way back with wedding cake for our neighbors up and down the Kendal Road.

——A bull.

——I don't think I ever forgave my mother for denying me the love I wanted. I suppose we share that, you and I.

When I don't respond, she says,

——You ought to have told Graham of your mother's connection to Ainsley's End from the start, Allison. But perhaps at this point you will let it go?

——Let what go, Bea?

——The anger at your mother.

——I'm not angry. How can I be angry at a dead woman?

Bea assures me she's right beside me. I needn't raise my voice.

——Your mother forgave you, I say. My mother never did. Hope and Sammy never knew their grand-mother or their grandfather because my mother never forgave me for marrying Jim.

——But Allison, Bea says, it isn't our mothers who need to do the forgiving.

12

Nutkin made a whirring noise to sound like
the wind, and he took a running jump right
onto the head of Old Brown! . . .
Then all at once there was a flutterment
and a scufflement and a loud "Squeak!" . . .
Nutkin was in his waist-coat pocket! This looks
like the end of the story; but it isn't.
——from **The Tale of Squirrel Nutkin**
by Beatrix Potter

ANNA PAGE WAS IN A BIT OF A CLEARING, THE
fingernail moon a light beam on her, standing
frozen between the long stretch of adder snake
and the shadow up the path. There were no such
things as ghosts, she told herself. It was only
another hiker in the woods, who perhaps knew the
way out. She would walk quietly and carefully in
his direction. He wasn't poisonous.

In the moment of that thought, the snake
slithered behind her, and a beast streaked at her
from ahead, a primitive snarl filling her with the
same terror she saw on the faces of patients
learning their hearts were bad. She turned to flee,
forgetting the snake altogether. It all happened so
quickly, she wasn't thinking about running, she
was turning to run.

Her foot slid on the slates. Both feet came out from under her. She screamed as she hit the hard ground, from the terror, or from the pain of her hip landing on the sharp edges of stone, or from both. The beast continued charging, its monstrous head reaching for her with each stride.

"Bloody hell, what is it!" The deep voice sounding as the beast tore past. "Napoleon!"

"Graham?" Anna Page said. "Oh my God! Graham?"

Napoleon barked terrifyingly, a throaty peel echoing against the hills. The snake was already gone, leaving the awful animal to return to Anna Page. It poked its broad, slobbering snout into her, right up against her heart whacking hard and fast against her sternum as Graham came running, calling out, "Anna Page?"

She tried to remain perfectly still, to avoid the dog's eyes lest he find challenge in her gaze.

Graham clicked on a flashlight to reveal the dog with his snout right in her crotch. "Napoleon, lay away, you bloody mutt," he commanded. There was some lay in Napoleon—he went down on his belly—but there was no away. "Good God, Anna Page," Graham said, "are you hurt?"

He ran a flashlight beam over her, finding a nasty tear in the arm of her jacket and in the shirt beneath it, a raw and painful scrape on her skin. "Hold the torch," he said.

She took it—a weapon against the dog's black mouth, if not much of one.

Graham lifted her arm carefully and bent it, a sensation shooting through her. Pain. Yes, surely it was pain.

"Are you hurt elsewhere?" he asked. Then to Napoleon, "Oh good Lord, Napoleon, lay away!"

The dog's expression in the beam of the flashlight was so pathetic that it made Anna Page laugh with relief, and the dog licked her, a big sloppy tongue on her cheek.

Graham unstrapped the pack from around his waist and pulled out the emergency kit she'd been so quick to make fun of. He extracted a small pair of scissors and cut away the torn edges of jacket and shirt, which were as soaked and dirty from the forest floor as the rest of her was. He unfolded a moist cloth and touched it ever so gently to her arm. "That's going to be a nasty bruise, but I don't think it's broken," he said.

Clearly, he'd forgotten she was the one with the medical degree.

He set aside the cloth and opened first a tube of topical antibiotic, then a package of sterile gauze and tape. Napoleon settled on the ground and plopped his massive head on her thigh. The dog looked up at her as Graham's steady hands dressed her wound, and she set her free hand on his fur—surprisingly soft—thinking of the last heart she'd worked on before she left California, a sixty-year-old African-American woman who'd had a massive heart attack. A widow-maker, it's called, although it ought to be a widower-maker, with more women than men dying from heart disease, more blacks than whites. What had provoked the memory? The dog's massive head? Graham's hands so carefully tending her own wound? As the dog nuzzled her hand, begging action, she replayed the last moments she'd spent with my mother, all the signs she must have missed.

"Do you suppose you'll be okay to stand?" Graham asked after the dressing was in place.

"Well, perhaps I won't stand on my *hands,* but I don't think I need my olecranon to flex my *articulatio genus.*"

He smiled slightly, a glimpse of unstraightened teeth, and still squatting beside her, he offered her a hand. In the gesture, she felt the shame and the bitter loss, the failure all over again.

"Oh, you're hurt there as well," he said, turning her palm that had been on Napoleon's head toward his face. "Right there on the . . . that would be the metacarpus, wouldn't it?" He touched a finger gently to the scrape. "It's the muscles and ligaments we focus on more in the hiking world, but we enjoy sounding clever, too." He brought her palm to his face as if to look closer. For an odd moment, she thought he might kiss it to make it better, the way Jamie was forever kissing whatever part of Oliver he had landed on, the way she supposed her own mother might have kissed her.

Graham lowered her hand. In the reflection of the flashlight beam off his glasses, she couldn't read his expression.

"What on earth are you doing out in the woods by yourself?" he said. "What if you'd gotten lost?"

She turned away before he could see his admonition stinging as surely as a physical slap, before he could see the truth in her face, too, that she'd been horribly lost. Was she not lost? She pushed herself up and brushed the leaves from her slacks, her ears ringing with the remembered pitch of that last patient flatlining, the heart on the heart-lung machine emptied of blood, yielding to her touch where it once beat strong and sure.

"What on earth are *you* doing in the woods by *your*self?" she demanded, anger filling the void left as she tucked the shame deep inside.

Though he looked taken aback, he only set an easy hand on Napoleon's head and blinked at her from behind the wire-rims. "I suppose it's what I do when I'm grieving, isn't it?"

The dog sat unmoving under the weight of his unmoving hand, as if he recognized that Graham needed his steadiness, as if they'd shared this moment before. The two of them reminded her somehow of a photo she'd been sent recently, a transplant recipient pictured with the family of the donor. The donor had been a Teach for America gal killed by a drunken driver, the recipient a thirtysomething game developer who'd wasted some part of his fortune and all of his heart on cocaine, who didn't deserve another heart but was the first match on the list. Months after Anna Page had all but forgotten them, the girl's family sent her a photo: the mother and father, the brother who might have been Anna Page's own brother, the sister who might have been Lacy, with whom Anna Page hadn't spoken in a year. The dead girl's parents stood touching the chest of the man who hadn't deserved their daughter's heart, in whose body it continued to beat. Just the photograph in a plain white envelope, with the name of the surviving sister on the return address. That was all that had come to Anna Page. She was living in Maine, the sister was. That was where the parents lived, where the transplant team had tracked them down to say that their daughter's heart was beating but the rest of her was gone.

Graham reached his hand from Napoleon to move a strand of Anna Page's wild hair from her face, the way her daddy sometimes did.

"I think my mother would like you," she said, the words tumbling out with some force that she knew was too much. "You, too, Napoleon," she said, stooping to the dog's level, taking his face in her hands.

Graham loomed above her, tall and sturdy.

"She's coming up from London next week," she said.

"Up here to the Lakes?"

She rubbed the dog's ears, saying, "She always meant to come, to see Aunt Ally's other life." She stood and peered down the dark path, Napoleon rising with her, rubbing against her leg, unwilling to let all that affection go. "Yes, I do think Ma would like you," she repeated, "and I think you would adore Ma. Everyone does."

He turned away, snapping at Napoleon, "Oh, good Lord, mutt, go chase your bloody snake."

The dog moved to him, nudging his hand to pet him. "Good Lord, mutt," Graham repeated, but he set a hand on the dog's head, let it rest there. "I might open a room for your mum at Ainsley's End, if that would do," he offered.

Anna Page fingered her bandaged arm, thinking there was no place to put her mother in the cottage, but uneasy with the idea of her staying at Ainsley's End.

"That would be nice," she said finally. "Hope will be relieved not to be crammed into the cottage with her mother's ashes and her anger at Ma." She stuck her hands in her pocket, her fingers meeting the tiny silver box. Napoleon made a hrmmmping sound, as if it were her presenting her mother in a bad light rather than the loss of attention that disappointed him.

"Well," she said. "I should get back."

She was relieved when Graham suggested he accompany her.

"Mind, step in the torch beam," he said. "And do let Napoleon lead, so he won't trip us up."

13

I do not often consider the stars, they give me a tissick. It is enough that there should be forty thousand named and classified funguses.
——**Beatrix Potter, in an April 1896 journal entry**

HOURS LATER, ANNA PAGE GOT JULIE TO WALK down to the pier on the excuse of needing to check in at the hospital. As they stood outside the cottage door fastening the lock, she whispered, "Did you ever cheat on Noah, Jules?"

Julie's expression startled Anna Page: the slightly raised brows over clear eyes so like the expression with which Jamie had greeted each pronouncement that Anna Page had a new guy.

"I'll take that as a no," Anna Page managed.

"It's over, Anna Page. It's done. You can't convince me to get back together with my husband. If my mother put you up to this, you're welcome to tell her I said forget it. I'm not going back to Noah. I want to go forward."

Anna Page nodded as if this were exactly what

she'd expected Julie to say. "Why don't you, then, Jules?"

"Why don't I *what?*"

"Go forward."

"You—I *am* going forward, Ape. The damned papers are filed. I'm supposed to . . . what? Go out in the middle of the night to screw total strangers in dirty boats, like you do?"

Anna Page looked ahead toward the dilapidated boathouse sitting sadly at the water's edge. "I thought *you* might screw him," she said, the word awkward in her mouth. It was Julie's word; Anna Page was just serving it back to her. It was, she remembered, the word that I'd used.

"You thought *what?*"

"I thought a good screw"—again trying not to stumble over the word—"might do you some good."

"Hell, Anna Page, if you think I need *you* to find me lovers—"

Anna Page held her breath, but if Robbie was there, Julie hadn't spotted him.

"Why don't *you, Anna Page?*" Julie demanded.

"Why don't I what?"

"Move forward."

Anna Page didn't know exactly what Julie was asking, except that it had more to do with Jamie than it did with men or sex. "Do you think Ma would find Graham attractive?" she asked.

Julie's bark of disbelief rang brittle. "You want

to do an Anna Page Woodhouse on your own mother? No. No, I cannot in a million years see your mother with Graham. Can you?"

But Anna Page thought it would serve her daddy right to have her mother fall in love with someone else. "Isn't it funny what our moms didn't tell each other sometimes, even as close as they were?" she said. "Like your mom. Can you imagine one of us not telling the other we'd been diagnosed with cancer?"

Julie could imagine not telling us all sorts of things. It was surprising what you could hide even from people who'd known you forever, or thought they did. If people didn't expect a thing, they wouldn't see it even when it was right in front of them.

Oliver's soccer game, that's where it started. Not the lies, but the rest. On a day when Jamie was having a dreadful morning but she'd promised Oliver she would go to his game. It was just a soccer game, and Oliver would be running around the field; he wouldn't know it was Julie rather than his mom. It might easily have been Jamie's idea, that's what Julie said when she first told me this story. Julie had come to bring her sister groceries, and Jamie said she simply couldn't do it that morning, that Oliver had been so disappointed when Isaac had taken him to the game alone.

"I'll take your hat," Julie had said. That's what

she told me. She'd wear Jamie's hat and sunglasses. She'd drive Jamie's car. And maybe Jamie had agreed or maybe she hadn't. She hadn't disagreed. So after she was comfortable again, after she was sleeping, Julie changed into Jamie's jeans, took Jamie's hat and her sunglasses, her car. Not the wig, though. The wig was styled like Julie's own hair, made from what she'd had cut off after Jamie's fell out.

When Julie arrived beside Isaac at the field, it was already the second half of the game, and Oliver was running toward the goal with the ball, his father cheering. Isaac didn't notice Julie until Oliver was at the goal, as they were both jumping in excitement. "Hey!" he said, and he put his arm around Julie as Oliver's little foot whacked the ball.

"Yaaaaay!" Isaac called out. "Yay, Oliver!"

He kissed Julie then, a big smacker on the lips, a fun kiss rather than a serious one, but still, it stunned her.

"Oh!" he said. "Oh my God. I'm . . . Shit, Julie. I'm sorry. I thought you were Jamie."

Oliver raised his boy fists in victory and, searching the sidelines for his father, saw Julie. "Mommy!" he called out. "I made a goal!"

Isaac looked stricken. Julie felt stricken. But she put her hand around Isaac's waist and waved, and Oliver ran off happily to the far sideline for a cup of Gatorade.

Julie slipped away before the game ended, before Oliver could run over to them. She returned to Jamie and Isaac's house, changed back into herself, and told Jamie about her son making a goal. That's what she told me, that she shared the details with her sister, as if Jamie had been there. But not the kiss. Not that brief moment of Isaac's lips on hers before he realized she wasn't Jamie. Not the putting her arm around Isaac and waving to Oliver, imagining he belonged to her.

For the sake of normalcy that Christmas, a month after Jamie died, Isaac asked Julie if she would help him host the annual Christmas Tree Lane gathering at his house, where Jamie had hosted it for a decade. It was a few weeks after her funeral, and Isaac and Oliver were home from Thanksgiving with Isaac's family on the East Coast. The rest of us could bring cookies and goodies, and we could make hot chocolate, like we always did. We would walk the two-block stretch of Fulton south of Embarcadero that, each holiday season, becomes an extravaganza of lights and trees and displays: the requisite manger and child, and Santa and Mrs. Claus kissing, but also—because this is Palo Alto, where a bit of everything thrives—multicultural "Peace and Joy" holiday dancers and enormous and endangered polar bears sitting on drums. My favorite is a very realistic dummy hanging from a gutter, with his ladder fallen back against a nearby tree as if it slipped from under him, the lights he was trying to hang when he lost his balance dangling down the front of the house.

When Julie arrived early, as promised, to help Isaac set up, Oliver was napping, having managed to stay awake after school just long enough to cut out and decorate the sugar-cookie dough he and his daddy had made the night before. He'd spent so much time on a single cookie that Isaac finally asked if he didn't want to decorate another, but Oliver had looked up at him with gray eyes that were Jamie's eyes, her straight, serious brows, and said, "This is the way Mommy likes cookies." It was an angel with red sprinkles in the middle and tiny silver sugar balls carefully spaced around the edge.

The minute the cookies went into the oven, Oliver lay down on the floor and stuck his thumb in his mouth—something he hadn't done in a year, until his mother got sick—and fell into an exhausted sleep. Isaac, almost as exhausted, carried him to his bed and sat stroking his soft hair. By the time he smelled the cookies burning, it was too late.

He set the tray on the kitchen counter and lay down on the couch. He couldn't much sleep in those first weeks after Jamie died, so when Julie arrived, he was lying there staring up at a crack in the smooth, flat ceiling that Jamie had managed to create out of developer cottage cheese.

"You don't happen to have an angel with red in the middle and those sugar balls around the edges, do you?" he asked her.

Julie uncovered a whole tray of beautifully decorated stars and angels, unburnt. She'd woken early to make them, before her shift at the library.

She went into her dead sister's kitchen and opened her dead sister's refrigerator, extracted the gallon of milk, and poured it into her dead sister's pan. The burnt cookies were still on the cookie sheet, sitting on hot pads on the center island. It was the first time she'd been in her sister's house since Jamie died.

Isaac went to wake Oliver, calling, "Guess who's here, Owl," leaving Julie alone with Jamie's toast crumbs in the toaster, her stained dish towels, the dust collected in her refrigerator grate when she was alive. It was worse than the funeral, her sister's absence more intimate here where she ought to have been. There were only ten cookbooks on the shelf; it didn't take Julie a minute to alphabetize them.

Isaac returned with a half-asleep Oliver in his arms. He set his son down in the kitchen and turned him to see his Aunt Julie standing at the stove, pouring chocolate syrup into the warm milk. There was nothing to the boy. He was so thin. They were both so thin. Cookies and hot chocolate would do them good.

Oliver's face lit up, and he ran and leaped into Julie's arms, shouting, "Mommy!"

As she caught him, her elbow knocked the cookie pan, which clanged to the floor, the burnt cookies crumbling to pieces at her feet and on the countertop, on the stove, in the sink.

"Where have you *been,* Mommy?" Oliver demanded, his little head still buried in Julie's shoulder.

The milk in the pan boiled over then, and the doorbell rang. It was the beginning of a very long night that never did see any Christmas lights or decorations, any dummy man hanging from a decorated-house gutter, trying not to fall.

Julie was out on Lake Windermere with Robbie, remembering that afternoon at the soccer game and the hours she'd spent in the library afterward, searching the triple 0s—Generality, Knowledge, the Book—unable to find a single misshelved volume. Remembering those Christmas cookies crunching under her shoes, the smell of burning milk, and Oliver realizing she was not his mother, the poor kid throwing the good cookies onto the floor with the burnt ones, sobbing, "I hate you I hate you I hate you."

I hate you I hate you I hate you. Which of course he did. Of course he should, even if he didn't understand why.

She blinked up at the starry-bright sky above the

boat and the water and Robbie lying back on one planky thing as she lay on another, their heads propped up against one side of the boat and their knees bent so their feet rested on the other. They weren't touching or even talking. They were staring up at the stars, the two of them floating in the darkness in the middle of the lake.

Anna Page had whispered, "Rowers do it with long, hard strokes," as she'd urged Julie toward the pier, "or that's what their T-shirts say— although to be honest, I've found they often leave whatever 'it' they have out on the water. But you never know, Jules. And I think this guy is for you."

This guy is for you. That's what Anna Page had said when she introduced Isaac to Jamie, after showing Isaac a photo of Jamie that had turned out to be a photo of Julie. They used to joke about it when Jamie was alive. They used to joke that Isaac had married the wrong twin.

Robbie said, "That constellation there, see the—"

"I'm seeing someone, actually," Julie interrupted. "I'm involved with . . . with someone at home."

He hadn't said anything romantic; she had no reason to explain herself, no reason but the soft water and the soft night, the soft curve of Robbie's body, his head turning toward her lying there and staring upward, feeling awkward and foolish but glad to have it out there, to have this little Anna

Page–concocted romance brought to its natural end.

"More's the pity for me." His tone more playful than disappointed. Then, "See the stars up there that form a sort of sprawling W? That's Cassiopeia, the queen."

Turned to stone when she looked at the Gorgon's head, Julie remembered. But since her daughter was to marry a son of Zeus, the gods took pity and hung her as a constellation.

"She's hanging upside down, suffering," Robbie said. "You fancy lasses always do scald your lips on the porridge."

She couldn't see that well in the darkness, but the grin was obvious in his voice.

"How do you see them, the formations?" she asked. "They just look like random stars."

"Do they now?" He pointed, saying, "Start with that shiny one there. That's Segin, where the queen's robe touches her calf. She's the far left star of the W. And that's Ruchbah, her knee. Shedir, her breast."

"What about that one? The other end of the W?"

"That's Caph, or palm."

"Her hand."

"Ah, but it's part of her chair, idn' it? The whole of Cassiopeia was described in pre-Islamic Arabic as *al-kaff*, 'the stained hand.' "

"Pre-Islamic Arabic?"

"A hand painted with henna. I haven't a baldy

how it came to mean the one star, Beta Cassiopeia alone."

"What else is out here?"

"That one, then that and that." He pointed to a series of stars. "That's Andromeda, the daughter of that boastful but nonetheless beautiful Cassiopeia and her poor sap of a husband, Cepheus."

"Andromeda who was chained to a rock as a sacrifice to Cetus."

"The sea monster," he agreed.

"She was saved by Perseus, who dispatched the sea monster by driving his sword into his throat, then turned Andromeda's suitor and his men to stone by using Medusa's head."

"Bit messy in your toolbox, a severed head," Robbie said, and he laughed that way he did, and she did, too. "You know quite a lot about the stars for a lady who doesn't know the sky," he said.

"You know a lot about pre-Islamic Arabic for a man who spends his days on the lake."

In the silence, the only sound was the soft lap of water against the wood of the boat.

"*D'Aulaires' Book of Greek Myths*," she said finally. "A library staple."

"You know all the books in your library that well, now, do you?"

She inhaled deeply, the fresh scent of the lake and the memory of the smooth pages in her fingers. "For Halloween one year I was Hermes, with wings taped to my shoes," she said. "One year I was Zeus, with a tinfoil thunderbolt. I wanted to be Athena, but my mom couldn't figure out a costume for her, so I was Artemis with bow and arrows instead."

He reached over and touched her hair, saying, "And surely you'd have been Aphrodite, now. All you'd have needed was a crown and a cushion of foam."

She could see that page in the book: the West Wind as a human figure blowing in on the pearly white of dawn at the horizon, the three graces and their golden chariot drawn by four doves. Aphrodite, the beautiful goddess of love. The year she'd asked to be Aphrodite, she'd somehow ended up as Ares, the god of war, who was tall and handsome but vain. Ares with gleaming tinfoil helmet and sword, rushing into battle, not caring who won or lost as long as plenty of blood was spilled. That year, Jamie had been Hephaestus, Ares's brother, who was as kind as Ares was cruel. Hephaestus went with Ares, and Jamie never did need to separate herself from their sameness the way Julie did.

"No, I never wanted to be Aphrodite," she said to Robbie, the lie coming easily to her lips.

14

11.11.2009, Ambleside. We spent the morning in the studio, Graham painting and me writing as if we'd done it together all our lives. Afterward, we set off to Moss Eccles Tarn, where I sat on the rock outcropping imagining Bea and Mr. Heelis rowing, with a fishing line in the water and the two of them occasionally kissing companionably rather than passionately, the way Jim and I seem to kiss these days.

——I'm having quite a time understanding Bea's relationships with Heelis and Warne, I told Graham. How did Heelis live in the shadow of Warne all those years?

——Allison! Bea protested.

——But really, Bea, I'm not talking about your fame now. I'm talking about how you kept Mr. Warne's umbrella at Hill Top Farm for the rest of your life.

I told Graham,

——Even after Bea married William Heelis, she wore Norman Warne's ring. She writes in her journal about it slipping off her cold finger once while she and the hired men were lifting the bundled corn.

She'd untied the threshing floor and ruined her woolen stockings, crawling on her hands and knees in the dirt. She wrote that she should have had just one consolation if she hadn't found it: "It was a pretty, sheltered field to lie in."

——But she did love Heelis, Graham said.

——Of course I did, Bea said.

——I don't know, I said. Perhaps he was just . . . convenient?

——Allison! Bea protested.

Convenient. Well, for all the things Jim has been to me, he wasn't that.

——You can't love someone who has doubts and not see them there on some level, I said to Graham. Even if you choose not to see.

I want to tell poor Kevin that Hope does love him, that it's just hard to know if you'll love someone forever when you don't even know yourself. I can't say that to him, though. Saying it would leave Kevin knowing my daughter means to leave him, or thinks she does. And I can't let Hope say it, even to me. I know from watching Kath that a marriage can be over long before anyone admits it, but I also know that once you start saying aloud that a marriage might be over, it almost always is.

I tossed a pebble into the tarn, and Graham and I watched its sad plink radiate out into perfectly concentric circles. Concentric circles——the term made me miss Brett. It made me miss all the Wednesday Sisters. They were my family, with Jim and the kids and my sister and her gang. They'd stepped in to replace as best they could the kind of family that can't be replaced. Funny that when I married Jim, I hadn't actually imagined my parents wouldn't come around. Until the day Mother died, I was waiting for her to come to her senses. Even after Father died. Even then.

——I was in love once, Graham said.

Across the water, the sun edged toward the clouds coming in over the hills.

——I don't doubt that first love would haunt anyone else I might love, he said.

He'd met her in his final term at Oxford. She was reading law, which few women did in those days. He was depressed at the time, he sees that now. His father was sick, was dying actually. He'd already lost his mother and he had nobody else.

——I was quite inexcusably wild, he said. I drank too much and I drove too fast and I gave off as moving from one party to the next, there was no fun I wouldn't have, when the truth was that all my life I'd been excluded from the invitation lists. It's a small world, and my parentage was the stuff of scandal. I see that now.

My parentage was the stuff of scandal, he said, as if I ought to know exactly what he meant.

The crowd he traveled with were not young men his father approved of, he said, nor men whose company he much enjoyed——not that he admitted that even to himself.

——She asked me to consider coming to Dublin with her when the term ended, he said.

——Dublin?

——I asked her to come home to Ainsley's End, but that wouldn't do for her. There seemed no compromise. She couldn't leave her world, and I wouldn't leave mine. I meant to inherit my father's fortune and live out my life as a proper English gentleman.

——If she loved you, if she'd been the right woman for you——

——I expect if she'd wanted a mess of a man without ambition, there were enough like me for her back home, he said. Sometimes it's those who love us most who have to turn away from watching us destroy ourselves.

In the silence, Bea whispered,

——Poor Mr. Wyndham. He does remind one of Mr. Jeremy Fisher, doesn't he?

——She saw a better me than I ever saw myself, Graham said. She used to say that. She used to say I needed to step outside myself and have a look. Wrote it in a letter, she did. After my father died, which I suppose was the reason I gave her for having to return to Ainsley's End. A letter I didn't answer.

——It's not too late, I said.

——With my father dead, I had no reason not to go to her.

——It's not too late, I repeated.

——She's been dead for years.

We sat together looking over the tarn where Bea and Mr. Heelis used to row companionably. It's not too late to find love, it's never too late, that's what I'm forever telling Kath. But maybe I'm wrong. Maybe the risk of love is too high beyond those foolish early years. Maybe the best the rest of us can hope for is this. Friendship. Understanding. A companion to sit at the water's edge and listen while the sun sets beyond the hills.

15

I am not married. . . . If there were a "Mrs. Jeremy Fisher" she might object to snails. It is some satisfaction to be able to have as much water & mud in the house as a person likes.
——Beatrix Potter, writing as Jeremy Fisher in an undated letter to Drew Fayle

THROUGH THE WAVY-GLASSED DOORS OF THE Ainsley's End dining room the next evening, geometric patterns of low hedges enclosed clusters of herbs while, through the doors opposite, soft landscape lighting illuminated a winged and flower-draped cherub standing in a large rectangular pool, a narrow stream of water shooting upward from his stone platter and falling back on itself. As Graham poured wine smelling of dark berries and sage—"Three Choirs Vineyards, England's finest"—Anna Page remarked on the etching on the decanter. Graham turned the crystal for us to better see, the tilting wine dripping thickly behind three dragon heads like blood dripping from a predator's mouth.

"We're perhaps overly fond of our family crests," he said with a self-deprecating smile, "etching them into our crystal, needlepointing them onto chair cushions, painting them on turtle shells."

"Turtle shells?" Anna Page said.

"I exaggerate. Only half of our crest found its way onto a turtle shell."

As Mrs. Anders cleared the remnants of our salads—"made from the last of the season's lettuces from the estate's kitchen garden," she'd assured us, leaving no doubt that she'd personally bent low to find the best of the tomatoes, to harvest radishes that were softer and sweeter than the spicy American ones—I wondered how many times my mother sat in this same chair, eating meals seasoned with these same garden herbs, so many herbs waiting for the winter frost to knock them down.

Graham, refilling our glasses already, asked Mrs. Anders to bring the second bottle he'd opened and fetch a third from the cellar. He returned to the turtle shell then, explaining that an ancestor who'd married the daughter of the explorer Sir Francis Drake had received as a wedding gift a giant green turtle shell Drake brought back from his adventures, which he'd had painted with half of Graham's family crest and half of Drake's. Somewhere along the way, the shell was lost. "And it had the good sense to remain lost over the centuries necessary for such a thing to become legend," he said, "so it could be found again in the 1980s and restored, rather than tossed in the rubbish, as it might have been."

"A restored turtle shell," Julie said with something akin to a giggle. Our social emergency brakes were slipping from the locked and upright position with each sip of wine. Yes, mistakes were made that night, and we prefer to blame jet lag and alcohol rather than ourselves. Jet lag had been our excuse earlier that day, too, when we'd closed the door to Mom's cottage and all the packing up that needed to be done there, and walked to Wray Castle for the public launch to Ambleside, and spent all day exploring stores and eating scones.

"A giant green turtle, though," Graham said. "An ancient one."

Mrs. Anders returned with a second decanter and two uncorked wine bottles. She handed one to Graham and set the other on a silver wine coaster—a pierced-border coaster made by J. Hoyle & Co. in 1770, Graham said. He collected silver, with a special interest in Old Sheffield, a process of plating silver over copper used before the mid-1800s.

"I've a lovely little box I meant to show you, Asha—a silver puzzle box. But it seems I've misplaced it somehow."

Anna Page studied the beautifully roasted

chicken and new potatoes and vegetables Mrs. Anders had served.

"Mom collected puzzle boxes," I said, an unease settling over me.

"Yes," he said. "Did I not say that? It was a gift from your mum."

I took a bite of potato, starchy and tasteless, while outside, a few drops from the fountain were wind-carried beyond the turbulent small pool of the platter, splashing onto the lily pads and fall leaves mingling in the water below. Graham let Mom use his pier. He helped her make coal fires. He kept an eye on her cottage when she wasn't here. Of course she might bring him a thank-you gift, an expensive one, because what else would you bring a man who wanted for naught? She would have seen it somewhere—a silver puzzle box—and remembered him going on and on about silver in his pompous way, and she'd have bought it as a thank-you for his help.

He began decanting the second bottle—not British but a 1991 Silver Oak cabernet, Mom's favorites for special occasions. Had she brought him that, too?

"This wine comes out of a facility in Geyserville, in Sonoma Valley," he said. "It isn't as charming as their Napa facility, but it's powered almost entirely by its own solar panels."

A man who liked to know things, and to have people know he knew. Not the kind of man Mom would have been drawn to. That's why Anna Page had taken the box, though. She hadn't wanted me to see that Mom had given it to this arrogant Brit.

"You've toured the California wine country, then?" Julie asked him.

Graham's dark eyes blinked behind the wire-rims, as if the question were confusing. "Asha's mum—*Hope's* mum—was going to have me to California," he answered. "She meant to take me up to see proper wine-making one weekend last fall when Jindas would be at his law firm's annual retreat, but then—"

Anna Page knocked her empty wineglass over, and Graham righted it, then filled new glasses from the second crested decanter as I sat trying to absorb his words: "to see proper wine-making one weekend"—the emphasis on "end" rather than "week." End. End. End.

"But then my sister died," Julie said.

"Was it your sister?" Graham asked. "I'm sorry. I hadn't known who precisely it was, only that it was the daughter of her chum Linda. You would be her twin, then? I'm so sorry."

Mrs. Anders came in with warm rolls.

"So you did know about Uncle Jim, then," Anna Page said after the woman and her quiet disapproval had disappeared again.

"About Jim?" Graham leaned back in his chair, closer to the cold fireplace behind him, a

134

needlepointed screen of off-white peonies hiding the sooty brick.

"Ally's husband," Anna Page said.

"You mean . . . did I know that Allison's husband was . . . she called him Jindas."

"And he knew about you?" Anna Page said.

"Did Jindas know about me?" Graham looked past her to the cherub outside the window, standing lonely in his pond. "Not at first, but I do imagine Allison . . . well, it was awkward, wasn't it?"

"Awkward?" Anna Page said.

Graham's eyes flashed a hint of ire behind the wire-rims. "For years, everyone thinks the world is one way, that this idea of themselves is true and always has been. Then it turns out they are someone else entirely, or that's the way it seems."

"That's the way it seems," Julie echoed.

Graham's eyes softened as, outside, a gust of wind scattered the cherub's stream of water. "Yes, exactly. You do see what I mean, don't you, Julie? The whole world looks at you differently, but you aren't a tittle different. That isn't what people see, though. People see the scandal of it all."

"The scandal," Julie said, more to herself than to anyone else.

" 'Scandal' is too big a word for it all anymore, but Allison . . . It was hard for Allison to contemplate telling everyone about me."

"Hard for Mom," I said.

"You do understand that, don't you, Asha? It was all so difficult. Your mum needed to get used to the idea of me before she could tell anyone."

I tried not to think of my mother's slipper tub in the middle of the cottage, of all the things parents never tell their children, all those years and years that Aunt Kath had fixed Sunday-morning breakfast for Uncle Lee, and read the paper with him, gone to church as a family so the children could believe their parents were together, when all that time Lee was keeping house with the other Kath.

"Did my mother . . ." Did my mother what? Ever think how devastated Dad would have been? How many times had I seen that devastation on Aunt Kath's face once I was old enough to recognize what it was? "Were you . . . Did she love you?"

"Well, yes, I think she did. I hope so. Not at first, of course. At first she was simply curious. She came here looking for the truth about her family, and what she found was me. I might be a nice surprise, but still I was a surprise, wasn't I?"

"She found you," I said.

"I wasn't what she was looking for. But I think I was better than nothing."

Anna Page let out a "phfff" of exasperation, as if it were her father rather than mine whom Graham had betrayed.

"I think you must not know what it's like to be . . . well, to be lonely, Anna Page," Graham said in response. "Lonely in the way that I was before Allison and I—"

"You think I don't know what loneliness is?" Anna Page demanded. "I grew up with the loneliest mother in the world, whom you clearly didn't know, and if you didn't know Ma, then you didn't know Aunt Ally."

"But your mum . . ." Graham put a hand to his graying hair. "Kathleen? She's an editor. She and Allison have been . . . well, they've been Wednesday Sisters for years, haven't they? Wednesday Sisters who meet Sunday mornings. I don't think there is a person in the world whom Allison loves more than your mum"—he looked to Julie—"or yours, Julie."

As if he knew us, as if he knew everything there was to know about us all.

"Loved," he corrected himself.

Anna Page stared at him. Julie stared. I looked past them both to the fountain and the cherub, the wide expanse of dark sky beyond, thinking, *Kept a bicycle. Didn't need.* Wanting to say this was all wrong, this didn't make any sense, I didn't believe it, I wouldn't believe it, but sitting as numbly as a train wreck victim pinned under the weight of the conversation.

"I don't think Allison loved even Jindas better than she loved your mum, Anna Page," Graham said. "She certainly didn't love me better." Then, almost as an afterthought, he added, "Of course

137

she loved you and Santosh more than anyone, Asha."

Anna Page fingered the soft cotton napkin in her lap. She reached for her wineglass, took a substantial sip. "And Uncle Jim," she said.

"And Jim?"

"Aunt Ally loved Uncle Jim more than you, she means," Julie said gently, her gray eyes tearing up, as if she understood the pain that this would cause Graham and wanted to ease it.

"Certainly," Graham said. "They . . . Well, they had a whole lifetime together, didn't they? Allison and I had . . . We've only known each other for . . . hardly more than months." He turned to me, saying, "She was an amazing person, was your mum, Asha."

Anna Page ran a hand through her wild hair. *"Hope,"* she insisted. "Nobody calls her Asha."

Except my parents. "Asha, Asha," my mother would say when she was exasperated with me. And sometimes, "Asha, our love."

"1997," I managed, the sadness bubbling over into anger. He was taking my mother and making her someone she never was. "Mom's journals, they start in 1997."

"1997?" Graham said. "You must be mistaken. Your mum and I, we didn't meet until the fall of 2009, did we? Yes, November of 2009, it was— right before the flood. She'd only been coming to the lakes . . . well, I'm not certain, but it hadn't been a decade. It hadn't been a year, I shouldn't think."

"Leave the poor man alone," Julie blurted. "Does it matter? Who cares when they—"

"Oh, good Lord, Julie," Anna Page said.

"Like *you've* never slept with a married man, Anna Page," Julie said.

Graham took a substantial gulp of the wine, as if for fortification.

"This is *Aunt Ally* we're talking about," Anna Page said, "and . . . and of course not! Me? A married man?"

"Oh, bullshit. After Jamie died, you told Isaac—"

"Isaac told you about that?" Anna Page's brown eyes uncharacteristically uncertain. "I didn't *know* he was married. I broke it off the minute I found out." She looked to Graham, her face pale, then to Julie. "But when did Isaac tell *you* that, Jules?"

Between his job, his grief, and his son, Isaac had little time for any of us, and none for Julie even though she was family, because Julie was too much of a reminder of his mom for Oliver.

"You see Isaac?" Anna Page insisted. "When do you see Isaac, Jules?"

Julie sat back and stared at the herb garden beyond the doors as if she meant to deny something but knew she wouldn't be believed.

"Lord, Julie," Anna Page said. "You can't be."

"Can't be what?" I asked.

Somewhere in the house, several clocks began ringing the hour: nine soft gongs from the front entryway, and from the library, and from somewhere upstairs, like the bells of Florence all chiming at the same time but not exactly together.

"You're *sleeping* with Isaac?" Anna Page asked.

In the absence of the gonging of the hour, the hush was complete.

"Not before Jamie died," Anna Page said. Almost as a question but not quite.

Graham said, "You don't think—" He turned to me. "I . . ." He laughed, a single bit-back syllable of disbelief.

Julie sank back in her chair, relieved to have the spotlight turned from her.

"But Allison was my sister," Graham said. "Your mum came to England, Asha, in search of the truth about her mother, and what she found was me. She was my *sister.* I'm sorry. . . . I thought you . . . Good heavens, I never imagined you thought anything else."

16

I sometimes sit quite still in the boat and watch the water hens. They are black with red bills and make a noise just like kissing. . . . One evening I went in the boat when it was nearly dark and saw a flock of lapwings asleep, standing on one leg in the water. What a funny way to go to bed!
——Beatrix Potter, in an August 7, 1896, letter to Noël Moore

PEOPLE WILL JUDGE, THAT'S THE THING, THE reason Julie would have said she and Isaac kept their relationship private. Not secret but private. They didn't need anyone butting into business that wasn't theirs. It wasn't like they didn't know each other well enough; it wasn't like they were two people who had just met. Isaac had known her as long as he'd known Jamie. Longer. Almost a year longer by the time we went to the lakes. And Julie had known Isaac almost as long as she'd known Noah, who had tendered a ring to Julie not long after Isaac started seeing Jamie. Isaac was almost as tall as Noah was—six-one to Noah's six-two—and good-looking in a similar way: dark-haired and oval-faced, with regular features, a distinguished nose, thin lips that, on

Isaac, came to a funny bow, where, on Noah, they remained straight. He wasn't quite as funny as Noah, who used to make Julie and Jamie both laugh so hard that they nearly peed their pants. (Same genes. Same inadequate urethral sphincter.) But Isaac understood so much more than Noah ever would. Isaac never questioned her decision to have a mastectomy despite there being no disease in her breasts.

Even that first time Isaac called in the middle of the night, Noah and Julie were already having problems. They'd gone to bed angry—he'd wanted to blow five hundred dollars on towels, for God's sake. When her cellphone vibrated on the nightstand, while her mind leaped to the kind of bad news that always comes with phones ringing in the dark (her dad having a heart attack, maybe), Noah only grumbled as if it might be an inconsiderate friend.

Isaac was on her front porch.

She hadn't questioned him. She'd stopped in the extra bathroom to brush her teeth and her hair, and had gone out into the night. She was wearing one of Noah's old white oxford-cloth shirts. Noah had told her it was the sexiest thing he'd ever seen, her sleeping in his shirt and nothing else, and if it was what Anna Page wore to bed, Julie didn't realize it. She'd almost thrown something over the shirt, but then she hadn't. It was a warm night, and Isaac was her brother-in-law. He'd seen her in much less at the beach.

That was the night of the day Jamie had been diagnosed, although Isaac and Jamie hadn't told anyone yet. Isaac couldn't cry with Jamie, he had to be strong for her, but he needed to cry, of course he did. He told Julie, and Julie sat with him on the porch swing, under the overhang of the beaded-wood porch ceiling Noah had wanted. They cried together, Isaac and Julie and the smell of the roses that had just that day opened up in the garden, bright red and white and yellow and pink roses that were all indistinguishable in the moonlight, in the night air. After a while, they stopped crying, and she went inside and got them a blanket, and they huddled together under it for a long time, the small bit of warmth each of them had to offer combining to give them strength.

Sitting side by side with their arms around each other, they talked about what Jamie should do: the surgery and the chemotherapy would be grueling, but what choice was there? She would lose her gorgeous hair, Isaac said. She would lose her nails. But they wouldn't lose her.

"She's in denial," he said. "She's hoping this is a nightmare and the test results will be wrong. She's hoping if she gives it time, it will all go away."

He closed his eyes and slumped against the soft cushion of the porch swing, and she stroked his head.

"Of course she is," she said.

"But she needs to schedule the surgery tomorrow." Still with his eyes closed, still accepting the comfort of her touch. "Will you talk to her? Talk her into it? Tomorrow, first thing?"

Julie said of course she would. Of course she would.

"Without letting her know I told you? I swore I wouldn't tell a soul until she was ready."

"Without letting her know," Julie said.

Julie knew how Jamie thought; they shared the same everything, and they always had. It was nothing for Julie to call her twin the next morning and ask her to have coffee—to talk about their dad's birthday, she said. They should do something special for their dad's birthday. "Let's meet for coffee at Il Fornaio to discuss it. We can sit on the patio and have cappuccinos and bran muffins."

She let that sit there for a moment, let Jamie consider whether it would be a private enough place to tell Julie what she didn't know her sister already knew. The quiet end table, separated from the inside world by the glass doors and from the street by the clear wind-blocks, where they liked to sit together for coffee, just the two of them, or for the cocktails Lexi poured in the evening, with Noah and Isaac and sometimes others of the Wednesday Kids.

As if Julie had just thought of it, she said, "Or better yet, how about I get us muffins and make

144

cappuccinos, and we can sit on my front porch. The roses are blooming. They're magnificent this year. You should smell them in the night air. Last night . . . last night I sat out and . . . and smelled them."

It was nothing for Julie to say, when Jamie arrived to find her already sitting on the porch swing, cappuccinos and bran muffins at the ready, "Hey, you look tired. Are you okay?"

Of course Jamie looked tired. The doctor had given her a sleeping pill, but when she woke, the nightmare hadn't gone away.

Jamie took a deep breath, and she lifted her little Deruta cup with her long fingers like Julie's fingers, her simple wedding band where Julie wore several rings, her unpolished nails, and she pressed her bare lips to the edge, and sipped. Still holding the cup, she told Julie. Lumps and mammograms and needle biopsies. She was pretty sure there had been some mistake.

"But Mom . . ." Julie said.

"Mom was only the one lump," Jamie said. "This isn't just one. But they have to be wrong. How can I have advanced cancer? My mammogram last year was perfect. My mammograms have *all* been perfect."

Julie took the cup from Jamie's hand and set it on its saucer, and she did what Jamie would have done for her: she took her hand.

Before Jamie left that morning to pick up Oliver,

they'd made the appointments together. They'd called Uncle Lee, who arranged for the best surgeon to do the surgery two days later. Say what you want about Uncle Lee as a husband—it's all deserved—but he's never failed to be there for his children, or for any of the Wednesday Kids.

"You'll tell Mom and Dad for me?" Jamie said.

"I'll take care of everything."

"Can you take time off from the library to watch Oliver while I'm in the hospital?"

Their mother would want to take care of Oliver, Julie assured her. All the Wednesday Sisters would. It would give them something to do. They'd take him and all the Wednesday Grandbabies to Eleanor Pardee Park, like they used to take the Wednesday Kids.

"Don't let them come to the hospital," Jamie said. "I can't bear the idea of the whole neighborhood huddled in the surgery waiting room like they're sure I'm going to die."

"I'll get them to take Oliver to breakfast."

Jamie started crying then. "Not waffles with strawberries and whipped cream."

Julie squeezed Jamie's hand that was identical to hers except for the rings. Their mother had turned out okay, but neither of them had eaten a waffle since that breakfast when she'd told them about her breast cancer surgery, when they weren't much older than Oliver. They weren't much for strawberries, either. They didn't care to

146

go to New York. Some memories aren't worth revisiting even when they work out okay.

"Mom was fine, and you will be, too," Julie said.

And we will be, she'd almost said. They shared the same everything, the good things and the bad.

"Isaac is beside himself," Jamie said. "He was up all night. He was out walking. I don't think he slept at all."

"I know," Julie said, and then, remembering she wasn't supposed to know, "Of course he's beside himself. He loves you. But this is all going to work out. This is all going to be fine."

"I'll lose my hair," Jamie said.

"I have enough for both of us. I'll cut mine, and we'll make you a wig, and we'll style it the same, and we'll go out shopping for identical clothes."

Jamie had hugged Julie then. She'd set her head on Julie's shoulder and left it there for the longest time, the same way Isaac had in the middle of the night. Not knowing what else to do, Julie fingered Jamie's hair the same way she'd fingered Isaac's. Was that when she'd first thought how odd it would be, Isaac fingering Julie's hair on Jamie's head? Memory, it's such an unreliable thing. It all runs together and blurs, the things that happen and the things you only imagine do, the things you want and the things you have.

17

Writing from about the age of fourteen until she was thirty, Beatrix Potter kept a journal in her own privately-invented code-writing. It appears that even her closest friends knew nothing of this code-writing. She never spoke of it, and only one instance has come to light where it was mentioned.

——Leslie Linder, in her introduction to
The Journal of Beatrix Potter, 1881—1897

The extant journal begins on 4 November 1881 when she was 15, but there is evidence that she began her code writing at least a year earlier, and destroyed those pages at a later reading, judging them unworthy. The last entry in the journal is dated 31 January 1897, some fifteen years later, when she was 30. In between there are some 200,000 words.

——Linda Lear, **Beatrix Potter: A Life in Nature**

A FIRE BLAZED IN THE COTTAGE FIREPLACE, and Anna Page, Julie, and I all had enough coal dust on us to mark the fact that we'd had a hand in getting it lit. It was late, but none of us could imagine sleeping. Julie, pen in hand, was settled on my mother's love seat with one of Mom's journals, her straight-across eyebrows knitted as she frowned down at the page. I sat back against propped pillows on the bed with a second of Mom's journals unopened in my lap, my out-stretched legs suggesting an easiness I didn't feel. The buzz from the wine I'd drunk at Ainsley's End had fizzled with Anna Page's suggestion about Julie and Isaac, and Graham's words. He was Mom's brother? No doubt there was some logical explanation: he was Mom's "brother" the way Aunt Kath and Brett and Linda and Frankie were her sisters, perhaps, Wednesday Sisters who weren't sisters at all, but friends so close they liked to imagine they were. That dinner had come to such a crashing halt—Julie saying she needed air and walking out the dining room doors to the fountain, me stammering apologies and following lest she head off into the woods, and Anna Page hurrying after me—that I hadn't begun to think of the questions I might put to Graham until we arrived back at the cottage, returned to Mom's secret world.

"This is a very bad idea," Anna Page said. "Aunt Ally clearly did not want these journals to be read."

I wanted to say she had no idea what Mom would want, but in truth, she probably did. She'd had conversations with Mom that I hadn't. She knew Mom in ways I never would.

I opened the journal. Deciphering the gibberish seemed an easier thing to endure than more of the argument we'd had on the short walk back to the cottage: Anna Page's inquisition meeting Julie's stoic silence on the subject of Isaac. Or not quite silence. "It's none of your damned business, Ape," she'd insisted. "And I'm certainly not taking advice about men from Miss Screw-a-New-Man-Every-Week-and-Pass-Them-Along."

Now Julie glanced up from Mom's journal, saying, "There's a six-letter name that appears here a lot: F-q-z-g-z-l."

Anna Page, with a glance in my direction—was this what I wanted?—opened the third journal. She didn't take paper or pen to hand; she expected us to be her scribes. Always the oldest of the Wednesday Children, Anna Page is in the habit of expecting us all to do her bidding without realizing she does.

Julie said, "It's probably a name—a person or a place—because it's capitalized. Not everywhere but mostly. Not Hope or Sam or Samuel or Jim."

"Sam isn't Samuel, he's Santosh," I said.

"Maybe one of the Wednesday Sisters?" Anna Page suggested, but when we went through them, none of them had a six-letter name.

"Jindas is six letters," Anna Page said.

Jindas, my father who used to sing to me even before I was born.

Julie wrote "Jindas" above Fqzgzl.

150

I'm not sure I'd realized how disturbing I'd found the idea that my mother might have lost her mind until I saw the gibberish of Mom's tidy handwriting with something that might make sense of it written above. How could she have lost her mind without me even noticing?

"There are two Z's, though, and Jindas doesn't have any repeated letters," Anna Page said.

Julie said, "It could be some kind of changing code. Or maybe it's Kevin—except that doesn't repeat a letter, either."

"And it's only five letters," Anna Page pointed out.

It was only five letters, and none of us had known him a dozen years ago.

Anna Page said there was no point in trying to work out a name because that could be anything; we should focus on the short words that repeated. There was a three-letter word that kept appearing, "adz," which Julie thought might be "the" until she turned the page and found it capitalized in the middle of a sentence.

"So that's probably Sam," Anna Page said.

Julie wrote "Sam" over "adz," then flipped forward, scanning a few pages. "Unless it's a changing code, I don't think it's Sam," she said. "If D is A, then there should be single D's sprinkled about the journal. But the only single-letter words I see are H and Z. So one of those is probably A and the other I."

Anna Page wondered why Mom didn't capitalize properly or use punctuation. It didn't seem like her.

"If you don't capitalize, or if you do it randomly," Julie said, "it makes a stronger code."

Anna Page draped a throw blanket over my extended legs, taking care of me the way she has ever since she babysat me: boosting me up the slide in the park or getting me balloons at the May Fete, giving me her old lunch box, taking me to see my classroom before I started kindergarten, when she was already sixteen and going on dates. Everything she'd ever done, I wanted to do, to be like her. Everything she said, I believed.

"Why did my mother want her ashes brought here?" I asked her. "Sam is right: she belongs back home with Dad."

Anna Page sat beside me, the batik bedspread creasing under her weight. "The people I operate on, when I give them the you-may-die speech and get them to sign the consent, their eyes . . ." She took my hand. "Hearts are as individual as people—no two are the same even if there is nothing about the heart itself that will tell you its owner is Caucasian or Asian or African-American or anything else—but almost everyone I operate on asks his or her children or spouse or someone to do some last specific thing for them. Just in case, you know? As if a kind of clarity they've lacked in their lives comes with the immediate threat of death. The things they ask for don't always make sense to me, but I know they make sense to them."

We sat there with the books around us and the darkness outside, the smells of old paper and of burning coals. Anna Page seemed a different person in that moment. If I'd ever imagined what she did every day, it was all competence and technical skill, stainless-steel surfaces and blood and machines. I never thought about what it must be like for her to wake every morning to the possible consequences of having a bad day, to having her hands on a heart that would continue to beat, or not.

"I so took Mom for granted," I said. "She was . . . My father, I adored. He would go off to the office, or on trips to take depositions or whatever, and I would miss him, and I would want him to be home. And when he was home, I would do anything he wanted—even wash the car or clean out the garage."

"Oh, Hope," Anna Page said in a gentle voice, "it's different, the way we feel about our daddies." She rose and went to the tub, turned the faucets. The water spouted cold and rusty. "Our mamas grew up imagining someday being like their mamas, while their brothers imagined being like their daddies, but our generation . . . All of a sudden girls are supposed to dream of careers, and our mamas don't have careers, so of course we idolize our daddies."

My dad had given me his *Black's Law Dictionary* the night before I started law school. He'd given me a leather briefcase for my first legal job, a summer clerk position after my second year in law school, for which I'd never needed to take work home, or anywhere. "But your mom had a career," I said to Anna Page, remembering the heavy weight of carrying that empty briefcase back and forth to the office every day for those long three months, the pages and pages of journals I filled with that weight.

Anna Page rinsed the soot from her hands in the water running into the tub, finally clean and warm. "Ma didn't become an editor till later. She was a secretary when I was a kid, and that only because Daddy didn't want her anymore."

She wiped a smudge from my face, the gentle touch of her wet fingers bringing back the memory of Mom and me in the bathtub together when I was a toddler. Mom's shallow, discolored-grout tub at home had been crowded with loofahs and soaps, lotions, always candles burning at the tub's edge and on the back of the toilet. If the bubbles were still high when I found her in the bath, I would drop my shorts and my T-shirt and my white cotton panties on the floor, and she would slide down to the faucet end of the tub so I wouldn't bump my head, and I would sink into the warm water, the tickling vanilla bubbles, my mother's pale hands against my darker skin as she soaped my face, my shoulders, my hands.

"Your ma knew you loved her, Hope," Anna Page said. "Don't you go talking yourself into thinking she didn't. Don't imagine her last thought was anything but how very much she was loved."

I stared down at the tidy handwriting in Mom's journal, the cacophony of non-words.

"I still remember the day she and your dad brought you home from the hospital, Hope," Anna Page said. "I don't think I've ever been loved as much as we all loved you that day. Remember that, Jules?"

Julie didn't answer her or even seem to register what Anna Page was saying. She stared down at Mom's journal as Anna Page recalled how I'd nearly died when I was born, how even after I came home, I was kept in isolation, too vulnerable to visiting-kid germs for the other Wednesday Kids to be in the room with me. "We sat on the front porch, and your mom took a Polaroid, that's how we first saw you," she said. "In a photo with the bear we'd given you."

"Mr. Pajamas," I said. "I still have Mr. Pajamas."

Julie said, "These journals must have something to do with whatever Aunt Ally was working on. Why else would she have old journals here in England, rather than at home with the rest?"

Anna Page said, "The Beatrix Potter biography?"

"Shit!" Julie said.

"For a librarian, you sure have a potty mouth, Jules," Anna Page said.

Julie was too busy scribbling in the journal to respond. A moment later she exclaimed, "Beatrix Potter! A three-letter name with the third letter A. Beatrix Potter!"

Anna Page, looking at her as if she were as batty as Mom's journal gibberish, put up fingers for each letter, saying "B-E-A-T-R-I-X. That's seven letters, Jules."

"Hell, it's simple!" Julie said, still scribbling, ignoring Anna Page. "It's all one letter different. A is B, and Z is A. Shift one letter in the alphabet. But look, it works. Adz. Bea."

When Anna Page leaned forward to look, Julie shielded the journal with her arm the way you might hide test answers you didn't want your classmates to copy. She wrote quickly, and in a minute, she said, "Listen." She held up the journal and read,

7.0.1999, first night at the cottage. bea is making herself comfortable in the slipper tub, never mind that there is unpacking to be done.

——youd be more comfortable in the big house, she says. The bed here isnt big enough for us both.

——if you think the big house is so very comfortable——

——some of us have reputations that would be at risk if we stayed unchaperoned in a gentlemans home, Bea says. And it isnt me hes invited, allison.

"Julie!" Anna Page interrupted.

"But Mom wasn't here in 1999," I said. "Even Graham said that. Mom didn't start coming here until a few years ago. That can't be right."

"And she wasn't exactly here with Beatrix Potter," Anna Page said.

"She must have been, Hope," Julie insisted, ignoring Anna Page. "It makes sense. Look." She turned the journal to Anna Page and me. "The gibberish turns into words."

"'Peter Rabbit' is underlined the way a book title is supposed to be," Anna Page said.

"'Peter Rabbit' is underlined," Julie agreed.

"But Mom didn't start coming here until a few years ago," I repeated, as if my insistence might make it so. "I'd have *known* if she'd been coming here all those years. Wouldn't I have?"

18

When I was young, I had the itch to write, without having any material to write about. . . . I used to write long-winded descriptions, hymns(!) and records of conversations in a kind of cipher shorthand, which I am now unable to read even with a magnifying glass.
——**Beatrix Potter, just weeks before she died, in a November 15, 1943, letter to Caroline Clark**

ANNA PAGE WAS STUFFING MOM'S UNDER-wear into kitchen garbage bags the next morning so I wouldn't have to, while Julie and I tackled the less heartbreaking sweater drawer—only to come across a powder-blue cardigan Aunt Frankie knit for Mom when they were both younger than we are now, when I was in middle school and Anna Page, a medical student already, seemed to have everything I didn't: striking alabaster skin and breasts and all that wild hair, guys forever flirting with her while I spent Friday nights at the gymnasium's edge. I was grateful for the studied silence we seemed to have settled into on the subjects of Graham and Isaac; bagging Mom's life up to dispose of it provided all the emotion one day could bear.

Anna Page draped the sweater gently over my shoulders, the smell of not quite damp wool embracing me. When I slid my arms in, it was itchy in a good way. Anna Page touched a bit of yarn dangling near my chin, where the top pearl button was missing. "It's lovely how the Wednesday Sisters took care of each other, isn't it?" she said. "Maybe I should learn to knit."

"If friendship doesn't go both ways, it doesn't go anywhere," Aunt Brett says—not quoting anyone, just being herself. But Anna Page never liked us to take care of her the way our moms took care of each other. She might knit for me, but she wouldn't let me knit for her.

"I don't get any of this," I said quietly. "Why did Mom write these crazy coded entries in her journal? Why does she write about Beatrix Potter as if she's some traveling companion, as if they're sitting by the lake together taking off their shoes?" I picked up one of the journals and read the last few lines I'd decoded: " 'No amount of trying to persuade her to trade her full-length skirts for slacks works, either'—as if they're college roommates and Mom is trying to avoid the embarrassment of being seen with a dowdy friend."

Anna Page took my hand. "Oh, Hope, I don't think that's craziness, I think that's—Ma is forever saying the best way to understand a character is to climb inside her and look out at the world. Maybe that's what your ma is doing in the journals? So that when she writes about Potter, she comes alive."

"That's for fictional characters, though," I said. "That's for novels like Aunt Frankie and Aunt Brett write. That's for trying to make someone who isn't real seem like they are."

"Is it different for a biography? The fact that Potter is a real person doesn't mean your ma knew her well enough to write about her without . . . imagining her there. Aunt Frankie knew our moms so well by the time she told their stories that she could have told them in her sleep. That's easy. But your ma didn't know Beatrix Potter."

"It's her *journal*," I insisted. "It's supposed to be about her. It's supposed to be all personal, and instead it's about Beatrix Potter's damn sheep."

"That's just that one entry," Anna Page said.

"It makes Mom seem like a nutcase."

It made me seem so self-absorbed that I hadn't even realized she needed help.

"Let me see the journal," Anna Page said, and she took it from the nightstand by the bed and found a pencil in the desk. She scribbled away as Julie and I finished emptying the sweater drawer.

"Here," she said finally. "Listen to this—"

Julie's hand stilled on my shoulders. I felt myself tense, wanting the writing in Mom's journal to return to me the Mom I'd known, the one who wrote at the dining room table where everyone could see her while it was her bathtub that was hidden away. But who was that woman? One working on a book about Beatrix Potter that wouldn't be published, who lived her life through my dad and my brother and me.

"No. Wait," Anna Page said. "Give me another minute."

She flipped forward a few pages and started decoding again. As she worked, I wondered what it said about me that my dying mother cared more for a long-dead children's writer than she did for me, that my husband cared more about having kids than spending a life together, that even my Ama had always wanted me to be something I had no idea how to be. Was that why I loved my father more, because he never seemed disappointed? Is that why I became who he was, spending my days tending to other people's business, packing a briefcase to arm myself with work even at night? Dad had loved the small intricacies of the law, though. He'd done it for the doing, rather than for the veneer of success it brought, the belonging it allowed. Or maybe he hadn't. Maybe he, too, would have chosen to write if there hadn't been bills to pay.

"Okay, listen to this." Anna Page started reading: " 'The delight in her blue blue eyes'— Wait." She skipped down the page. "Here. '. . . the stories I wrote when I was pregnant with Hope.

Such silly things, heavens to Betsy, but Hope loved them nearly as much as she loved Bea's.'"

"'Heavens to Betsy,'" Julie said. "Now, that is definitely Aunt Ally."

"Listen, there's more," Anna Page said. "'How Hope loved Bea's stories. *The Tailor of Gloucester.* "NO MORE TWIST."'" She turned the page and continued, "'The line could make her giggle in the grocery store, or in the bath, or when she would come home from kindergarten looking like the world's end had come.'" Anna Page flipped back to the prior page and handed me the journal, and I reread to the end of the page, the tears welling in my eyes.

"'NO MORE TWIST,'" I said, hearing the words in Mom's voice, the expression she often used when I hadn't quite gotten something done: a scarf I meant to knit for my dad, the yarn on the needles in a closet somewhere; a story for my high school literary magazine; the college applications I signed "Asha Tantry," my legal name, on which I'd forgotten to check the "race" box, or that's what we pretended, that I'd forgotten rather than become overwhelmed. No more twist.

I hadn't changed my name when I married, and Kevin hadn't presumed I would or even asked me to, but right after the ceremony, every one of the Minnesotans called me "Mrs. Gallagher." We survived that, though, and we survived the early compromises: his television and his kitchen table, his pans, my couch and china and rice cooker. My bed in the master, his in the spare. Our books and music together, alphabetized. Paint colors we agreed on, contrary to what Anna Page always says about me picking the colors and Kevin nodding along. Then I had gotten pregnant—or thought I had—and for those brief few weeks, it had seemed as if even my body were no longer mine. Kevin began questioning my working late. He purged the kitchen of junk food. He changed my riot grrrls out for Brahms, shocked that I might like anything punk or feminist, much less both. How could he have married me without realizing what music I liked? It had been a relief when the whole thing turned out to be a false alarm, a missed period. "You're too skinny," my doctor had said.

"Kevin is too compulsive," I told Anna Page and Julie as we sat out on my mother's Lake District terrace, the powder-blue sweater Aunt Frankie had knit for Mom warming me. Julie had found a teapot and loose tea—the kind Ama used to send from India—and we'd taken our cups outside to sit in the chairs Mom would have sat in. The stones and the ground beyond the patio were the dark of after-rain, and it was chilly, but the last of the slanting sunlight through the few remaining clouds warmed our faces as we talked.

"*He's* compulsive, says the woman who alphabetizes her spices?" Anna Page said.

I tried to sort out how to explain it, but reduced to words, it sounded silly even to me: I couldn't load the dishwasher without him suggesting a better cup placement. I should smooth the bottom sheet before I make the bed. I couldn't even drive with Kevin in the car because he was forever telling me to watch out for this or that, sure I would crash, even though I'd never gotten so much as a parking ticket.

"It takes ten minutes to alphabetize spices," I said to Julie and Anna Page, "and it saves you a minute every time you cook for the rest of your life."

"And her books and CDs," Julie said.

"You're one to talk about alphabetizing books, Jules," I said.

"But you alphabetize your *underwear*, Hope," Anna Page said.

"I do not alphabetize my underwear."

"You keep them in a tidy stack," Julie said, "with your favorites always at the top."

"Kevin *loves* you, Hope," Anna Page said.

"I can't wash a damn pan without him telling me how to do it better!"

We sipped our tea and looked out at the gray water, trying to pretend I'd said that with less emotion than I had.

"He's a teacher," Anna Page said. "He spends all day herding ten-year-olds. Tell him—"

"But I have, Anna Page. I've told him, and he knows how much it bugs me, and still he tells me how to wash a pan, like I haven't been doing it for thirty years. And when I say, 'You're not really going to tell me how to wash a pan, are you?' he says no, he wanted to suggest how to save the *sponge*."

Anna Page laughed, and Julie looked amused. When I didn't join them, Anna Page said, "He was joking about the sponge, right? It's part of his charm, the self-deprecating humor."

I tried to rewind the memory, but my back had been turned to him. If there had been humor in his voice, I'd missed it.

"He sang to the baby. Kevin did," I said. Like my father had done when Mom was pregnant with me, although the songs Dad sang were Hindi songs, words even Mom couldn't understand. Thank God we hadn't told our parents about the baby. "'Imagine there's no heaven,' that's what he sang," I said. "He would rest his head on my stomach and sing to the baby that wasn't there." I said it easily, as if it were cute or laughable rather than the terrifying thing it somehow was to have him so invested in what I'd expected him to think of as a few dividing cells, something that in any event wouldn't have a soul, because Kevin doesn't believe in souls. He believes in rings of universes preceding the big bang and the possibility of cold fusion, particles moving fast enough through space to allow humans to travel forward and back through time, but he can't get his head around any god of any sort, anywhere.

Julie put a hand on my chair, and Anna Page covered my fingers with hers, and we looked out across the lake, no longer talking, just listening to the extraordinary silence and thinking—or at least I was thinking—about going to the beach when we were children, the Wednesday Gang piling into Aunt Linda's Volkswagen van and Aunt Brett's station wagon, our dads carrying us out into the water, teaching us to bodysurf, building sand castles with moats that would fill as the surf came in. My dad was the master castle maker; while the other dads made dumped-bucket towers with finger-prick windows, he oversaw foot-wide steps up to raised castles with high center towers and winding stairs. When, as grown-ups, we'd all started going to the beach together again, Dad and Kevin would help the Wednesday Grandkids build Taj Mahals, shaping the central domed marble tomb, the unequal octagon with its chamfered corners, its spindly outer towers. "He's going to be an amazing father," Mom would say of Kevin. "He gets children in a way so very few grown-ups do." And sometimes, "You're a partner in your firm now, Hope, you can do what you want," as if my career were nothing and children were everything, as if anyone could birth the dozens of businesses every year that I helped bring into the world, even if no one could save a heart like Anna Page could.

"I think, if my mother's ghost is still on this earth, she's soaking in that slipper tub," I said.

Anna Page said, "I used to love the smell of her bathroom. Not Ma's Chanel No. 5, but warmer, almost edible."

The smell of her bathroom. In the words, I saw Anna Page as a fifteen-year-old creeping into my parents' private place after she'd gotten Sammy and me to bed, opening Mom's bottles and smelling them, lighting her candles, perhaps even taking a bath in my mother's tub while my parents were out at a party, not expected home till late.

"For God's sake, Ape," Julie said.

"What?" Anna Page said.

"You wanted to claim my grief when Jamie—"

"Jamie was my *best friend*." Anna Page turned her gaze to the hills across the water, the reddening bracken and the stone walls, the certainty in her expression draining as quickly as it had filled. "Jamie was my best friend," she repeated. "Aunt Ally was the only real mother I knew."

I looked down at my hands, dark hands like my father's, that spent their days turning the pages of legal documents, like his did.

"Why didn't your mother ever publish Mom's

books, Anna Page?" I asked. "Why does she want the damn Potter book now, when publishing it does Mom no good?"

"That's Ma," she said, her eyes her mother's, her substantial chin her mother's as well. "That's not me."

Across the water—a hard gray under the overcast late-day sky—a hint of peach underlined the clouds. The sheep on the hillside were growing fainter, the stone walls forming their maze.

"My mom wasn't your mother, Anna Page," I said quietly.

Her eyes that were her mother's eyes were full of the memory of all the things my mother had done for her when her own mother was working a job, earning money they might need to pay the mortgage—who could have known back then what Uncle Lee would do? The term-paper help and the meeting of boyfriends. The baking together. The honest conversations she had with Mom.

She looked to the blue cottage door, the geraniums, the old bicycle moved from the kitchen to the protection of the mossy roof over-hang. "But I wished she'd been my mother, Hope," she said. "My whole life, I wished your parents who loved each other were my parents, that I had that to live with instead of this screwed-up thing Daddy and Ma tried to pass off as a marriage. Does it lessen your grief for me to be grieving?" She wiped her eyes, her nose. "Can't you see how I might need to tuck little bits of what's left of your mama into my pocket, too?"

19

I write carefully because I enjoy my writing, and enjoy taking pains over it. I have always disliked writing to order; I write to please myself.
——**Beatrix Potter, in a November 25, 1940, letter to Bertha Mahony Miller**

WHEN ROBBIE SHOWED UP IN HIS LAUNCH TO ferry us across the lake for our cookery lesson the next morning, Julie balked for no reason having to do with the boat itself: a gorgeous polished wood with a cabin of wide glass windows and a long stretch of bow that allowed for a lovely view, if not for hearing the quiet of the evening coming up. Anna Page only shrugged and whispered, "It's a boat taxi, Jules. We need a boat taxi. You want to miss 'Afternoon Tea and Temptations'?"

She had been haranguing Julie again about her relationship with Isaac while we waited, saying she knew Julie and Isaac's relationship was none of her business, but—

"You don't know anything about Noah or me or

our marriage or any marriage, Ape," Julie insisted. "You think you know exactly which guy each of us should love. You want to make a match for your own damned mother, for God's sake! Well, if you're so brilliant at picking out men, why can't you find one for yourself?"

"Brilliant." A word Mom had brought back from the Lakes.

As Robbie eased the boat to the pier, I looked uplake to Wray Castle, where the two hands of a clock set in the stone tower both pointed straight down, too weary to keep time if no one was there much to care. I knew I ought to stop Julie from saying too much, going too far, but she'd already gone too far, hadn't she, sleeping with Isaac? And not telling even me, her closest friend.

"You'd have me screwing Robbie in his damned rowboat, Ape," Julie whispered, one last shot at Anna Page as Robbie hopped from boat to pier and began to tie up. She gathered her humor, then, and patted the lovely polished wood hull of Robbie's launch, where the boat's name—*Argo*—was painted. "What prophesy you, oh bow?" she asked.

"We're too busy living in the moment of having three beauties on board to worry about the future," Robbie answered, his short hair a bit wild with the wind, his face the red that some blonds turn in weather of almost any kind. "We're imagining we might grow up to be a constellation someday."

"You'd be unwieldy," Julie said.

"We'd be broken in three," Robbie agreed. "Three beauties."

Anna Page, who had no more idea what they were talking about than I had, told him we were going to Ambleside to learn to cook cross buns and scones.

"Lucy's on a Plate, that'll be in Ambleside, sure it will, along with her grocery," Robbie said. "But Lucy Cooks will be in Staveley, out the A591. You'll have a car waiting across the lake?"

He sailed us to Bowness rather than Ambleside, where Anna Page, without a thought of doing otherwise, took the front passenger seat of Robbie's old Aston Martin—"a DB5, James Bond's favorite," he said, as if that would make his car any bigger or safer. Anna Page called the hospital from the car while Julie, squeezed into the tiny backseat with me, directed Robbie, never mind that she would have taken us to the wrong *town*.

The logo on the door to Lucy Cooks—sporting the same charming woman-chef-holding-whisk icon Julie had found on the Internet—was a surprisingly good representation of the black-aproned blond woman who introduced herself as Lucy and handed us identical aprons. "You'll be wanting your apron as well, Robbie?" she asked, not giving him a chance to say no. She introduced Janet, a dark-haired, dark-shirted woman in her own dark apron, whom she described as "the head of the BBC." Breads, Bakes, and Cakes.

Lucy and Janet showed us into a brightly lit room where several kitchen stations with cooktops and stainless-steel sinks were set in granite counters dotted with cheerfully colored canisters, cutting boards, colanders, and utensils. We all donned the black aprons—all but Robbie, who sported a black-and-white-striped one.

"These'd be me prison stripes," he said.

Lucy said, "You'll think our Robbie is just your average Irish wordsmith, but he's cracker with a hob as well. His speciality is afters, but he does a fine chunky beef and swede pasty as well."

"A wordsmith?" Julie said with a lift of her straight-across brows.

"You can drop me pasties down a mine shaft or take them out on a boat to see the stars," Robbie said, whereupon Lucy explained that pasties were meant originally for miners, who held the folded pies by the crimped edges to eat around their dirty fingers.

We were measuring out 450 grams of flour for hot cross buns when Anna Page's phone rang. She excused herself to take the call, leaving us to explain that she was a heart surgeon. She did not look happy when she returned, but by then Lucy had left us in Janet's hands, and Janet was directing us in sifting the flour with salt and cinnamon and "mixed spice"—some British combination with nutmeg and something more I couldn't identify.

When we had it all together and set out to rise, Robbie went with Janet to swap out the dough we'd made for some that was already risen, which we could punch down and shape. The minute they'd left, Anna Page said, "That was Ma on the phone, Hope. She's coming up tomorrow, on the first train."

"But she wasn't going to come until next week."

"I know, but listen, Graham offered to put her up at his—"

"It's not up to her when she comes."

Anna Page leaned back against the countertop. "I tried to tell her that, but she's got some bee in her 'proper lady's hat.'"

Julie said, "What could possibly be so important that—"

"I don't know, Jules," Anna Page interrupted. She crossed her arms over the cartoon Lucy on her black apron. "Maybe she's been talking to Isaac. Maybe she's learned about that."

Julie's silver-ringed fingers went to the several small silver globes in her right ear, her eyes crescenting and the cords of her neck tightening. "Isaac is none of her business and none of yours, either."

"But it *is* our business, Jules," Anna Page insisted. "It's all of our business, because of Oliver. Fine, have a rebound relationship. I would,

173

too, if Noah had left me the way he left you. But not with Isaac."

"The way Noah left me?"

"We all think he's behaved terribly," Anna Page said. "I'm on your side about that. He's changed his mind, and I know your parents think you should take him back, but I don't think you should if you don't want to."

"*Behaved terribly?*" Julie pulled an orange spatula from a red canister and examined it as if judging its effectiveness for beaning Anna Page's head. "You don't even know what you don't know. Noah didn't leave me. I left him." She returned the spatula to the canister and selected a yellow slotted spoon. "Unwed sisters always used to marry their widowed brothers-in-law," she said.

"You're going to marry Isaac?" Anna Page's voice the quietest whisper.

"That's worse than screwing him and walking away, like you did?"

"What are you talking about? I would never do that to Isaac. God, even if I would have, I don't look exactly like Oliver's mother!"

Julie paled. "You slept with your own sister's fiancé."

"Lacy was going to marry that turd," Anna Page said.

"So you slept with him and told her."

"Not *then*. Before they met."

"Exactly."

"Exactly *what?*"

"You want to feel sorry for me, Anna Page. You want to think I'm devastated because I have silicone where you have breasts. But I chose these breasts. I feel liberated by these breasts. I'm not sitting around waiting for them to betray me. I feel more sexy with them, not less." She stared at Anna Page's breasts behind the cartoon Lucy on the apron, and didn't say anything. It was unsettling, Julie who'd had her breasts removed looking so directly at Anna Page's chest. "If you want to feel sorry for anyone, Anna Page," Julie finally continued, weighing her words like she was weighing the slotted spoon, "feel sorry for your jealous little self."

Before Anna Page could respond, Robbie and Janet returned with bowls of yeasty-sweet pre-risen dough, and Julie, as if to prove her point about feeling sexier, smiled and arched her back, stretching her long body. Her new same-sized breasts pressed against the top edge of her black apron, leaving me thinking that Henry VIII had married his dead brother's widow, and in the George Cukor movie *Wild Is the Wind*, the widower had married his wife's sister, although that, too, hadn't ended well.

Julie took one of the bowls of dough from Robbie, saying, "So you get hungry out at night in a boat, do you?"

Robbie, clearly sensing the tension but with

nothing to hang it on, set his second bowl on the countertop Anna Page still leaned against. She turned to it and stuck a fist in, punching the dough down before Janet could show us how.

"Now, for midnight, midlake stargazing," Robbie said to Julie, "I prefer a two-course pasty, one end savory and the other end sweet. Where the savory and sweet mingle in the middle, that's the best part, idn' it?"

We pulled ourselves together long enough to follow Janet's instructions for punching down the dough and sprinkling flour on the countertop.

"You're a writer of some sort, Robbie?" Julie asked as she turned her dough out from the bowl.

"You can't believe everything you hear about me," he offered with an untrustworthy grin. "Despite what Lucy said, my speciality is not afters *or* beef and swede pasties. My speciality is a fine bit of fry on a silver tray, with a pot of tea and cross buns, and a single flower in a bud vase."

"A moonflower," Julie said.

"A morning glory, to be sure. It's bang on with the kippers and eggs."

The suggestiveness in his tone made Julie and me laugh, even if Anna Page only frowned.

We spent several minutes choosing rolling pins and rolling the cross bun dough flat.

"'His tail is sticking out! You did not fetch enough dough,' Anna Page," I said to her, hearing my mother quoting that line from *The Tale of*

176

Samuel Whiskers—mischievous Tom Kitten nearly ending up in a pastry made by Samuel and Anna Maria, but saved by John Joiner, who could not stay for dinner as he had to finish a wheelbarrow for Miss Potter. Mom had always substituted "Anna Page" for "Anna Maria," even when Anna Page wasn't there.

Anna Page, leaning hard into her rolling pin, responded in a subdued voice, " 'I fear that we shall be obliged to leave this pudding. But I am persuaded the knots would have proved indigestible.' " She knew the lines from all those afternoons baking with Mom and me while Aunt Kath was at work.

"But I am persuaded *that* the knots would have proved indigestible" was the line, and she'd skipped the part about the dough smelling sooty.

" 'Make it properly, Anna Page, with bread crumbs,' " I said.

" 'Nonsense!' " she replied. " 'Butter and dough.' "

We'd shaped the buns and set them on pans to let them rise again, and Janet was starting to talk about how to make scones when Julie leaned close to Anna Page and whispered, "You've always been jealous of Jamie and me."

Anna Page straightened a hot cross bun so that her pan was perfectly symmetrical, and laid a cloth over the dough. "Robbie," she said, with her gaze fixed on Julie, "what kind of writing do you dabble in?"

Robbie glanced from Anna Page to Julie. "I write beef and swede pasty recipes," he said lightly. "And I'm starting a show for the telly: 'Chef Robbie.'"

"'Nonsense! Butter and dough,'" I said.

"'Nonsense!'" Anna Page repeated. "'Butter and dough.'"

20

But upon the table—oh joy! the tailor gave
a shout—there, where he had left plain cuttings
of silk—there lay the most beautifullest coat. . . .
Everything was finished except just one
single cherry-coloured button-hole, and where
that button-hole was wanting there was pinned
a scrap of paper with these words—in
little teeny weeny writing—
NO MORE TWIST
And from then began the luck of the
Tailor of Gloucester; he grew quite stout,
and he grew quite rich.
—from **The Tailor of Gloucester** by Beatrix Potter

EVENING WAS FALLING FAST AS ANNA PAGE set off uphill from the Ainsley's End pier—to steal a few herbs from Graham's garden for an omelet, she claimed, although what she really meant to do was to get Graham to renew his offer of accommodations for her mother. She needed to walk off the tension she still felt despite the soothing taste of scones and hot cross buns, anyway. What Julie had said in the Lucy Cooks kitchen about Anna Page being jealous was true—not in the way Julie had meant it but in other ways, even she would grant Julie that. Anna Page would grant Julie anything, really: that Julie understood better than anyone how Isaac's grief felt, that they shared the want of Jamie's touch and smile and laughter, the press of her lips against her Deruta cups. That loving Jamie's husband and son sometimes felt like loving Jamie, that it was the closest any of us would get to having Jamie back. That filling the void felt better than leaving it empty, except when it didn't. That there was nothing to do when it didn't except crack open a chest and pull out the sick thing that was someone else's heart, and pour your grief into that small saving act.

Graham was in the garden when Anna Page ducked through the passage in the stone wall, between the rose garden and the too-perfect geometry of the herbs. Napoleon came bounding over to greet her, and she stooped down to return his affection, a far easier thing than looking Graham in the eye. This would be awkward; none of us had seen him since the dinner disaster. But it would be less awkward than shoehorning her mother into the overcrowded cottage or convincing her to stay across the water, in Bowness or Ambleside.

Graham held a sprig of rosemary out to her, and she inhaled the sweet-spicy aroma she knew from the community garden back in Eleanor Pardee Park, where we played as kids. It was the herb her mother used to put into scalloped potatoes, which she made only for Sunday dinners, when Anna Page's father was sure to be home.

She stood, and smiled, and apologized for the abrupt way we'd left the other night. She thought to try to explain the misunderstanding about him, but there was no way to do that without scraping at the hurt of us having had no idea of him before we came. She thought to try to explain the rest—Julie and Isaac—but he wouldn't know who Isaac was. So she told him about Lucy Cooks and making hot cross buns.

"My mother comes tomorrow," she said finally.

"Tomorrow?" Graham replied.

"Earlier than originally planned," she said.

"I've a room ready for her anytime," Graham said. "What time is she scheduled to arrive?"

"Sheduled" rather than "skeduled."

Anna Page said she would be on the first train.

"And she's traveling without your father?"

"She's here on business," Anna Page responded, surprised that he didn't know about her parents' odd situation when he knew so much else about us. She supposed it was something the Wednesday

Sisters had ceased talking about years ago, even among themselves.

"Pardon," he said. "I didn't mean to—Your father, he hasn't passed, has he? I can't recall Allison speaking of him."

Passed. It meant such different things in different contexts, but in her life, it so often meant what he meant here, that someone was dead. She'd known when she went into heart surgery that some patients would die in her hands, but it's one thing to know it and another to face it every morning when you scrub.

"Why don't you come for breakfast at the cottage tomorrow morning?" she said, thinking she would need to do something to bridge the gap opened at that dinner, although she had no idea what.

In Graham's dark eyes she read concern. "I'd like that," he said. But she hadn't fooled him by changing the subject.

"Daddy and Ma have been separated for decades," she said.

He nodded. "I see."

He couldn't see, of course; not even the Wednesday Sisters understood why anyone would stay in a marriage that was such a sham.

"Daddy had affairs," she told Graham, feeling the need to explain that it wasn't her mother's fault, that he ought not to think less of her mother for what her daddy had done.

She ought not to have loved her daddy for doing that to her ma, she knew that, and yet she'd always loved him best.

"Not affairs. Another woman. When I was growing up."

Napoleon returned to Graham's side and nudged his hand.

"My father took a second wife," Graham said. "He was married to Mum, but he took a second wife."

"Married her?"

"Purported to."

"My daddy only lived in sin," Anna Page said. "He still does, actually." She twirled the twig of rosemary in her hand. "We all pretend it doesn't matter."

Graham stroked Napoleon's head with a tenderness that surprised her. "It's what one does, isn't it?"

Your heart will beat three billion times for you, Anna Page likes to tell people. "Even if it's sick, if I take it out to replace it," she says, "it will beat on the tray, trying to keep going for you." It's something she learned from her father even before she started medical school, before she chose heart surgery, and Stanford, the world of her father and the other Kath.

She didn't want to be a pipe layer, she wanted to do transplants, and Norman Shumway was at

Stanford, she will tell you. "It's easy to forget everything but the patient on the table with the whole team looking the same under the surgical gowns and caps, the shoe covers, the masks," she'll say, as if it's easy to ignore that the person with whom she most often shares the OR is her father's lover. Once, when Jamie responded to what she called "Anna Page's faux toughness" by pointing out that in all that getup, nothing covers a person's eyes, "the window to the soul," Anna Page assured Jamie that the surgeons wear Clark Kent glasses with magnifiers on them. "Thick black plastic rims," she said. "I think that was when I knew I wanted to go into heart surgery: when I realized I'd never have to wear mascara to work."

The eyes may be the windows to the soul ("life's *dim* windows *of* the soul," Julie would correct us, with a lecture on how the saying probably originated with some French poet we'd never read but should), but if the soul is anything more than a construct of religious literature, the heart is where it resides, Anna Page also likes to say. Even doctors used to think the heart couldn't be operated on, lest the soul be set loose from the body. Anna Page rather likes that: the idea that it's up to her to set souls free.

She loves the whole routine of surgery and has from the start, from the first operation she ever did, assisting the other Kath in a mitral valve repair. She had arrived at the hospital before dawn to find Catherine eating yogurt on a bench by the door nearest the parking lot; Catherine had wanted Uncle Lee to be with Anna Page when she walked that first terrifying walk to the OR, but Lee thought Anna Page would take his presence as a reminder of what she had to live up to. So Catherine was the one to insist that Anna Page eat a second yogurt Catherine pretended to have brought for herself. They might be in the OR for five hours, or ten, or fifteen, she said. Always the last thing you did before you scrubbed was fill your stomach and empty your bowels.

Catherine had been the one to scrub with Anna Page—seven long minutes of nails, hands, wrists, forearms. "Ablution, is that the word?" Catherine had said as she knocked the faucet off with her elbow. "The scrubbing is my psychological passageway into the OR."

"Like a warrior putting on armor," Anna Page said. "Blood sport."

"Except the goal is to shed the least blood possible rather than the most." Catherine laughed then, her gentle, sophisticated laugh that Anna Page tried to emulate. Jamie used to tease Anna Page about that. Jamie was a big believer in the beauty of an openmouthed guffaw.

Catherine introduced Anna Page to their "congregation": Nurses who draped them in sterile gowns, tied masks on their faces, slipped latex gloves over their clean, short-nailed fingers. Anesthesiologists who smiled behind their own masks. Two fusionists on the heart-lung machine whom Catherine called "my favorite confusionists." At least they weren't refusionists, one had answered affectionately, and Catherine's cheek pads had lifted slightly under her mask and loupes and headlamp, leaving Anna Page wondering if the two had ever slept together, or might. Wondering if the other Kath was faithful to her father, and if he was faithful to her.

Anna Page knew which suckers saved the patient's blood and which didn't, she'd observed countless times, and she knew how to work with the hair-thin suture material so like the fishing line on which she used to string bait all those summers they spent in South Carolina with her ma's family and her daddy's. But everything seemed new that morning. All these things that were supposed to be so familiar seemed overwhelmingly real.

As they worked, Catherine explained all the things Anna Page knew and had practiced, all the things she wouldn't need to be told if she weren't as overwhelmed as she suddenly was. "A razor-straight incision on the outside is a good omen you can control," Catherine said as she marked the patient's skin in two places. She had Anna Page hold a piece of dental floss to mark the line—unwaxed, so it wouldn't slip against the latex gloves—before calling out "Incision!" to let the room know as she began to cut. In what seemed both an eternity and no time at all, Anna Page was suturing the cannulas in place for the heart-lung machine, her fingers shaking as she remembered the first time she'd held a fishing line, her daddy shouting at her and her being so startled by the fish flopping that she'd dropped the rod off the pier, losing both the fish and all opportunity to catch another that long, hot summer.

"See, it's as easy as sewing spaghetti end to end," Catherine said. She de-aired the tubes and connected them to the bypass circuit tubing and told the room, "Go on pump." She turned to Anna Page and said, "You have your father's fingers, long and graceful and strong. You're going to be great at this."

And she is. Anna Page is a terrific surgeon. She's one of those people who, through sheer willpower, would be good at anything she committed to, even if there weren't the element of needing to be better than her father's lover. But as often as she tells that story, she never seems to realize how often she does tell it, how badly she needs to be great at what she does. She never stops to think that she had her choice of colleges and medical schools, her choice of residencies and internships and fellowships and jobs, and every time she picked Stanford. She picked cardio-thoracic surgery at Stanford, knowing she would have little choice but to learn how to mend a heart from the woman who had broken her mother's. Anna Page, she is at least as complicated as her parents are, and probably more.

She never tells the end of the story, either, not since the night she told my mom at our dining room table while I watched from the stairs. Home on break from Smith, I woke to Mom's and Anna Page's voices in the dining room, and I headed down in my nightgown, imagining myself grown up enough finally to join in their intimate conversations. But something in the sight of Anna Page's blood-blackened scrubs made me settle on the stair where I'd so often eavesdropped on them as a child.

". . . a bottom-drawer adventure, that's what my friend John calls it, as if he's talking about a carnival ride," Anna Page was saying. "A mitral valve repair ruptured in the surgical ICU, and I was the first doctor there."

I could see Anna Page sitting at the table, but Mom sat tucked behind the wall, a disembodied voice that gently chided, "A mitral valve resting by its poor little self in the hospital bed?" But she didn't suggest Anna Page take a deep breath.

"The chest-cracking cart was there, at least," Anna Page said, "but I had to slice the chest open in the bed, with a kid waking up in the guest chair and me yelling at him like he's a nurse who ought to know how to help. I've got three fingers on the left atrium, and still blood is pouring out with every damned heartbeat, running warm all over my hands."

She'd climbed onto the bed for better purchase, trying to stem the bleeding for so long that her thighs burned from holding herself in place. By the time she was doing the bed ride to the OR, a male nurse was running alongside her, holding her up because her thighs had quit.

"Her blood starts running cold on my hands, then—no time to warm the stuff from the blood bank, so it's going in cold and it's coming out the same way, it's not inside her long enough to warm up. And this nurse is holding me, and I'm holding this damned heart, I'm palpating the aorta and it's softening and I'm communicating that to the nurses calmly, like I'm not screaming inside, I'm trying to stay calm because for one thing the kid is following us, and anyway, if I panic, everyone else will. I'm talking like it's a dinner-party conversation, saying I need a bigger pop of epinephrine and we're only in the elevator, the door closing on the kid who looks like he knows it's the end. Then we get to the OR and we all breathe out, we all think, *Thank God, thank God.* And it . . ."

The whole house was so quiet that you could almost hear Anna Page trying to gather breath to form the words.

". . . it quits," she finally managed to whisper. "This heart I've been holding in my hands for all

188

that time, that kept going all the way to the OR where I could maybe do something, it just quits."

Mom said nothing, Anna Page said nothing, no sound of weeping although my eyes were pooling at the ache in Anna Page's voice, or at the sight of their fingers intertwining, Mom's untidy nails laid over Anna Page's, which were cut to the quick, and clean, no trace left of all that blood.

"And I . . . God, Aunt Ally, I was so exhausted that all I could do was lie back on the bed next to the bitter, metal smell of losing that heart."

"Of course you did," Mom said.

Anna Page closed her eyes and sat back in the dining room chair, her fingers still intertwined with Mom's, Mom leaning forward slightly so that her forehead occasionally bobbed into view only to disappear again behind the wall. The dining room table beyond them was the usual mess of Mom's writing, all that failure that had begun to mortify me sometime in middle school. Are we all uncomfortable with our mothers when we're young? Was that why Anna Page confided in my mom rather than her own?

"I'm lying there, too tired to imagine telling the kid," she said. "I'm not even thinking of the kid. I'm just empty. I'm thinking I will close my eyes and nap for five minutes. Just five. And that's when Catherine shows up."

The quiet moment of Mom absorbing the name—

Catherine—gave way, and she gently squeezed Anna Page's hand.

"She was the other Kath's patient," Mom said, not quite a question.

"Catherine stands there at the door to the OR. She doesn't say a word. She just stands there and stares at me like I'm crazy to be lying beside a corpse, and she turns and walks away."

Mom leaned forward, a bit of her face visible to me. I quietly slid down a stair to see her short dark hair, her pale face. Rain began falling gently on the roof as she reached up and traced a finger along a patch of dried blood on Anna Page's right arm, the one that had pressed for so long on the dying heart.

"There was nothing left for me to do but pull the sternal wires from the bottom drawer," Anna Page said. "You can close the skin over the open bone, but I put the breastbone back together over the heart. I know it was dead. I know it didn't matter. But I couldn't bear to leave it unprotected."

"Tell me her name," Mom said gently.

In the silence, tears began to pour down Anna Page's cheeks.

"She's not a heart, Anna Page," Mom said. "She's a whole life. And you didn't help her any less because she was Catherine's patient, don't go talking yourself into thinking that. You'd have saved her if she could have been saved. Now name her, and honor her, and let her go."

"Alice Memmer," Anna Page sobbed. "Mrs. Memmer, but I called her Mrs. Memorable." With tears streaming down her cheeks, she whispered, "Her heart tried so hard for her."

Mom put her arms around Anna Page, pulling her head to the chest she'd forever covered with a washcloth when I'd intruded on her baths, tucking her face down into Anna Page's wild hair.

"Nobody can save everyone," Mom said. "You can't and Catherine can't and your father can't, either. Most of us can't even save ourselves."

"But that poor heart," Anna Page said. "That poor, generous heart tried so hard."

21

From the Journals of Ally Tantry

12.11.2009, Ambleside. **This is what Graham says. I'm writing it down the way he's told it to me. It makes no sense, and yet the pieces fit as smoothly together as the sliding panels of a personal secret box.**

Graham is half Indian, like Hope and Sammy are; that's how the conversation started. His father went to India in the 1930s, like many British second sons needing to make fortunes they weren't in line to inherit, and he fell in love there, and he married. An Indian

woman, a Brahmin, from a good family, like Jim and me, only decades earlier and in reverse.

Like Jim and me, his parents——Graham's grand-parents——declined to recognize the marriage. They accepted that Graham's father had taken an Indian woman as his lover; he wasn't the first British man to do that, or even the first British man from a prominent family to. But that was all. He was called back to Britain under threat of being cut off financially, so what choice did he have? India hadn't provided even the prospect of a reasonable living, and this was all before his brother's death in World War II left only him to inherit Ainsley's End. So when Graham's grandparents insisted his father marry a proper British wife, Graham's father began attending balls.

He selected an appropriate young lady and proposed to her. He stood at the altar and said "I do" a second time, and in short order, his brother died and the newly minted second Mrs. Wyndham moved into Ainsley's End. She moved into his house and into his bed, thinking she was his wife, not knowing Graham's father already had a wife and daughter. They were living in Manchester, where he spent most nights.

Well, what could the British wife do? She had been living all la-di-da upper crust with this man she thought she'd married——who turned out to be already married. Married and with a daughter diagnosed with polio. That was when the British wife learned of the Indian one, when the half-Indian daughter was put in the iron lung in which she would die.

Passage on a ship was quietly arranged, and the British wife was given money, and she set off. It was foolish: the world was at war; the seas weren't safe. But what choice did she have? To bear the shame of living with a man who was not her husband even legally, and who did love his legal wife? Graham is quite clear on that: the British wife was taken on only to be able to keep the Indian wife and child comfortably within reach. Graham's mother is the wife his father truly loved.

Graham's father, not the British wife, was the one who should have been shamed, and perhaps he would have been if the truth were made public. But it never has been the same thing for a man to have an unwed woman as it is for an unwed woman to have a man.

Let her disappear from the face of the earth. Let the whole world think she abandoned him. Let her disown this life and start over in some new place, where nobody would know of her shame.

Graham's father hadn't imagined any other narrative, the rumors of the British wife being buried somewhere in the woods.

When his father and his daughter died in the same week, not long after the British nonwife left, Graham's father moved his Indian wife into Ainsley's End, never mind all the gossip. He loved her too much to hide her anymore. And so it was at Ainsley's End that Graham was born.

——Graham Wyndham V, son of a long line of respectable Graham Wyndhams, I said to him.

193

——Precisely, although it was my uncle for whom I was named, my father's older brother who was killed in the war. That was what was always said, although no doubt my father meant by the name to establish that his son belonged in proper British society despite my mixed heritage. So much harder to dismiss a Lord Graham the fifth than a Martin Junior. But of course that was seen to be the dog's bollocks it was.

Martin Wyndham. His father's name was Martin Wyndham, the groom's name on the marriage license I'd found. Mother must have stood at an altar here in England with Graham's father, pledging until death did they part, thinking she'd live out her years in the wealth and respectability of Ainsley's End, only to discover she'd married a bigamist. Mother must have been the proper British wife who disappeared, the wife people think was murdered and buried somewhere in the Claife Heights woods.

——Your mother is not so very unlike mine, Bea tells me.

We are back at the inn, and I've written this all in my journal, and still it doesn't seem real.

——My parents were the children of tradesmen who'd risen up to a place in London society, Bea says, and I was giving up all the respectability they'd gained, tossing it away for the sake of love just as you were tossing off all the respectability your mother had reclaimed in fleeing this place.

——I don't know, Bea.

——It isn't so improbable, you know, Allison, Bea says. It's the answer you came here looking for, after all. What you came for again and again. Did you not think you'd find it?

22

And because the Mouse has teased Miss Moppet—Miss Moppet thinks she will tease the Mouse. . . . She ties him up in the duster, and tosses it about like a ball. But she forgot about that hole in the duster; and when she untied it—there was no Mouse!
——from **The Story of Miss Moppet**
by Beatrix Potter

"LUCKY DAMNED DUCKS," JULIE SAID TO Robbie. They had remained tossing crumbs from the bird-crap-covered pier after we returned from the cookery lessons, while I went back to the cottage and Anna Page walked up the hill for herbs. "How often do you suppose this pair gets fresh hot cross buns?" she asked.

"Lucky damned *swans,*" Robbie said as the pair surged at the bread, then backed away.

"You don't actually cook anything but pasties, do you?" Julie said. "You're the type to make a homemade dessert and get everything else takeout

195

from Lucy's. I know your type. You put it on your own china and pretend you've made it all yourself, to impress."

"You think I have china?" Robbie said.

Julie laughed. She couldn't help herself. "You use paper plates and plastic cups on your silver tray with the moonflower, I guess?"

"I'd have a silver tray with no china to put on it?" he said.

She laughed again.

"It wasn't a moonflower, either, it was a morning glory," he said.

"You're stretching it," she said, the thought that his hair couldn't be more tousled in the morning than it was coming off the lake surprising her. What did she care how he looked in the morning, or when he served his damned tray?

"Well, you might be right about the moonflower. 'Gone and not gone. Is this garden the one we walked in hand in hand,'" he conceded, something in his voice or his weathered face not quite of him, the way Aunt Brett was when she was quoting, like she so often was.

Robbie kissed her then, the lingering taste of raisins from the cross buns and almonds and lemon from the scones catching her off guard.

"Oh, sorry!" he said in a chirpy voice that wasn't the least bit apologetic.

"You are not!"

"I'm not," he admitted, "but I thought I ought to

get that in before you find I don't even have the moonflower."

Flustered, she said, "Or the takeout from Lucy's—"

"The takeaway? They do make a fine beef and swede pasty, does Lucy's, and brilliant puddings. But I only try to pass those off on foreign girls like you. The locals, they know Lucy's when it's served to them."

Julie laughed again, she didn't know why. He was making fun of her, and she was laughing. "You were flirting with Anna Page all through the cross buns and the scones," she said, "and now you think you can kiss me just because you want to."

Robbie had such an impish face when he laughed: his lake-blue eyes widening and the lines between his nose and lips deepening, a thin scar stretching on his chin, some last vestige of a childhood cricket accident, perhaps. "But I can, now, can't I," he said.

He tried to kiss her again, but she pulled away, thinking of Isaac.

"Who were you quoting?" she asked. "The line about moonflowers."

"I was quoting, was I?" he teased.

"'Seventeen and insane,' that's Ray Bradbury," she said. "That was a quote, and you didn't correct Anna Page on it. She said Vonnegut, and you didn't correct her."

He reached out and touched her hair the way Isaac sometimes did when he knew what she wanted to say but couldn't, when he wanted to save her from having to say the words.

"Don't you bother yourself with being jealous of Anna Page," Robbie said gently. "She's a fun one to take the mickey out of, that's all."

"I'm not jealous of Anna Page," she said.

His blue eyes searched her face, as if there might be some explanation for her feelings in the tilt of her straight nose.

"She wants to fix her mother up with Graham, never mind that he's creepy," she said.

"Our Lord Wyndham?" He smiled, the creases around his mouth and his eyes deepening. "But he isn't at all a creeper. He'll rabbit on, he will, but he's a regular bloke under all that poof. Surely he likes to have a pint at the local same as anyone. A Hawkshead Bitter, I'd think."

"The suspect defending the suspected," she said, feeling somehow that he was talking about her even though he was talking about Graham. "A single man who cooks nothing but pasties defending the recluse from the big estate."

Robbie dipped his head toward the water, toward the faint reflection of his body next to hers over the straight line of pier. "But things aren't always as they look, are they?" He considered her, the memory of his wife damp in his eyes despite all the intervening years. His wife and his daughter both, like Isaac and Oliver. Except Isaac still had Oliver, and Robbie had nobody.

"Take you, Julie, you'll be telling the whole world what to do when you haven't got a baldy yourself." He touched her elbow, his two fingers pressing at the joint making her arm relax, leaving her aware of how tight her shoulders were. "Your grief is here in your elbow, idn' it? In the way you hold yourself so carefully, lest anyone see." Still holding the elbow, he touched a finger of his free hand to her forehead, ran it down between her straight brows to her nose. "It's there in the bridge of your nose, though you do a fine job of making all that grief look like something else."

He stared across the darkness that was the lake now, to the small islands in its middle, all but one uninhabited. "Have you ever seen the stars in the Southern Hemisphere?" he asked. "There's no pole star there, no simple way to get your bearings. There's a Southern Cross, and there's a false cross. What you do is you find the brightest star—Alpha Centauri—and from that you can find your way to the Pointers. And from the Pointers you can determine south."

He touched her shoulder, easing her back until the hard wood slats pressed cold against her shoulder bones, relieved only by the gaps and the softer moss, and all she saw was the starry sky. How long had they been talking?

"People call Alpha Centauri the brightest star in Centaurus," he said as he lay beside her.

"Half man, half horse," Julie said.

He propped himself up on an elbow. "You're wrong about me, you know," he said. He touched a finger to her lips before she could say anything. "The rocket with parm salad. The beef and swede pasty. The pudding. I make it all."

He traced his finger over her chin and down to the base of her throat. She swallowed, feeling the ridged insides of her neck against the press of his touch. "And the silver tray?" she whispered.

He lay back on the pier and looked upward toward Andromeda and Cassiopeia, leaving Julie free to study his face, the roughness of acne scars marking what might have been a more difficult youth than his charm suggested. Maybe that was why he'd learned to be charming, to make up for the acne.

"My silver tray, it'll be fierce tarnished," he said. "I might manage a proper morning coffee, though, for the right lass."

A meteor shot across the sky, but by the time she said "Look," it was already gone.

"The Orionids," he said. "If you watch between Orion's head and Gemini's feet, you can see twenty-five shooting stars in an hour this time of year."

"It was for your wife?" Julie asked. "The silver tray. The morning glory."

In the long pause that followed, Julie knew the answer.

"And sometimes the both of them, when Erin was old enough to climb from her bed and into ours. That's years ago now, though."

Julie closed her eyes for a moment, wondering how Isaac would have survived losing Oliver, too.

"What do you write, Robbie?" she asked.

"Everyone writes something in the Lake District, except those that are painting," he said.

"Janet said you cook almost as well as you write."

He sighed slightly. "Well, I was a journalist, wasn't I?"

In the upturn of the question, she heard Isaac's voice: *Without letting her know I told you?* The betrayal already begun.

She whispered, "Why do you turn everything into a question, Robbie?"

He whispered back, "Why do you tamp all you want to know down to a whisper not a soul can hear?" He studied the sky, small bright points fighting against the dark. "That was how I met Cornelia, covering the Troubles from the sidelines while she was deep in them, trying to change the world."

"Cornelia," Julie said.

"And you?" he said. "Why do you ask so many questions of others without answering any yourself?"

"What do you write *now,* Robbie?" Julie insisted.

They watched together as a second star shot off from the princess chained to her chair.

"It isn't a single star you're seeing when you see Alpha Centauri," he said. "It's a binary system, Alpha Centauri A and Alpha Centauri B, two stars the human eye can't separate. Gravitationally, they're a single object, aren't they? A third star hangs with them as well, Proxima Centauri, a red dwarf that can't be seen with the naked eye at all.

"Red," he said. "It's such a brutal color."

Julie peered up at the red dwarf she couldn't see.

"A dozen years ago now, it was," Robbie said, "in the Omagh bombing."

"In Ireland," Julie said.

"All the time Cornelia put herself in harm's way, but never with Erin. Then the Good Friday Agreement is signed and the Troubles are said to be over, and they go off for a day's holliers, the two of them, and a car bomb explodes."

Another star shot across the sky, fading to nothing. In the darkness left in its wake, Julie remembered that first evening, Robbie talking about the Crier killing his wife. She imagined that he might have been talking about himself somehow. Not that he'd killed his wife but that he ought to have kept her from dying. Thinking that was how she felt about Jamie, not that she killed her but that she ought to have kept her from dying, she ought to have seen that Jamie wasn't herself before it was too late.

"I have scars," she said quietly. She was glad not to have him turn to her, not to worry if he was looking at her face or her chest.

"We all have scars," he said. "How's a person to be interesting without her scars?"

"I'm in love with someone," she said.

Robbie considered this, again without turning to her. "So it's love now, not just 'involved'?"

Julie didn't answer.

"And he's in love with you?"

The question so direct that she hesitated.

"You've awfully lovely lips for them belonging elsewhere," he said, his voice teasing, not judging. He smiled at her, turning only his neck and head, his body still flat against the pier.

She didn't move away from him, but she kept her gaze fixed upward, thinking of Isaac, thinking it was daylight in California, he couldn't see this extraordinary sky.

Robbie studied the stars with her, the two of them feeling the cooling night air, and hearing the quiet.

"He's a good man, I hope," Robbie said finally.

Julie heard in his words what he was asking: Who is he?

His name is Isaac, she thought. She could tell him. What would it matter, a confession to this man she would never see again? But she couldn't bring herself to say the words.

He fingered her hair the way she'd fingered Isaac's the night he told her about Jamie's cancer, the way she'd fingered Jamie's the next morning as her sister told her the news she already knew.

"Proxima Centauri, she's a flare star," he said. "She undergoes random dramatic increases in brightness from magnetic activity. She's the star closest to the sun, but she won't likely support life on any nearby planet, because of the flares."

23

From the Journals of Ally Tantry

15.11.2009, Ambleside. I went down to Liverpool to have a look through the ship passenger records. It took me the whole day, but then I found it: Caroline Anne Crompton——my mother——set sail from Liverpool to New York in January 1943. 1943. The year I was born.

Bea says we are who we choose to be, and nothing of where we come from has the power to take that from us. "Family history is little more than expectation to be overcome," she insists. "A straitjacket of limitations on who we otherwise might be."

24

"I will not have Mr. Jackson;
he never wipes his feet."
—from **The Tale of Mrs. Tittlemouse**
by Beatrix Potter

KEVIN AND I ONCE LOOKED AT A HOUSE WITH A
double tub, imagining ourselves bathing side by
side in the same warm water, then climbing out
to wrap ourselves in warm towels. He wanted to
put in a bid, but the house was expensive; we
were only poking around, the way people do in
Palo Alto. At home that night, he drew a bath for
me, the bubbles overflowing the top of the tub
even before I got in. He turned off the lights and
lit candles, saying in a funny-sexy whisper,
" 'But they did not keep "self-fitting sixes": it
takes five mice to carry one seven inch candle.' "
He washed my hair, his fingers slow and
soothing on my scalp. "Close your eyes," he
said, and he rinsed the shampoo away with clear,
warm water from a pitcher, and washed my face
slowly with a clean washcloth and the face soap
I always use. He washed my neck. My shoulders.
My breasts. My stomach. Between my legs. We
had no towel warmer, but it didn't matter. He

lifted me from the tub—soaking his rolled-up sleeves, his shirt buttons that were cool against my bare, wet skin—and carried me to bed. And the next morning, I found him at his computer long before dawn, working on a story. "About a couple who think of buying a house with a double tub," he said. I suggested I ought to write my own version of the story, and he said he hoped I would.

I plugged the rubber stopper in my mother's tiny cottage sink and turned the hot-water faucet, which ran cold at first, leaving the pool tepid as I washed my hands and splashed my face. I looked up to see myself in the mirror only to find the blank wall. The hand towel smelled of my mother's soap, the smell of Mom when I came down to the dining room table where she was writing to say good night. Her bubble bath here, as I opened it, was a blue vanilla, where at home it had been pink, but I closed my eyes to see Mom in her dank little developer bathtub at home, pulling her knees to herself and setting a wet washcloth over her small breasts, smiling as if a daughter who couldn't leave you alone for the time it took to bathe was a delight.

"Mommy, I need bubbles," I'd once barged in to inform her—not a memory I can recall but a story Mom told on me so many times that it feels like memory. I'd tendered a plastic teacup from my doll tea set, and Mom, relieved that I didn't mean to climb in the tub yet again, put in a few drops of bubble bath for me.

"Only for the sink," she said. "And take your shirt off so it doesn't get wet."

I had boats I liked to float in the sink, pretending the bubbles were icebergs and I was an Arctic "'plorer"; I struggled with X's when I was young, and S's as well.

I pulled off my T-shirt and dropped it on her bathroom floor. "Mr. Pajamas and Mrs. Tittlemouse are having a party and they invited everyone 'cept they won't have Mr. Jackson," I informed her.

"Why don't they want Mr. Jackson to come to the party?" Mom responded, no doubt after she stirred up the water—trying to create more bubble coverage, I realized as I stared into her empty slipper tub. How had I never realized that as a child?

"His feet are muddy! Mrs. Tittlemouse doesn't like him, 'cause she just cleaned and cleaned, so it's all nice and shiny."

"Her floor?" Mom asked.

"Her whole house!"

"I see," Mom said. "Well, why don't you ask him to wipe his feet?"

"*I* can't ask him, Mommy. It's a pretend, and I'm not in the pretend. Only Mr. Pajamas and Mr. Jackson and Mrs. Tittlemouse are in the pretend."

"I see." She turned the water on again, adding more warmth and more bubbles. "Perhaps Mr.

Pajamas could ask Mr. Jackson to wipe his feet, then."

"He doesn't want to."

"I see," she said once more. "Perhaps they could hand him some tea out the window in one of your teacups, then? Not that cup with the bubble bath in it, though."

I giggled and said, "He would make bubbles when he talked if he drank bubble-bath tea!"

As I ran off, Mom called after me, "Remember, only in the sink!"

She was relaxing in the tub to the sound of the water running in our bathroom. Sink volume, not bathtub rush. I wouldn't drown in the sink. I would have my step stool pulled up to the vanity, and I would be—

"Heavens to Betsy!"

She hopped from the tub, threw a towel on, and bolted into my bathroom to find poor stuffed Mr. Jackson already submerged in a sink full of bubbles from which he never did recover.

In Mom's cottage, I stepped into her empty slipper tub and lay back against the cool white porcelain. I was still clothed, with only my feet and my hands bare, my neck, my face. "Who was my mother?" I asked the cold unvanilla emptiness.

I climbed from the dry tub, collected my journal and pen, and climbed in again. I stared at the first page for a long while before writing the date at the top of the page. A date and nothing else.

"Beatrix?" I said the name aloud, trying it out on my tongue, whispering to the cold, empty tub, the cold, empty cottage. To the same imagined Beatrix Potter my mother wrote to in her journal, the same Bea my mother imagined herself with here, when she was away from us.

Outside, it was dark, all the things that might be beyond the window shaded, indistinguishable from the trees. Only the smooth surface of the lake bumping up against the shore was clearly visible.

I wrote the first words that came to me then, before I could question the writing of them:

> It never struck me until I was grown up myself how often the Wednesday Sisters tell me what to do.

"Is this how you do it, Bea?" I asked. "Is this how you start writing a thing you both want to write and don't?"

The only response I got was the smooth press of porcelain against my unmanicured toes, the cold tingle of it above my shirt collar, on the bare skin at the back of my neck.

25

From the Journals of Ally Tantry

19.11.2009, Ainsley's End. Heavens to Betsy, it's raining so much that the roads to Ambleside have been cut off, and the inn I'm staying at has flooded, and Bowness is largely underwater as well. You can row right through the trees around the lake. Bea and I would have been wading through it ourselves if Graham hadn't sent a rescue boat and offered accommodations higher up from the lake, at Ainsley's End. He would offer us the cottage so we might have more privacy, but it, like the inn, is in danger of taking on more water than one can sleep in unless one is a fish. It's quite awful: so much ruin. And yet it's fascinating.

I had a crazy notion this morning that we should hike up to Stock Ghyll Force, to see how the falls look after the storm. The road between Ainsley's End and Ambleside is flooded, so we got the old fellow who hires boats to come fetch us. Graham doesn't keep a boat, he hates being on the water, but I dragged him with me. Napoleon, who is no fonder of boats than Graham is, stayed home.

Beyond the revolving gate, water poured over the weir in a frightful torrent, but fools that we are, we braved the slippery stone path to the lower walking bridge across the beck. It, too, is a falls now, submerged in rushing water except for the railings, so that if we'd tried to cross, we'd have been washed away. And yet we continued on uphill, Graham urging me to turn back but following me. You'd have thought I was Hope, the way I wanted to be in the midst of all that turmoil. Hope or Anna Page. The path itself had turned into a small stream so that we had to wade out to the overlook. The falls aren't three separate falls anymore but a single deluge, the pool where we might have gone for a dip indistinguishable from the splash.

——Now, Allison, Bea said. Ask him about your mother.

——I think that was my mother, I said to Graham.

The words out before I realized I was saying them aloud.

——Pardon? Graham said.

——My mother, I repeated.

I told him then about the marriage license with my mother's name and his father's.

——That's why I came to Ainsley's End, I said.

——But you were getting out of the rain, he said. You'd been wandering around Wray Castle, and you were caught in the rain.

——That's what I wanted you to think, I said.

——And now the rest, Bea said.

Standing in the heavy mist of the rushing water, holding tightly to the rail and hidden by the hood of my raincoat, it did seem possible to say the thing aloud. I could claim Graham misheard——the rushing water and the wind and the spray distorting my words——if he looked appalled.

——I think we might be siblings, I said. I think you might be my brother.

He didn't say anything, he just turned to me, and he didn't seem . . . disgusted, I guess was what I'd been afraid of. That he would think I was sick. So I kept talking.

——Half siblings, I said. I think my mother was your father's British wife. I think she was pregnant with me when she left England.

That's the timing. That's what the date on the ship passenger records I found in Liverpool suggests. Like all of this, it doesn't make sense. And yet it does.

Half siblings. I had put it to Bea first, trying it out, afraid even to commit it to paper. It explains so much about Mother. Why she never talked much about her life before she married Father. Why she never did accept Jim and Hope and Sam.

Had she known she was pregnant when she fled? She must have suspected by the time she met Father——on a ship during the war. No one waited to marry during the war, Father always said. No one waited for anything. You met and you fell in love and you had the ship's captain marry you.

Had he known Mother was pregnant? Was that something Father would have done? Met a pregnant young beauty——my mother had been beautiful—— and wanted to take care of her, even if she was pregnant with another man's child? He couldn't have failed to know for too long, unless he chose not to, which is easy to imagine as well. Father was pock-faced and quiet. He had bad teeth when he first met my mother. In the pictures of them before he got his dentures, he looks a bit like a mutt she's brought home to care for. But perhaps he was the one who did the caring.

Had Graham's father known Mother was pregnant when she left, that he had another child somewhere? Mother might have kept this secret her whole long life, even from the man who raised me as his daughter. She might have gone to her grave denying the truth. Or she might have spit it at Graham's father as she left him. She wasn't beyond bitterness. She wasn't beyond wanting to make sure people who hurt her felt pain, too.

——Come stay with me, Graham said.

This was much later, at Ainsley's End. Hours and hours of talk later, about how we wouldn't have discovered each other or any of this if I hadn't gone in search of some reason for Mother abandoning me, if I hadn't found that marriage license and not much else. About how it felt to Graham to suddenly have a half sister when he thought he was the end of the line. About how I would ever explain this to Jim and Hope and Sammy when I'd barely mentioned the name Graham to them, when they thought of him, if at all, as just some British gent I'd met.

——Come stay with me, not only now, not only until the floodwaters recede, he said. I've so many empty

213

rooms here. Or you can stay in the cottage. I could have the cottage fixed up for you, for whenever you come.

And later,

——You take the house, and I'll take the cottage.

That made us both laugh——it's all so unreal.

——You'd be his oldest, he said.

"His," not "our father's," although when he said it, I tried to imagine what the man must have been like. I'll ask Graham; he'll tell me all he knows. But there is time for that.

——You'd be his oldest, he repeated. You ought to be his heir.

The words spoken as if Graham wanted to give me everything he had, now that he had family to share his life, or something like family.

——Except, of course, that I'm female, I said.

And Bea whispered to me that I should take the cottage, that I should let Graham give me that. It was much cozier than the big house, she said. She could sleep on the love seat. I could have the bed. We would both love bathing in the slipper tub.

26

When Mr. McGregor returned about half an hour later, he observed several things which perplexed him . . . he could not understand how the cat could have managed to shut herself up inside the green-house, locking the door upon the outside.
——from **The Tale of Benjamin Bunny**
by Beatrix Potter

I DREAMED THAT NIGHT THAT MY MOTHER'S puzzle box was empty. I sat by a warm fire in a comfortable chair and opened it, expecting to find Mom there, but when I adjusted the last panel and slid the Madonna and baby aside, the box was swept clean. I woke with such a start that I turned to Kevin, only to touch an unfamiliar tangle of long hair that sent my heart into an even more frantic rush. I turned on the bedside light to see Anna Page stirring beside me, and Julie turning over on the love seat. Not wanting to wake them, I clicked the light back off.

When I'd finally settled out of the fright of it— just a dream, just a dream—I gathered the box and my journal, and I crept down the steps to the cottage kitchen, to the small window facing uplake to the darkness where Wray Castle was. I set a finger on the baby's gold halo and traced it over the edge to the third flower. Slide, click, adjust. Adjust, slide, click. The movements familiar. They should have been easy, but my fingers shook, and I lost the thread of the steps. I couldn't make it open.

I turned to Mom's journal and took up a pencil, decoding in light marks right on the page, above her writing. An entry about the flood she'd told me about, and my grandmother being married to Graham's father, who was already married to a woman from India. About my grandmother being pregnant with Mom when she fled to the U.S. to start over.

Was that why my grandparents had refused ever to see me, because I evoked something from my grandmother's past that she couldn't bear? I closed my eyes, remembering a conversation I'd had with Mom after I'd read a *New York Times* piece about kids like me. Multiracial. At college campuses, it said, kids were taking back the term "mulatto," but did it work that way? Is it like what they say about banana peels: if you slip on a banana peel, everyone laughs at you, but if you *tell* people you slipped on a banana peel, you own the joke? They have student groups for multiracial kids now, sort of like EKTA, the South Asian Student Association that had just started at Smith when I was there, that I never did belong to, since I never felt exactly Asian, even if I never felt exactly not. The Asian kids always saw me as not quite Asian, and the white kids saw me as nothing but. I was glad for those kids in the article and maybe a little jealous of what I hadn't had. A little confused about it all, though: if you don't belong anywhere, then you belong with us?

"Remember when you took me to meet your parents?" I'd said to Kevin one night the week after Mom died; we'd settled on the benches facing *The Gates of Hell* in the Rodin sculpture garden at Stanford, passing a thermos of margaritas back and forth. "The first thing your mother said was 'Oh, you're Indian!' And you said I wasn't Indian, I was a half, my dad was Indian and my mom was white."

"That's the way you say it, Hope," Kevin said. "I just explained it the way you say it."

"It didn't feel like that. It felt like you were trying to distance me from my dad. You know, 'She's not *all* Indian.' " I reached for the thermos and took a sip, staring up at the bodies falling toward damnation. "Like you were telling them not to worry, your Irish blood would dilute my Indian so their grandchildren would look Italian, at worst."

"Hope. You know I don't think that."

"But your parents did."

"My parents didn't, not really."

I passed the thermos to him, but he only held it.

"Why was your mom so surprised, Kev?" I asked.

"She was just meeting you, Hope. She was meeting you for the first time. She didn't mean it like you think she did."

"You never told her before that? You never told your parents, 'Hey, I'm dating this terrific woman, she's half Indian'?"

"Oh, good Lord. For all the white girls I brought home, I didn't say, 'I'm dating this terrific girl. She's white.' That isn't who you are any more than the fact that I'm so pale I'm practically see-through is who I am."

"But you—"

"I didn't tell them, Hope. I didn't think to tell them." He lowered his voice as a student passed on the sidewalk by the road. "It isn't the way I think of you."

"Isn't it?"

"You know it's not, Hope."

"We'd been engaged for months, Kev. We'd dated for a year."

"But you were busy at work, Hope. You were the one who had this deal to close, or that meeting or partners' weekend, or a damned hair appointment that you couldn't miss, for God's sake! We were supposed to go at Thanksgiving, then you had that deal that didn't close on time. We had the plane tickets, you know we did."

"Over a year, Kev! Over a year! We'd dated for over a year, and we'd been engaged for months, the wedding invitations were out, and you'd never even shown your parents a *photograph* of me?"

Kevin took a drink, tipping the thermos high. He lowered it, his eyes fixed on *The Three Shades* at the top of *The Gates*, the same distorted figure replicated three times, all pointing to the graceful *Thinker.*

I'd known this about Kevin when I walked down the aisle, that he'd been embarrassed to have me meet his family.

"Hope." He set the thermos on the ground and turned to me, his face pale in the darkness, like an early moon. "Hope, you can't not know how much I love you. You can't not know that."

Out in the direction of the science buildings, someone laughed, a male voice that went unanswered.

"Nobody loved your dad more than I did, Hope. You know that. You can't think I've ever thought of either of you as 'other.' "

"Not one photograph—"

"Okay! Okay, I take your point. I understand. Don't beat me to death about it."

"Now it's my fault?"

"For God's sake, Hope, tell me you've been wearing this like a hair shirt for the last five years. Is this why you don't want to have kids, because my parents might not have wanted to take them to the freaking zoo? Why did you marry me, then? Why didn't you walk away?"

"I don't know."

"Oh, Hope." He leaned forward, forearms to thighs, hands clasped between his knees, and stared at the pavement. "Don't say that, Hope," he said, his pale eyes in his pale face devastated as he turned to me. "Don't say that. Don't think it. You love me as much as I love you. You know you do." He pulled me to him and wrapped his arms around me. "This isn't you talking, Hope," he said. "This is the grief at losing your parents. It's the weight of the grief."

I set Mom's journal down and picked up my own, opened it at the scarred wooden table in my mother's cottage kitchen, and wrote, *Is it just the weight of the grief?* I stared at the puzzle box I couldn't open. *It doesn't feel like that,* I wrote.

Mulatto. Quadroon. Octoroon.

Would that be better for my kids, to be able to say to people demanding to know what they are, "I'm a quadroon"? The terms all have the ring of not belonging, of being neither one thing nor another. "Other." That was what Dad and I both were most of our lives. It sounds so innocuous, but it's dehumanizing when it's the only description left to you. You aren't white. You aren't black. You don't belong.

I tried to talk to Sammy about it once, but maybe it's different for him, or maybe he's convinced himself it is. He doesn't look at all

Indian; he looks like Mom, but in a bigger, like-Dad version, with skin that is darker than hers without actually being dark. His friends, when they meet Dad and me, often aren't great at masking their surprise that we aren't white. When faced with a box to check, Sammy doesn't hesitate. We were raised by a white mother in white neighborhoods where everyone sees us as white even if we're part Indian, he says. But I check both boxes now, because I finally can.

Yes, I'm white, I wrote in my journal. *And yes, I'm Asian. Here I am, finally, thank you very much.*

It isn't even that I want people to see both of my races. It's that I want them to see beyond my race. I want it not to matter. I want them to see the person I am.

One in seven marriages now is a mixed marriage, the *New York Times* article said, but less than three percent of Americans are multiracial even now. When I showed it to my mom, she said, "You wouldn't believe the stares your father and I used to get." As if I'd never been stared at, even before I started seeing Kevin. As if my children and I wouldn't be stared at, too.

I wrote: *But it would have made Mom hurt to hear me say that.*

Is that why reading Mom's journals is so disturbing, because of all the conversations I never did have with her? It didn't feel like that, either. It felt like Mom was a different person in those journals, at the Lakes by herself, planning to write a biography when she'd always written children's books.

"I wrote the books for you and Sammy," she told me—this when Sam was a grown man who didn't much like being called Sammy. "They're your books. You two decide what to do with them."

As if there might be something to do with them other than box them up and stick them in an attic. Save them to read to the children I wasn't sure I would ever have. Yes, Sammy and I had loved them as kids, but what three-year-old doesn't love everything her parents do? Even the Wednesday Sisters used to laugh at them. Even my mother did. "Remember that first story you wrote, that one about the duck?" Aunt Frankie would say, and Aunt Kath would say, "That duck, she wouldn't quack even for a loaf of bread fresh out of the oven," and they all would have a big old laugh.

Still in my pajamas, I slipped on hiking shoes and a jacket, found Anna Page's international phone, and went out into the night. It was utterly quiet this late, even the insects silenced, only my footsteps on the path and on the mossy planks of the pier, where I sat and pulled my knees to me, trying to keep warm, and dialed home.

"Hey," Kevin said. "I was hoping you'd call. I miss you."

"There's no phone reception in the cottage," I said, glad of the excuse not to have called in the long days since I'd called from the airport to say we'd arrived.

"I see," he said. "All right. But are you okay?"

"Anna Page is being all Anna Page," I said.

He muted the sound on a television in the background. He'd be leaning against the pillow, waiting to see where I was going with this. Or not in bed yet; it was still early evening there. He was sitting in his favorite chair, images from the *NewsHour* flashing silently across the screen.

"There's this guy here, Robbie the boat rower," I said.

"Anna Page is sleeping with him?" Kevin said.

I could hear a small smile in his sigh; he's quite fond of Anna Page. Had they slept together before I met him? Should I care if they had?

"She's doing the Anna Page Woodhouse thing, trying to match him with Julie," I said.

"Anna Page doesn't know how to grieve," he said. "She soldiers on in the same way her mother does, refusing to have emotions she can't address. But she loved your mom. You can't think Anna Page didn't love your mom."

"Mom was *my* mom, not hers."

"Of course she was. It's okay, Hope. It's okay. But be easy on Anna Page, she's—"

"She's what?"

"Nothing. I'm sorry."

"Aunt Kath called Anna Page. She's coming up from London earlier than we agreed, on the first train tomorrow."

"Called?" Kevin said. "But there's no phone reception."

"While we were out at our cookery lesson," I said.

"Tea and Temptations?" he asked, his voice lingering on "temptations," intimate.

"With the added temptation of Robbie the boat rower in an apron."

He laughed gently and said, "Don't you let any crazy Brit tempt you, Hope."

"He's Irish, actually."

He laughed more loudly. "What have I done, letting my lover go off on an adventure with the recently liberated Julie Mason and the ever wild Dr. Anna Page?"

Julie Mason. She hadn't changed her name when she married, saving herself the need to change it back.

"I can't get the box open, Kev," I said. "I can't get the box open." And I started weeping.

"Hey," he said. "Hey. Why don't you let me come? I can be on the next plane."

I pulled my knees in more tightly. The lake was so still. If the swan pair was out there, they were hidden from sight.

"I'm just tired. I had a nightmare." I wiped my eyes. "And now I can't open the box."

"You started at the baby's halo?" he said. "Traced around to the flower?"

The pale perfect baby's perfect like-the-mother face under the perfect damn halo.

"Then you adjust the thing at the left forward, and then the almost farthest right bottom panel."

"I know how to open the box!"

The silence at the end of the line matched the silence of the lake, Kevin counting to thirty-three the way he does. Thirty-three, his lucky number. The age we were when we met.

"I'm just tired," I repeated. "I'm exhausted. We're all in this one tiny cottage. We're on top of each other."

"Of course you are," he said. "Of course you are, Hope."

"I don't want Aunt Kath to come. She's only coming to get her hands on my mother's stupid book, the stupid Potter biography that isn't even here."

There was a long pause on his end, Kevin perhaps distracted by some image on the TV screen. Then he spoke in a soft, soothing, serious voice, saying, "You need to let her come, Hope. Aunt Kath needs to—"

"None of the other Wednesday Sisters feels the need to intrude on this."

"Lee had a stroke, Hope."

"You're kidding." I reached in my coat pocket for a tissue, found only a residue of the dust of my mom. "You're kidding," I repeated.

"He's fine. He's doing okay, but Kath wants to tell Anna Page herself. You know how Anna Page is about her father."

Her "daddy," she still called him.

"The thing is, he wasn't with the other Kath," Kevin said. "He was at the house. At Kath's house."

"At Aunt Kath's?" Trying to get my head around what Uncle Lee would have been doing at Aunt Kath's when Anna Page and her siblings weren't there, and why it should matter.

"Apparently the other Kath has found another Lee," Kevin said. "Although I don't think his name is actually Lee. Apparently Lee has been bunking at the Palo Alto house until he finds another place to live."

"With Aunt Kath?"

"At the house, yes. Don't tell Anna Page, Hope. Let her mother do this."

"Of course. Of course."

"It was a small stroke," Kevin said. "A blessing, honestly. A wake-up call. No paralysis. No speech loss. Maybe he'll stop smoking now."

"He won't be able to operate, will he?" I said. "Not after having a stroke."

"I guess not."

"It's hard to imagine an Uncle Lee who isn't Dr. Montgomery."

"I know."

"How is everyone suddenly so old and dying, Kev?"

With Mom's death, I was the oldest in my family. There were my aunt and my cousin, Carrie, but I had no parents left, no grandparents. Just one younger brother, one nephew.

"Hope," Kevin said, "if you want to open the box, why don't you try it now, while I'm on the phone with you? I won't tell you how to do it. I promise. I'll just be here for moral support."

"But it's . . . I don't have it. It's back in the cottage."

"Where are you?" Kevin asked.

"I opened it fine earlier, Kev."

"Why don't you go get the box and bring it to the phone, Hope," Kevin suggested. "I'll hold. I'll wait right here for you."

27

The place is changed now, and many
familiar faces are gone, but the greatest
change is myself. I was a child then, I had no
idea what the world would be like. I wished to
trust myself on the waters and the sea.
Everything was romantic in my imagination. The
woods were peopled by the mysterious good
folk. The Lords and Ladies of the last century
walked with me along the overgrown paths, and
picked the old-fashioned flowers among the box
and rose hedges of the garden.
——Beatrix Potter, in a May 8, 1884, journal entry

AUNT KATH IS ONE OF THOSE PEOPLE WHO
seem to remain unchanged every day of their
lives. Yes, her hair is a striking silver-gray now
where her daughter has just a sprinkling at the part
line, and her face is lined and jowled, but what
you see is her strong chin and her strong
cheekbones, her strong eyes that are determined
and caring all at once. "I'm not one to gripe with
a hand under each arm," she likes to say, which,
when you parse it, means she's pretty happy with
her editorial job (which, even at seventy, she has
no thought of relinquishing) and with her children

(although she wouldn't mind if Anna Page and her sister made up).

"Robert Smythe?" she said when we introduced her to Robbie. "Do go on."

"Robbie," he insisted. "Those who know me call me Robbie."

He'd taken us on the *Argo* again, this time across the lake to the train station in Windermere. Graham had come as well, to meet this stranger he'd somehow agreed to put up at Ainsley's End for a few days. We were standing inside the spare station, the train outside at the end of the line, about to head back the way it had come. Aunt Kath smiled warmly and extended a hand to Robbie, their palms and fingers lingering together. "Well, I'm tickled pink to meet you, Robbie," she said.

"And this is Graham Wyndham," Anna Page repeated, so anxious to get her intended romance started that she missed the surprise in her mother's voice at Robbie's name—surprise I'd dismissed as surely as I'd dismissed the idea that Robbie might have known Graham when we'd introduced them at the Ainsley's End pier.

They were about the same age, Graham and Robbie, which surprised me. Robbie seemed so much younger. That introduction had been more awkward than I'd imagined. The disaster of who was who to whom that had erupted during dinner at Ainsley's End still hung over us, despite our tacit agreement over a boiled-egg breakfast at the cottage with Graham that it would not. Robbie's usual charm seemed to have abandoned him, laying bare his curiosity, while Graham drew back from Robbie's prying questions as if from a snake he couldn't bring himself to step across. Graham was the "lord" here, something like royalty—not the type of person Robbie met on a daily basis, I supposed. And Graham had said when they were introduced, "Robbie Smythe, it's a common name, isn't it," with some emphasis on "common" that did make him seem arrogant. Robbie hadn't seemed miffed, though; with a glance at Julie— who was watching the exchange with surprising attention—he had replied that it was not as common as you might think. Even when Graham had said, "You're a boatman? That's how you earn your living?" Robbie had only studied Graham for a moment longer than was comfortable before answering, "It's an honest enough living, idn' it?" He'd said he knew of the Wyndhams, everyone in the Lake District knew of the Wyndhams even if almost nobody claimed them as friends. "It'll be hard to collect friends when folks hold you in awe, now, won't it?" Robbie had said. But then he'd surprised us by going on at length about Graham's family—which was only Graham, and had been for all the time Robbie was talking about. The Wyndhams had contributed more than anyone but Beatrix Potter to the preservation of the Lakes, he told us, going on in detail with the kind of appreciation people who adopt a home often have when lifetime residents don't realize their luck. The Wyndham family had restored buildings and preserved the history, he said. Mended footpaths. Replanted native trees. It left me wondering why Robbie hadn't told us any of this before, why he'd shared only the story of the Crier of Claife.

Now, as the introductions to Aunt Kath were being made, Anna Page said, "Graham will be your host while you're here, unless you'd like to sleep on Aunt Ally's kitchen floor, Ma. And it's cold, hard stone, without so much as a rug by the sink."

I told her we planned to do a once-around-the-lake in Robbie's launch first.

"Graham," Aunt Kath said, seeming not quite to know what to make of him.

"If you're spent from your journey, Kathleen, we could instead have tea at Lindeth Howe," Graham offered. "It once belonged to Beatrix Potter—it's an inn now—and is a short hop down the road."

"There's not a view quite like that of the lake from a boat, though, is there?" Robbie said.

Anna Page and Julie and I exchanged glances. Graham had suggested all manner of alternatives to a boat tour when we'd proposed it back at the cottage, before he'd confessed to a hatred of boats; it wasn't until Anna Page had insisted that a boat tour of the area wouldn't be the same without his running commentary that he'd removed his glasses and wiped them, his lovely dark lashes and cheekbones so like my mother's, and agreed to come along.

Aunt Kath assured him the train from London had been no trouble at all, and she'd been in England for a week, so there was no issue of jet lag.

"Brilliant." Graham sighed. "Brilliant."

Robbie took Aunt Kath's arm and led us to the launch.

Graham looked up at the sky before he stepped aboard again: blue as blue could be, but it was very changeable here. He positioned himself up against the cabin, as close as he could get to the boat's exit ladder and still be a safe distance from the water. He leaned back as if casually, but his grip on the railing around the cabin was two-handed and as tight as it had been even inside the cabin on the trip across. He startled visibly when Robbie, who'd taken the helm, slid the front window glass open so he could hear the rest of us.

"Pretty as a pat of butter melting on wheat cakes," Aunt Kath proclaimed the upper lake as we circled it, charming Graham and Robbie both without appearing to be charming anyone. It was so odd to see this woman I'd seen only as a mom like my mom—older and vaguely asexual—here in this other life, free of my idea of her. She would have men other than Uncle Lee if she wanted them. Anna Page's ease with the opposite sex, which I'd always imagined came from her father, might have come from Aunt Kath. What did I know about Uncle Lee, anyway? I saw him primarily through Anna Page's eyes.

Graham plunged into a lecture on the origins of Cumbria, "which means 'brothers,' " he said.

"Brothers," Robbie repeated from the helm.

Graham, taking the tone as a challenge, said, "From the Celtic words 'cymri' and 'cumber.' "

Robbie watched him through the opening but said nothing more.

"The borders of this area—modern-day Cumbria—roughly equate to those of the Celtic kingdom Rheged." Graham's head dipped to Aunt Kath's level as he reluctantly let go of the rail with one hand to direct her attention to a white house on the cliff. "That's Brockhole, perhaps the Lake District's loveliest gardens." He pointed out Low Wood Bay, with all the sailboat masts in the foreground, and Storrs Hall, a Georgian mansion where in summer they deliver to your boat afternoon tea sandwiches and scones and cakes served on bone china.

"That's your favorite way to spend a summer afternoon, Graham?" Anna Page teased. "Tea on a boat?"

Graham laughed as he gripped the rail with both hands again. "Careful there, Miss Montgomery, or your ace tour guide will insist on being put ashore."

Don't go into Mr. McGregor's garden, Mom would have said. *Your Father had an accident there; he was put in a pie by Mrs. McGregor.* But there was something familiar in Graham's voice, if not in his words—a tone and a cadence. Or was that me looking for something of my mother that might survive?

"*Dr.* Montgomery," Anna Page said.

"*Dr.* Montgomery," Graham acknowledged.

He had the dates at his fingertips: The Romans arrived in AD 43 and established a fort at Ambleside. Hadrian's Wall was built on the order of the Roman emperor to separate the Romans from the barbarians. "So many tourists cycle and hike these roads with no idea of the history," he said. By AD 410 Britain was largely ruling itself, he told us, but it wasn't until the beginning of the Dark Ages that the Romans abandoned Cumbria.

Robbie left Graham to his soliloquy, remaining at the helm and saying little. He seemed to be listening for something more than was there in Graham's words. Aunt Kath stifled a yawn no longer attributable to jet lag or the travel fatigue she'd denied, although perhaps she could lay it off on the gentle rock of the boat. It's such a funny irony that when men are trying hardest to impress, they become their most tedious. I had half a mind to tell Graham to give up with Aunt Kath; she and Uncle Lee had moved back in together after decades of being estranged, for heaven's sake. I couldn't say that with Anna Page there, though, and I didn't have the sense that they were back together so much as Uncle Lee needed a place to stay and Aunt Kath was letting him use the guest room.

As it became clear that Graham was heading into the same kind of excruciating detail about the Anglo-Saxons and Vikings settling the Lake District, Aunt Kath said, "I do believe God must have taken as much pain creatin' the Lake District as he did creatin' the South." She suggested he might tell us about the Lake Poets, somehow deftly leaping centuries of history without giving offense. "Wordsworth," she said. "I adore Wordsworth, although that's like saying I adore Frost. It doesn't separate me from the other heifers quite so clearly as I like to imagine it does."

Graham adjusted his wire-rims with one hand, his other firm on the rail, and said, "Wordsworth lived here at Dove Cottage, then at Rydal Mount. His sister Dorothy, too. Also Samuel Taylor Coleridge, Charles Lloyd, Thomas De Quincey, and Robert Southey."

"Robert Southey?" Aunt Kath said, though more to Robbie than to Graham.

"'Once more I see thee, Skiddaw!'" Robbie

practically sang out from the cabin. " 'Thou glorious Mountain, on whose ample breast / The sunbeams love to play, the vapours love to rest!' "

"That's here?" Aunt Kath asked him. "Skiddaw?"

Robbie said it was, although his answer seemed directed at Julie rather than Aunt Kath.

"England's fourth highest peak," Graham said. "But it's farther north, near Bassenthwaite."

Anna Page, frowning at the little intellectual skirmish, ran her hand through her hair, which was limp and lifeless today, devoid of its usual wildness. She wandered into the cabin and to the back of the launch, where she stood looking through the clear glass to the receding shore. I wanted to join her, but I hung back, afraid I'd inadvertently say something about her father. How could Aunt Kath take Uncle Lee back after all those years apart? Were all our parents more complicated than we'd ever imagined?

Robbie said, "If you want closer to home, 'The leafless trees and every icy crag . . .' "

Aunt Kath said, " 'Tinkled like iron; while far distant' . . . hills? Lordy, I have no memory these days, Robbie. Though not for lack of loving poetry. That's Wordsworth, though. 'Hawkshead.' "

"Hawkshead is just over the hill," Graham said, nodding but not taking his hand from the rail to point.

"And 'hills' is right, Kath," Robbie said. " 'The leafless trees and every icy crag / Tinkled like iron; while far distant hills / Into the tumult sent an alien sound / Of melancholy not unnoticed, while the stars' "—he smiled at Julie on the word, but didn't pause—" 'Eastward were sparkling clear, and in the west / The orange sky of evening died away.' "

" 'Melancholy not unnoticed,' " Julie repeated. "That's lovely, isn't it?"

I wondered if Wordsworth had always written like that, or if it came with practice; if, as with everything else in life, one could become a better writer. How much difference did the place where you were writing make? Did Mom write better here than she did at home?

I would write best in Big Sur, I thought, and I wondered for the first time if Kevin missed living on the coast. It hadn't occurred to me when we moved in together that he might have been making a sacrifice for me. I'd assumed without asking that he'd lived in Half Moon Bay because he couldn't afford the Palo Alto side of the hills, and he hadn't dispelled me of that. But it would be different for him, spending the hour or two he took to write every afternoon at the Peet's coffee shop in the strip mall across from the high school rather than at some perch overlooking the Pacific. Was that why he sometimes wrote in the Rodin sculpture garden at Stanford, wearing fingerless gloves in the wintertime?

"It reminds me of 'The Crier of Claife,'
Robbie," Aunt Kath said. "Not the images, not the
whole poem, but that line."

Robbie said he didn't suppose there was an artist
or poet who wouldn't use the stars here, and he
started talking about several who had.

We were approaching the Ainsley's End pier
when Anna Page rejoined us, the motor already
cut, the boat drifting quietly toward the rubber
tire stops, Robbie at the ready with the docking
rope. As he bounded out first, his strong legs and
strong shoulders moving easily onto the pier,
Aunt Kath asked if he wouldn't join us tomorrow
for whatever we were going to do. "Perhaps a
Wordsworth walk?" she suggested to Anna Page
and Julie and me, as if she cared not one wit about
all the attention from Graham that Anna Page had
arranged to have showered on her. To Robbie, she
said, "To see 'the sunbeams play and the vapours
rest'?"

Anna Page looked from Robbie to Graham to
the stone chimneys of Ainsley's End, all you could
see of it from here.

"Yes, a Wordsworth hike," Graham said. "Rest
assured, Kathleen, that I know much less about
poetry than I do about Cumbrian history, and I'll
leave my lecture notes at home."

Aunt Kath smiled then, a big old smile.

"Shall we meet at Wordsworth's Wishing
Gate?" Robbie suggested. Then, with a glance at

Julie, "Perhaps a breakfast hike? We might find a morning glory in bloom."

"I don't believe they're in season," Julie said, her gray eyes under her straight brows more lighthearted than I'd seen them in a long time, her right hand unconsciously rubbing at the empty ring finger of her left.

"Aren't they, though?" Robbie grinned. "You might be surprised."

28

We had a pleasant dry spell, with the
occasional still days. Today is wild rain.
I have been in Little Langdale and Coniston
on days when the fells were very lovely. . . .
The fells are never twice alike.
——**Beatrix Potter, in a February 28, 1938,
letter to Josephine Banner**

THE OLD WOMAN WHO RANG OUR PURCHASES at the specialty grocer's the next morning was short and round—not five feet, with hair thinning to almost nothing, her visible scalp vulnerable and endearing. As Graham paid, Aunt Kath asked her whether anyone still used farthings (no) and how many there were to a pence. The clerk said to Graham, "I'm too young to know that, now, aren't

I, Lord Wyndham," giving us all our first laugh of the day even before we'd met Robbie at the wooden footbridge that crossed to Rydal Water and Grasmere Lake. As I laughed, I tucked an orange I'd chosen into the pocket with Mom's ashes, remembering her standing at the kitchen sink peeling them for me when I was young, the sharp, sweet citrus scent remaining on her hands later, when she read to me.

Robbie was at Rydal Water when we arrived, and we set off "like a herd of turtles on peanut butter," as Aunt Kath put it, pausing on the footbridge just steps into the five-mile loop, Robbie quoting a few lines about "the earth, and every common sight" seeming "the glory and the freshness of a dream." It was a glorious and fresh day, walkers offering "Hiya" greetings—one of those funny expressions Mom had so loved—as we made our way along a path between a small lake and a red-brackened hillside that rose up to a crag Graham told us was Loughrigg. The path crested at a stretch of rapids connecting Rydal Water and Grasmere Lake, where two men in a canoe dug frantically with oars only to be caught up on a protruding tree root and turned around backward—a metaphor for something, surely, Robbie said.

Aunt Kath responded in a fair mimic of the thin-haired clerk, "I'm too young to know that, now, aren't I?"

Anna Page would have done a better imitation than her mother if the exhaustion of her father's stroke hadn't settled so firmly into her brown eyes. Did it irritate her to have her mother flirting so easily while her father lay in a hospital back home? Not that Aunt Kath owed anything to Uncle Lee, but still, her easy interaction with Robbie and Graham did irritate me. I hadn't slept any better than Anna Page had. We'd all moved into big private rooms at Ainsley's End; Aunt Kath, after we showed her Mom's cottage, had turned to Graham and said, "You did say you have room enough for these girls and then some in that big ol' house of yours, didn't you? Three engines runnin' and not a one of them has the sense to drive." I'd spent much of the night looking out the leaded glass window to the Claife Heights woods, though, half expecting to see the light of the Crier looking for his wife's bones.

From the end of Grasmere Lake, we dropped down into the town where Wordsworth was buried. "He had two wives?" I asked, seeing two women's names on the tombstone: Dorothy and Mary—two wives, like Graham's father, who married Graham's Indian mother and my mother's mother both.

Robbie reminded us that Dorothy was Wordsworth's sister.

"He had five children, two of whom died in childhood," Aunt Kath said.

"Five with Mary," Robbie said. "He fathered a child out of wedlock as well, in Paris."

" 'Strange fits of passion have I known,' " Aunt Kath said.

" 'And I will dare to tell, / But in the Lover's ear alone,' " Robbie replied.

In the lover's ear alone. The words echoed as we wandered through the poet's Dove Cottage, an unassuming white stucco house that reminded me of Kevin's and mine—modest and in need of more windows. "My lover," Kevin always called me. Not "my wife" but "my lover." I had liked that so much, and then I hadn't. How does that happen in a marriage? The small irritations blister and scab as romance gives way to a more stable reality that finds you having given up some part of yourself that you can't bear to have lost.

"Your mama sure loved it here, didn't she?" Aunt Kath asked, taking my arm when we set off again, as if she had no idea how many discussions Anna Page and I had had about how to keep her from joining us at the Lakes. We were headed uphill and across a dirt path Graham and Robbie called "the coffin road," a path over which, in the days when the only consecrated cemetery in the area was in Grasmere, coffins from Ambleside were carried by hand. The deep red bracken below the high road stretched down to a green hillside, beyond which a wreck was being cleared on the road we'd traveled to get to the footbridge, a stretcher being loaded into an ambulance.

"What do you think when you see an accident?" Anna Page asked Graham.

Her mother frowned and said her name, a warning. I half expected Aunt Kath to tell her not to act ugly, as she had so many times not just to Anna Page or Little Lee or Lacy but to all of us Wednesday Kids. Anna Page, undaunted, told Graham, "I hope everyone involved will have completed organ donor registrations and will be matches for my patients." Strange fits of passion, indeed.

"Your grandmother was from these parts, you know," Aunt Kath said to me.

I stepped on a twig across the path, snapping it, catching a glimpse of the smooth blue of the lake below us before turning away from it. "From Manchester," I corrected.

"So you know about your grandmama disowning your mama," she said. "Your mama was so good at keeping focused on the plum in the pudding that I wasn't sure she'd ever shared that grief with you."

On the lake, a lone duck settled on the water beside an abandoned boathouse.

"I let your mama down," she said. "I didn't stop to think what she went through all those years of having lost her own mama but thinking somehow, if she were just a better daughter, her parents

243

would come back to her. It about broke her poor heart until she had you, I suppose. I do think you were all she needed in this whole world, though, at least for a spell."

I watched a second duck join the first as I tried to hold back a deep wave of sorrow, thinking of what Anna Page had said about needing to tuck some of Mom into her pocket, too, thinking of all the years Aunt Kath had been my mother's friend, more years than Anna Page had been taking care of me in her odd little way, decades more than Julie and I had been friends.

"It must have hurt Mom," I said. "Her parents disowning her." Several other ducks had joined the pair on the pond, while a yellow-beaked blackbird settled on the boathouse roof, watching them from a distance. "It hurt me, and they were only my grandparents," I admitted. "It made me feel . . ." I looked ahead to Graham, his skin, like my brother's, not light but lighter than mine. "It made me feel wrong."

Aunt Kath touched a hand to my back, saying, "Oh, Hope, there is nothing wrong about you, honey. Every dog has a few fleas, but even your fleas have great big ol' hearts."

Robbie and Julie, quite a ways ahead, paused beside a large, flat slab of granite. I began walking again, and Aunt Kath fell in beside me. "Who wouldn't like it here?" she said. "Especially some-one like your mama, who always did prefer a quiet sunset to fireworks exploding and falling to earth."

"And then Graham was here."

She looked ahead to Graham. "This little brother she'd not known she had was here to greet her. Imagine that."

We walked along in silence, catching up with the others at a large flat boulder tucked up next to a dry stone wall: Coffin Stone, or Resting Stone, a small white marker beside it explained. A place the porters rested their heavy loads on their sad journeys across the Coffin Road. Wordsworth's coffin would have rested here, I supposed, and his wife's and his sister's.

I fingered the orange in my pocket. My mother's little puzzle box would seem so insubstantial resting here.

" 'O there is blessing in this gentle breeze,' " Robbie said as a light wind kicked up.

"Wordsworth began writing *The Prelude* when he was twenty-eight," Graham said, "and it wasn't published until after he died, at eighty. Can you imagine that?"

Anna Page smiled at him, delighted for the first time that day, and responded in a nearly perfect imitation of the clerk's voice, "I'm too young to imagine that, now, aren't I?"

The two of them laughed together.

"The work of a lifetime," Graham said.

When everyone made ready to set off again,

Anna Page asked me to wait with her a minute. She thought I would welcome the relief from her mom. "Graham and Ma seem to be hitting it off, though, don't they?" she said.

She sat on the stone, and I sat beside her, the cold seeping up from under me.

"Ape, is it true what Julie said about you and your sister's fiancé?" I asked.

"Good Lord, where did that come from?" She looked down at the water, the ducks all floating together but the yellow-beaked blackbird no longer atop the abandoned boathouse. "It wasn't like that, the way Julie says it was," she said. "I didn't know Lacy and that turd were going to meet. How could I know they were going to meet?"

"You brought the guy to the beach."

Kevin had built sand castles that day. Dad was alive. Mom and Jamie, too.

"I was still seeing him myself, though," Anna Page said. "How could I know they were going to get together?"

"You brought Kevin to that tailgate party."

"Oh, Hope." She looked at her feet, the weedy ground around the stone. "It wasn't like that with Kevin. It wasn't like that at all with Kevin."

I stared toward the imposing crag across the lake. "What was it like with Kevin?"

"It wasn't like anything with Kevin! God, Hope, Lacy's guy was a jerk! Didn't you know that from the start? Of course I told her I'd slept with him. She might have married him! You dreaded that for her as much as I did. You know you did. I couldn't let her marry him."

"Because you'd slept with him."

"Because he was a jerk."

"You didn't sleep with him?"

She looked at me, but I didn't look back. "You think I made that up to scare my sister away from some guy I didn't want her to marry?" she said. "Jeez, Hope."

I stuck my hands in my pockets, found the bit of Mom under the orange, the ashes that weren't ashes, that I didn't want to share. "So you did sleep with him," I said.

"I slept with him before she met him, Hope. Before. And it's not like it meant anything. It was just sex."

"Why didn't you tell her when she first started seeing him? Why wait till they were engaged?" Wondering if she'd ever told Mom about all the men, or any of them. Thinking she wouldn't have, that she wouldn't have wanted Mom to know.

"I don't know, Hope. If I'd seen where it was going, absolutely I would have. And maybe I should have seen that. Maybe I should have known Lacy would fall for such an absolute jerk."

"One you'd had sex with."

"Would you want the wrath of the whole

Wednesday Gang coming down on your sex life before Kevin?"

"I *had* no sex life before Kevin!"

We looked down the Coffin Road toward the others, hoping they were far enough ahead not to have heard.

I had no sex life before Kevin and almost none with him in the past months.

"Not even with Rajiv?" Anna Page asked, the disbelief in her voice hurting more than I had imagined. But Rajiv wasn't the kind of guy who would marry a woman he'd slept with. Rajiv wasn't the kind of guy who would marry anyone who'd ever had sex.

"Pffft," Anna Page said, the way Jamie used to. "Rajiv was a jerk."

The kind of guy she was forever sleeping with and tossing off. But if she'd slept with Rajiv, she wouldn't have told me, any more than she would have told Lacy, except that Lacy had gotten engaged. And if she'd slept with Kevin, she wouldn't admit that, either, because she liked Kevin, because she didn't think he was a jerk. And maybe I didn't want to know. What would be the point? If she told me she'd slept with him, I could never turn away from that, and if she denied it, I would have no way to know whether she was telling the truth or protecting me from it.

29

I once had a mouse which must have been cross
bred. . . . It was all brown except a white mark
down its face. It was ferociously tame. I used to
let it run about in the evenings & when I wanted
to catch it I flapped a pocket handkcf. in the
middle of the room—or rooms—when it would
come out & fight, leaping at the hdcf.
I think I remember it was that same mouse which
got into trouble with the authorities by biting out
a circular hole in a sheet on my bed!
——Beatrix Potter, in a November 27, 1920,
letter to Jessie Wyatt

AFTER TEA IN THE PROSPECT BACK AT
Ainsley's End, I found myself following Graham
out through the perfectly geometric herb garden,
past the rose garden and the last of the fall squash
vines to a greenhouse I'd not seen before, inside
of which the only green was paint: watercolors of
rabbits and possums and ducks on small canvases,
Gabby the goose in her purple velvet vest from the
story Mom had written for Sam and me. There
were Petey the Parakeet and Oyster Joe, each on
an easel, and Aaron Anaconda, who was Sammy's
favorite. When Aunt Frankie had made me a

replacement stuffed Mr. Jackson, she'd made a stuffed Aaron for him.

"This is where my mother painted?" I asked.

"Your mum?" Graham looked as if the idea of my mother painting was as improbable to him as it was to me. "I wanted to . . . Your mum would have wanted you . . ."

He extracted a funny little book from an intricate chest of inlaid wood flowers and vines finished to a high polish—a chest very like my mother's puzzle boxes, which surely she'd chosen for this place where all her paintings lived. The book had no real cover; it was just pages hole-punched and bound together with yarn Mom might have gotten from Aunt Frankie. "The True Tale of Lolly Labradoodle," it was titled, and on the front page was a watercolor of the cutest brown Labradoodle. Really, you just wanted to pull him into your lap and bury your face in his fur, which was long and wavy, neither the tight curls of a poodle nor the straight short hair of a Lab. The puppy's eyes were buried under all that inviting fur, his ears floppy and furry, only his button of a nose and his bright pink tongue giving non-fuzzy texture to his face.

Labradoodle. I remember Mom's glee at first hearing that word. "You could name him Doodle," she'd said, "and call him Doo-Doo!" The Wednesday Sisters had laughed and laughed together over that. She never had gotten any dog, though. Sammy and I had talked about getting her one after Dad died, but she was already coming to England regularly by then, and who would have cared for a puppy while she was overseas?

Lolly Labradoodle. I turned the page and started reading. Lolly's mother was a chocolate Lab and her father a poodle. They all lived together in a falling-down old mansion at the edge of a children's park in Palo Alto, where, when Lolly was old enough—past the parvo vaccine? was Mom really writing about parvo vaccines in a children's book?—she and her parents began taking their humans for walks.

Eleanor Pardee Park. I recognized it in the illustration. The playground. The big sycamores that used to edge the park but had been cut down lest another limb fall, perhaps on a child playing on the playground this time. It had grieved Mom when they'd torn down those majestic trees and replaced them with twigs that would never amount to much in her lifetime; she'd been right about that.

The old house Lolly lived in was the mansion that used to stand in the park, I supposed.

"Nobody starts out being able to play the piano," Lolly's father assures her in the story. Since Lolly won't play with the other children— all the happy quacks and chirps and meows of the others seem to scare her—her parents have put an old upright piano in her bedroom in the old mansion, and they try to teach her to play. The poodle plays ragtime, and the Lab plays quieter classical. They are awfully good at it, especially for animals with thick pads and short toes. Really, they have extraordinary reach with those toes, even taking into consideration the additional length of their nails, which they don't much like to have clipped.

The other children in the park stop to listen at first—it becomes part of what they love about the park, the possibility of piano music wafting out from the upstairs windows. But Lolly plays so poorly, it sends everyone fleeing. She tries to mimic her poodle dad's ragtime. She tries her Lab mom's classical. The harder she tries, the more often she hits the wrong notes.

The Lab mom closes the piano and goes to an old-fashioned record player. "Close your eyes and listen," she says to Lolly, and she plays first one record and then another: pop and show tunes and jazz. Lolly just looks sad. Her floppy brown ears droop low, and she sets her head on her paws, giving her mother the saddest look you've ever seen. On the sixth record, though, Lolly's ears perk up, and in the last illustration, she's wailing on the piano while, outside the window, the other animal children have a grand time in the park. The sheet music on the piano has no text, only a familiar pattern of watercolor notes.

"It isn't quite done," Graham said. "I thought it

252

was, but your mum, she was still working on it. She meant to hold on to it until you and Kevin had your first child, I believe. She would have wanted you to have it now, as would I."

He would? This brother who didn't even mourn her?

He tilted his head slightly, considering me.

I paged backward through the book for an excuse to look away. I turned from the happy puppy piano player back through her struggle to learn the music, all the way to the front cover, the cute little Labradoodle. Lolly Labradoodle. When I'd told Mom that Sam and I considered getting her one, she'd said it was Kevin and me who needed a Labradoodle, they were wonderful with children and didn't wreak havoc with allergies.

"I'm very good at what I do," I said to Graham. "The law."

Graham slid the book back and opened it again, to the first few pages: the Lab mom and the poodle dad with their little Labradoodle in environmentally correct cloth diapers.

"It's comforting, that: having a defined role," he said.

Graham Wyndham V, lord of Ainsley's End. A role that had been defined for generations.

He turned the pages of the book, stopping at the last scene with the piano, and smiled. "The notes on the sheet music, your mum was quite particular that they be just so. I believe they are a few measures from a band named . . . was it Ruckus Girls?"

I shut my eyes to the sunlight streaming through the glass surrounding us, willing me to grow, like a plant. "Riot grrrls?"

Bratmobile. Bikini Kill. Music that, my last summer in college, Mom was forever asking me to turn down.

"It may have been," Graham said.

"I had no idea what Mom was doing here," I said. "I don't know that I gave it much thought, what life she might have that didn't revolve around me. I didn't even know she could paint."

He closed the book again, his touch lingering on the carefully drawn lettering of the title. "It wouldn't be the first time I would be wrong about a thing, but . . . Your mum, she once tried to draw here in the greenhouse, channeling Beatrix Potter the way she did. Quite honestly, I'm afraid her stick figures were a sorry sight. Stick figures, literally, as she was trying to draw a bare branch in a vase."

"This isn't her studio?"

"It is. Yes, of course. We shared it, your mum and I did."

The realization dawning: all my mother's characters propped up around me warmed in the sunlight, the possums and spiders, the goose in her purple vest at home against the backdrop of dying vines beyond walls of glass. "You did these, Graham? The illustrations?"

But he didn't even mourn her.

He turned to the glass wall and set a palm flat against it, the wall that had let in the sun but kept out the cold, the wind, the rain as he and Mom had worked side by side, in companionable silence. In his posture, I saw how wrong I was about him, about so many things. He was what he was: a proper British gentleman from a proper British estate, playing his role. A man who was expected to control his emotions and was doing his best.

"She used to say we were two different halves of one thing, in different bodies," he said.

30

From the Journals of Ally Tantry

10.7.2011, Near Sawrey. Bea took me to Hawkshead so she could show me Mr. Heelis's law offices today.

——I always feel very dumpy without my husband, she said.

She meant to comfort me, I suppose. She meant to be telling me she understood how dumpy I feel without Jim, and that she didn't mind keeping me company through my dumpiness. That she knew how I felt because she'd lost Norman Warne even if she hadn't lost William Heelis.

——I always hate to go to London because it takes me

so very far away from William, she said. Also, because no one there remembers to call me Mrs. Heelis.

I actually smiled a little; I never think of her as Mrs. Heelis, either.

William Heelis's offices have been turned into a gallery now, filled with Bea's art, but she ignored that. She spent forever taking me about the room that was his private office, which someone had the good sense to leave as it was when he was a solicitor, with his desk and his typewriter, his law books in an alcove across the hall. One could imagine the window view hasn't changed much from when he worked here, although I suppose the line of tourists in T-shirts with odd sayings do present a different prospect than Mr. Heelis enjoyed.

——I can't imagine why Mr. Heelis left his golf clubs here in his office, of all places, Bea said.

She was not thrilled with the idea of going upstairs; the top floor has been converted into space to show her drawings and paintings. Virtually all the originals belong to the gallery, although they show only part of the collection at any one time. Right now the things they have on display center around **The Tale of Mrs. Tittlemouse**, published over a hundred years ago.

Hope would love to see the original painting of the final scene in **Mrs. Tittlemouse**, where Mr. Jackson is leaning in through the window to participate in the tea party without getting dirt on Mrs. Tittlemouse's floor, being handed acorn cupfuls of honeydew. "Haycorn cupfuls," that's the way Hope used to say it. As I imagine her own daughter will say it someday.

——Allison, Bea admonishes. Let's not go into Mr. McGregor's garden, now.

We're nowhere near Mr. McGregor's garden, we're again at the charming tea shop down the road from Hill Top, but I take her point.

——I wish Hope would write, I say. Not for anyone but herself if she doesn't want to. Just to help her sort out how she feels.

I wish Hope had been with me to see Bea's original work. Somehow, if you imagine Bea creating her stories at all, you imagine she just pulled out her watercolors and painted, then penned in some text. In fact, there were many, many sketches of the characters——and everything else, but the ones I noticed most were the characters.

——And the mushrooms, Bea reminds me.

——And the mushroom drawings, Bea, I concede.

——People do underestimate how many years I spent drawing and painting my pet bunny, and the cabbages in the Fawe Park garden, and frogs and hedgehogs and anything else I could capture long enough to study and sketch. Oh, the hours I spent hunched over mushrooms as a young woman. I was only an amateur, but the paper I wrote about the symbiotic nature of lichens——

——Yes, you've told me about that, Bea, I say.

She looks out over Esthwaite Water, her favorite view, while I make notes about a quote from one of Bea's letters, which I'd seen hung in a simple frame on the wall of Mr. Heelis's offices——the most moving thing I've seen here yet:

Thank God I have the seeing eye, that is to say as I lie in bed I can walk step by step on the fells and rough lands seeing every stone and flower and patch of bog and cotton grass where my old legs will never take me again.

I said "Oh, Bea" right out loud, there in the place that had been her husband's offices, where she must have come often on any excuse to see this late-blooming love of her life. Such a stunning few words. So moving. I keep returning to them, trying to sort out why they're so effective. Maybe because the beginning carries the suggestion of going somewhere, as if she's just woken and is planning her day. Then the turn at the end: she's looking backward on a whole life rather than forward to an afternoon, and all that hopefulness and beauty at the start of the sentence belongs to a past she can't ever have again.

Very moving. And perhaps an argument for sad endings. I will have to think about this.

There were all her sketches, and her completed paintings, some with notes around the edges that you can see if the frame doesn't cut off the words, things like "Make his fur the same color as all the other paintings, but don't alter the picture when doing it." Lines across the bottoms of some of the pictures indicate the width should be, say, three inches, although the original picture might be larger.

—Some think I'm too particular, Bea says, but a

picture that is too small or too large can spoil an entire book.

——Hope is compulsive like that, I say. She gets it from her father. It makes her good at what she does, but it can be a challenge to live with.

——Can it?

I give her a look, and she sighs.

——Anna Page is more like I am, I say. Easier.

——Kathleen's Anna Page? Allison, I'm sorry to say that Anna Page is easier than precisely no one.

Well, perhaps not. And yet I imagine she would be easy with Graham. Why is that?

——Making the match for the matchmaker, Bea says. But do you suppose Anna Page would be good for Graham?

——She does seem to order the dinner plate she least prefers and leave it all behind for the waitress to clear, I concede, but he would be good for her if she would let him be.

I pour tea into our cups and return to my journal.

——Do you truly mean to write about me? Bea asks.

——I hope so, Bea.

——And Water Lily, she says. You can't write a whole book about me without including Water Lily.

——We'll see about that, Bea, I say.

She looks a bit niggly in response. Niggly. I love that word.

——All this talk about Hope and Anna Page, Bea says. Sometimes I have the sense that it's your own life more than mine that you've come to the Lakes to learn about. I used to imagine it was your mother, but now I see it was more than that.

I look out at the water again, trying to imagine my mother as a young woman who thought she would live her whole life here when she is in fact about to leave.

——If you must write about me, Bea says, I think I ought not to be dead in your book. What good comes of writing about a dead old woman sheep keeper?

——Beatrix Christ, I say. I was thinking more of a dead old woman who wrote children's stories that will long survive us all.

Bea basks in this for a moment.

——But I'm much more interesting alive than dead, you know, she says.

And the truth is, I can't disagree with that. The truth is that all during this conversation——all during this tea while I've scribbled notes and Bea has contemplated the view——I've been thinking about the quote I saw on Mr. Heelis's office wall, thinking it would be a lovely thing to take Bea up onto the fells again, if ever our old legs could manage the task.

31

The first thing I did when I arrived is go
through the back kitchen ceiling, I don't
think I ran any risk, it went down wholesale so
it was not scratchy to my stockings, & the
rafters were too near together to permit my
slipping through. The joiner & plasterer were
much alarmed and hauled me out.
——Beatrix Potter, after a visit to her newly purchased
Hill Top Farm, in a September 30, 1906,
letter to Millie Warne

"LOOK AT THIS, AUNT KATH," I SAID, NOT FOR
the first time since we arrived at Beatrix Potter's
Hill Top Farm the next morning, and paid the
ticket price, and passed the time waiting for our
turn to go in by wandering the lane where Potter
drew herself into *The Tale of Samuel Whiskers*.
Mom read me the book so many times that I
recognized at once where Potter had stood in the
background watching Samuel Whiskers and Anna
Maria flee with Potter's own wheelbarrow—
which they'd stolen and filled with bundles—after
being caught trying to make Tom Kitten into a
roly-poly pudding.

Our group—Anna Page and Julie and I, together

with Aunt Kath and Graham—were about as many people as they let into the modest little house at a time, so we had it nearly to ourselves when our turn came.

"Are those her shoes?" Aunt Kath asked, indicating a pair tucked under a chair by the fireplace—shoes my mom would have studied in detail, trying to make out some truth about their owner. Shoes she would have imagined walking in, for the book she meant to write. Shoes "Bea" wore in the pages of Mom's journal sometimes, and yet not. The shoes Mom wrote about were lace-up. These were gardening clogs.

"That's Potter's hat," Graham said, touching Aunt Kath's arm and directing her attention to a fedora hanging by the mantel. The touch seemed so easy, as if, in the space of two days spent getting to know each other, they'd become intimate. Anna Page looked even more discomfited by the touch than I was, although this was what she'd intended, her mother and Graham hitting it off. The uneasy set of her chin was very like when she tells the story of introducing Jamie and Isaac, a triple date of Julie with Noah and Anna Page with some guy whose name she no longer remembers, all at the outdoor tables overlooking the Rodin sculpture garden at Stanford, where Kevin and I like to go late at night.

A year. It had been a year since Jamie had died. It was the anniversary of her death.

"Is this Potter's umbrella?" Julie asked.

The docent answered that even after she married William Heelis, Potter had kept Mr. Warne's umbrella and pipe. She'd died with her wedding ring from Heelis on her left hand and her engagement ring from Warne on her right.

"Beatrix remained friendly with Mr. Warne's sister her whole long life," Aunt Kath said, "but do you s'pose that was truly friendship or simply shared grief?"

Julie looked a bit stricken by the words, but if Aunt Kath noticed, she didn't show it. "Lordy," she continued, "it's a hard thing to let go of a love who has died."

I took Julie's arm to comfort her, to comfort me, and I said, "Look: the clock from *The Tale of Samuel Whiskers*."

As if to assure me of my memory, the book itself sat beside the clock, opened to the page with Mrs. Tabitha Twitchit standing on the landing at the turn of the stairs, right in front of the clock. On the adjacent page: *Some of the walls were four feet thick, and there used to be queer noises inside them, as if there might be a little secret staircase. Certainly there were odd little jagged doorways in the wainscot, and things disappeared at night— especially cheese and bacon.* It was something, how Potter took disgusting critters who were destroying her home—rats in the walls, for heaven's sake—and turned them into adorable

263

storybook characters who charmed children and adults alike.

Upstairs, in the room to the right, Aunt Kath showed us a copy of a rejection letter she found on a desk in the corner. "Well, if that doesn't put pepper in the gumbo. How does an editor have the nerve to reject Beatrix Potter?"

In another room—a small bedroom with bed curtains Potter herself embroidered—I found a beautiful dollhouse, with Tom Thumb's ceramic ham inside. It was shiny yellow streaked with red, like the ham that jerks off the plate and rolls under the table in *The Tale of Two Bad Mice*, provoking poor frustrated Tom Thumb to have at it with tongs and a shovel. Tongs like Julie had thrust at Anna Page, opening up a mean little place in my heart. *Bang, bang, smash, smash! The ham flew all into pieces, for underneath the shiny paint it was made of nothing but plaster!* Tom and Hunca Munca had broken all the dollhouse food then: the lobsters and the fruit and the pudding, which I hadn't realized meant not just Jell-O pudding but any kind of dessert. They put the fish in "the red-hot crinkly paper fire" because it wouldn't come off the plate, but it wouldn't burn, either.

I'd smashed a plate once, in the middle of an argument with Kevin. Not smashed, exactly, but set it down hard in the sink so that it cracked—I'd meant for it to crack. What had that fight been about? It was hard even to remember. Was that the anniversary Kevin had prepared a fancy seafood gumbo and opened a bottle of champagne that had grown flat by the time I arrived home, hours after I'd said I was on my way? Was it the disappointment on Kevin's face or in my heart that had started that red-hot crinkly fire? I'd have called if I'd realized how much time it would take, if I'd been in my office instead of stopping by a conference room to check some closing-documents changes on my way out the door. A last-minute disaster of a problem for my biggest client—what was I supposed to do? I'd wanted a romantic evening together as much as Kevin had. I wasn't the one who'd grown so impatient as to open the champagne and drink a glass by myself.

Beside me, Julie reached a ringed finger toward Lucinda and Jane Doll-cook but didn't touch them. "Jamie and I had a dollhouse," she said, blinking and blinking.

"I remember that," I said.

"We each had our own dolls for it, but we shared everything else. The house. The furniture. The tea set."

I intertwined my fingers with hers and leaned my head against her shoulder as Anna Page joined us.

"You used to sit your dolls at the table and put real tea in the tiny cups," Anna Page said. "A drop each, that's all that would fit." She stroked Julie's hair like she stroked mine when she was comforting me. "I was too old for dolls when you got it, but I used to wish I weren't."

"It's funny how those few years that separated us grew less and less important over time," I said.

Anna Page smiled a little. "You both used to be envious of how old I was, and now I'm envious of how young you are."

Julie, too, managed something like a smile. "Isn't it weird to imagine that Beatrix Potter was once as young as we were, playing with dolls?"

"The dollhouse isn't from Potter's childhood," a docent informed us. She stood unobtrusively in the corner. We hadn't seen her there. "It belonged to a niece of her publisher, Norman Warne. Potter meant to visit Surbiton to sketch it for *The Tale of Two Bad Mice*, but her mother intervened, as there had been entirely too much visiting with Mr. Warne already." The docent lowered her voice. "Mr. Warne was in trade, you know." Then more brightly, "He sent Miss Potter photographs, as well as the dolls which became Lucinda and Jane, and later, some of the dollhouse furniture and a box of the food on platters. Miss Potter began sending miniature letters— ones that folded up to form tiny envelopes— to her favorite young people about then. Conversations between animal characters that continued the stories in the books, they were, weren't they? Squirrel Nutkin writing to Old

Brown 'Dear Sir, I should esteem it a favour if you will let me have back my tail, as I miss it very much. I would pay postage.' "

We all laughed at that.

Egged on, the docent quoted another letter: " 'Miss Lucinda Doll requires Hunca Munca to come for the whole day on Tuesday. Jane Doll-cook has had an accident, she has broken a soup tureen and both her wooden legs.' "

We all laughed again, Julie and Anna Page wiping tears from their eyes together. What a blessing humor is, what a balm for grief.

32

The dumpling had been peeled off Tom Kitten,
and made separately into a bag pudding,
with currants in it to hide the smuts.
They had been obliged to put Tom Kitten
into a hot bath to get the butter off.
——from **The Tale of Samuel Whiskers**
by Beatrix Potter

SOMETHING ABOUT TOM THUMB'S PERFECTLY intact little ham, where in the book he'd smashed it to bits, haunted me all the way home from Hill Top Farm. While everyone else settled in at Ainsley's End, I collected the Labradoodle book

Mom had done with Graham and escaped to her cottage, where I washed my face in the tiny sink that, I realized as I did it, was the sink in which Lolly washes her little piano-playing paws. With my face still damp, I stretched out on my mother's bed and opened the book again. The illustrations were very like Potter's and yet not. They were watercolors, and they were charming little animals in charming little settings, but they weren't derivative. I read through the text again— charming in its own way, except maybe the part about the parvo vaccine. Yes, Lolly Labradoodle was a ridiculous name, but so were Hunca Munca and Tom Thumb.

I looked up from the book to see the tub that was the slipper tub on the pages, the fireplace with its odd insert that was behind the tub in the book. Perhaps Mom had sat on this bed writing that scene. Perhaps Graham had sat with his back against these pillows and a sketch pad in his hands, the two of them chatting easily as he drew and she wrote. It was the kind of thing Sammy and I had done as kids: sat with our backs propped up against the same headboard, watching television in our parents' bedroom while they hosted a dinner party downstairs. It was what we'd done after the undertaker had come for Mom's body, sat side by side on the bed where she died. And it was what I'd done later the night Mom died, with Kevin—sat beside him on our own bed and talked about when I soaked the stuffed Mr. Jackson Aunt Frankie had given me, the first real memory I have. "Isn't it weird, Kev," I'd said, "that my first memory is about drowning some poor stuffed toad in a bathroom sink?"

"Your first memory is of your mother loving you, Asha," Kevin said, taking my hand. "The toad was just the medium for that, or maybe for the whole Wednesday Gang loving you."

If I left Kevin, if I started over with someone new, they would never understand that. They wouldn't know the sound of Mom laughing together with all the Wednesday Sisters, like Kevin does. They wouldn't know what all the Beatrix Potter quotes meant and had always meant, something beyond the books. They wouldn't have built Taj Mahal sand castles with Dad, making magic for the Wednesday Grandkids that I was always sure was meant for me as well. They would never laugh with me when I said "Heavens to Betsy." They would have no idea that "Heavens to Betsy" was my mom.

And yet the hurts had piled up between us: the snaps at each other when we were tired or crabby, the all-out arguments that weren't about what they appeared to be. "What kind of a child would Kevin and I have?" I'd asked my mother once when she was pushing me. "A redhead who looks like the altar boy his father once was but would quote Richard Dawkins—'You keep believing,

I'll keep evolving'—even to his poor great Ama if she were still alive." Mom had said I was being melodramatic, that no one had ever wanted me to be anything but who I was except maybe Ama, who couldn't be blamed for wanting her grand-daughter to perform *laxmi puja* the way she did. And maybe I *was* being melodramatic, like with cracking the plate. But there was hurt there, too, the hurt of my opinions being dismissed. My *feelings* being dismissed. Kevin was always so sure of everything, and he was always so reason-able. How could I care more about the color of a bike than the smoothness of its ball bearings if smooth ball bearings kept me safer? How could I argue with the idea that my clients should respect a lawyer who made dinner with her husband a priority? How could I defend in the face of men throwing acid on young girls' faces my amorphous belief that something somewhere must have started this world, my vague notion that God was a comfort, that the existence of some god somewhere was more humane than making those girls live without hope of some better afterlife. My compromise God might not make sense to Kevin or to anyone else, but it was the place where my mother's Christianity and my father's Hinduism overlapped. It was what I grew up with, what I had.

It was a way my parents had compromised that Kevin and I seemed unable to. I bought the safer bike helmet or lawn mower or car because it was easier than not doing so. I brought work home and did it after he went to sleep. I listened without contradiction to his soliloquies on religion that came with each new article on Afghanistan, each new pedophilia charge or proclamation against birth control. I'd given up trying to defend my compromise God against Kevin's barrage of science long before I needed a heaven for Jamie and Dad and Mom, before I wanted that comfort for myself.

I set the Labradoodle book aside, put the stopper in the tub, and let the water run. Mom's bubble bath was on the marble tabletop that had been empty when we'd arrived here, where at home the tub edge was crowded with the scents and textures of her. I uncapped the bottle and smelled—the vanilla of my childhood, almost without fragrance and yet as warm and comforting as the thin, crispy sugar cookies Mom and Aunt Kath used to make together. I'd almost forgotten that, all of us in Aunt Kath's kitchen, making those cookies. Aunt Frankie and Aunt Linda and Aunt Brett talking with Mom and Aunt Kath while they helped us cut the dough into shapes and decorate with colored sprinkles, silver candy balls, smashed candy-cane pieces that looked like Tom Thumb's smashed ceramic ham.

I recapped the bottle without adding any to the water and set it on the low marble table. Not bothering to light the coal fire, I took off my clothes, folded them carefully, set them at the end of the perfectly made bed that had been my mother's bed, where she'd slept alone. I stepped into the water, which smelled faintly of iron, and adjusted the faucet so that more cold mingled with the hot. I sank down, leaned against the smooth white slipper back, and closed my eyes. The water splashed warm on my feet.

The bath was growing cold when the cottage door opened and Julie barged in without apology, closed the door behind her, and stretched out on my mother's batik bedspread. "Can I talk to you for a minute?" she asked. "It's about that damned umbrella."

I looked for a washcloth to cover my chest, the way Mom always had in her bathtub, but there was nothing but the bubble bath bottle unopened on the table beside me.

"Do you think she loved him?" Julie asked.

I frowned at my unmanicured toes underneath the faucet, trying to figure out who "he" and "she" might be. "My mother and Graham?"

Julie's silver-ringed fingers went to her temple, her straight-across brow, and she said she was sorry, she shouldn't be bothering me. "God, aren't you freezing?" she asked.

She laid a coal fire, lit the paper in the grate, and flicked out the match. "Only one left," she said, holding up the burnt end. She blinked surprise. "That's the answer."

"The answer?"

"To the dates in your mom's journals. Like with the alphabet, the code. If you add one, it makes sense. The A is B, and the one is two. 1998 is 2009. 1999 is 2010."

I toed the cold faucet with my bare wet foot. "1999 would be 2000 if you add one to each digit."

"Not one to the whole thing, to—Oh, I see." Julie tossed the spent match on top of the coals, in the center of the fire-starter flame. "Your mom makes a mistake, then. If you'd been writing 2009 in your journal as 1998, when you got to 2010, would you stop to realize you didn't just add one to the prior code?" She settled on the bed, her back against the pillows. "So do you think she loved him?" she asked. "Not your mom. Beatrix Potter."

The umbrella, she'd said. "The publisher fiancé who died?" I asked.

"The other one," Julie said. "The husband."

I watched the smoke wafting up into the chimney, the ashes falling into the drawer at the bottom. "Because she wore the first fiancé's ring for the rest of her life, you mean?"

"And kept his damned umbrella and the doll-house food, but she married the second guy, and they used to go boating in the evening at that pond we hiked to. It sounds so very romantic. I think she did love him, despite what Aunt Kath said."

I looked to the fireplace, the paper burned up, the coals reddening. What had Aunt Kath said? "It's a hard thing to let go of a love who has died."

Julie stood and picked up the tongs she'd thrust into Anna Page's face. Uncle. Aunt. Second cousin thrice removed. She scissored up another coal and set it on the grate, then added another the fire didn't yet need.

I toed the faucet again. She'd never said it, but I supposed she thought if Jamie had lived, her marriage to Isaac would have fallen apart, too. Same genes, she might say. Same inability to be satisfied with what you have. It's perhaps the only advantage to dying early, she might say: you're left without the time to make the mistakes the rest of us eventually make.

"Jamie's been dead a year," Julie said. "In the Jewish faith, even children mourning their parents are supposed to set aside their mourning after a year."

I sank lower in the water, the smooth porcelain against my shoulders and a thin skin of water between the tub and the small of my back. Could Oliver let go of his mother? Could anyone expect him to? I was almost forty, I didn't need my mother every day like Oliver did, and yet it seemed impossible that I might love anyone who asked me to let go of her.

"Isaac still wears his wedding ring on his left hand," she said, "but Potter wore Warne's engagement ring her whole life."

I climbed from the water and went into my mother's tiny bathroom, pulled a towel from the towel warmer, and wrapped it around myself. It was cream-colored. The contrast to my skin made me think of my parents' hands intertwined. They'd held hands their whole lives. I wondered if Julie and Isaac ever held hands.

I returned into the main room and sat on my mother's bed, beside Julie. I took her hand. Her left hand, where there remained a pale indent from all those years she'd worn Noah's ring. "Oliver is only six," I said.

"But I love Oliver," she said, blinking back tears. "Nobody loves Oliver more than I do." She fingered a chain of silver beads at her throat. "He doesn't call me anything," she said. "I think he dreads making that mistake."

"Oliver?" Thinking of the Christmas cookies. I hate you I hate you I hate you.

She held the tissue box from the bedside table out to me, and we each took one. "Isaac," she said.

The light through the window cast a reddened softness on the wide-planked floor, the smooth white tub, the batik spread that Aunt Frankie must have made for Mom. So many things I'd lose if I left Kevin, all the things he understood that no other man would: the sound of my mother's laughter, the stories. But was that love, or was it, as Aunt Kath suggested, simply shared grief?

All the difficulties Jamie and Isaac had endured, they had survived. That tough first year, Jamie teaching and trying to complete her Montessori training at the same time. Jamie's pregnancy, when, let's be honest, no one in his right mind would have endured how crazy she was with all those hormones running rampant. Their marriage had lasted through the first year of nonsleeping Oliver, and his terrible, terrible threes. It had lasted through Jamie's diagnosis and her treatment. Till death did they part.

Julie's brows gathered, and she swallowed once, twice. "Before Jamie died—"

"But you both knew she was dying!" Not wanting to hear her admit it aloud, not wanting the certainty of a confession that she'd done that to her own sister while Jamie was dying. "Don't you think the grieving starts with the certainty that someone is dying, even if we fight against it?" I said. "That on some level we all accepted that Jamie was dying before it happened? That we had to, to get used to the idea of losing her before she was gone?"

"Oliver didn't," Julie sobbed. "Poor Oliver, he couldn't understand any more than Jamie and her brother and I understood what our mother was saying over those damned strawberry waffles."

A flutter of honking came from some geese down by the boathouse, leaving in its wake an awareness of other sounds that had been there before: the lap of water, the tapping of a woodpecker some way in the distance, the rustle of a bird in the tree outside the cornflower-blue door.

"The thing with Oliver, with the Christmas cookies, that wasn't your fault," I said.

Julie took the tissue box from the bedside table and extended it to me again. I tightened the towel around my chest. She pulled a tissue, blew her nose, and set the box on the table, beside the book my mother had done with the brother she hadn't even known she had.

"It must have been hard to lose your mom without any warning," Julie said.

I reached across her and took "The True Tale of Lolly Labradoodle" in hand, not turning the pages, only feeling the steadying weight of the open book. You get to say goodbye or you don't. Either way, the person you love is gone.

Julie wiped the tears from her cheeks with her fingers like her sister's fingers, and Oliver's. "At least you have Kevin," she said.

"I don't, not really," I said. "Indian-lawyer Barbie in her fancy home with the double tub has Kevin. The suits and pumps, the briefcase—all of it so much more attractive than the reality of a wife who doesn't always come home for dinner."

"He doesn't care about the suits and pumps," Julie said.

"He . . . keeps assuming I agree with him when

I don't, Jules, talking about things as if no one but a fool could disagree with him, the implication being that if I want to disagree, then I'm a fool. It leaves me wanting to retreat into the warm world of the Wednesday Gang."

Julie smiled just a little. "Where Aunt Kath can question your reading choices?" she asked. "Where my mom can assume you will do exactly what *she* wants to do—write, run, whatever—because who wouldn't want to be like her?"

I got up and traded the towel for my clothes, thinking: *Where Aunt Frankie says I'm beautiful, even if I'm not, and believes it. Where Aunt Linda admonishes everyone to focus on my brains rather than my looks.*

Dressed again, I sat beside Julie on the bed. It was more comfortable than the love seat. "I'm not sure I could go through losing all those babies, like Mom did," I said.

"You didn't miscarry, you were just late. There's no reason to—"

"I'm almost forty."

Julie shrugged.

"Mom took DES."

We both looked to the empty tub, as if Mom might be found there, as if this thing she never talked about might be explained without her.

"Is that what scares you, Hope?" Julie asked.

I traced the pattern in Mom's bedspread, where Julie's fingers had just been. "I don't know." I stood and poked at the fire Julie had built to warm me, then I sat beside her again. "Noah loves you, too, you know," I said.

"But I don't love him!" She tipped her head, stared up at the ceiling. "I don't love him. That was the thing I realized when I was breathing in the anesthesia before my mastectomy."

"You left Noah when . . ." I swallowed against the idea of her leaving her husband when she'd just had her breasts removed, when she must have wondered if she'd ever feel sexy again. "That must have taken courage."

Julie leaned back and closed her eyes. "It was just desperation, Hope. I was thinking that I might die and Jamie might die, both of us. I was thinking that she at least had love; she had a whole family. I was thinking that I'd never really loved Noah, that I'd only married him because . . . because I'd been seeing him for so long, because I was supposed to love him, everyone wanted me to love him. Because Jamie was going to marry Isaac, and I didn't want to have the second wedding, the afterthought."

"Jamie and Isaac weren't even engaged when you and Noah—"

"They were going to be. He was so head over heels for her."

At the end of the bed, the circle of darkness in my mother's bathtub was all that was left of my bath.

Where was the line between desperation and courage, or might they be the same thing? Julie was just like Jamie: The same long fingers, except that Jamie had worn only a simple wedding band while Julie covered hers with all that silver. The same breasts, except Jamie's had killed her and perhaps, in doing so, saved Julie. The same faces and hair and hands. Thigh muscles. Elbows. The same taste for Brussels sprouts, red shoes, men who told goofy jokes, or at least appreciated theirs.

"I never told Jamie about Oliver's soccer game," she said, tears welling in her eyes again.

"I know," I said soothingly. "You didn't want to—"

"That I was going to the game," she said. "That I was wearing her things."

She started weeping in earnest then, like I'd expected her to in the days after Jamie died. I wondered if I would weep like that eventually, too, if a whole year without Mom would be harder to endure than the first few weeks, if I could bear letting go of the loss and carry on with life.

"I made that all up," she said. "All this time I've lied about it even to you. I didn't tell Jamie I would do it. She fell asleep, and I did it. She never would have forgiven me if she knew."

"She might have—"

"But she wouldn't, and I knew that. She wanted me to be there for them after she was gone, but she

280

would never forgive me for trying to replace her in Oliver's heart before she died, even for that moment."

I intertwined my fingers in hers, her silver rings cold against my skin, remembering the way Mom had taken Anna Page's hand that night she couldn't save Mrs. Memorable. Not Isaac but Oliver.

I reached across her and pulled two tissues from the box. One for her, one for me. "Jamie would forgive you anything."

"I wouldn't have forgiven her," she said, blowing her nose again, wiping her tears with her like-Jamie fingers. "If Oliver were my son and she'd tried to claim him, I never would have forgiven her for that."

"You would have been glad Oliver has that memory of his mom being witness to his triumph," I said. "You would have seen that your wanting to be there—the best you could manage—would be for him a memory of his mother already lost. You would have been thankful that your sister, who loved your son as surely as you did, made possible what you wanted him to have but couldn't give him yourself."

We sat for a long time, watching the riddled coals. In the quiet of the evening coming up, I wondered how Julie had kept that secret for all this long, impossible year. But it's a hard thing, to share our shames, or what we think are our shames, even with our closest friends. We fear that admitting them will cost us the love of those whose love we most need. We forget that's why they love us: not for our perfection but for our humanity.

"It was impossible for Oliver after the holiday party," Julie said quietly, "and it was impossible for Isaac and for me. I used to go over, and we would just sit on the porch and have a drink together late at night, with Oliver asleep inside."

In the few words, I could see how it must have started. A warm evening, days or weeks or months after Jamie had died. A drink together, then a second. Cocktails, or a bottle of wine in Jamie's favorite wineglasses, the crystal ones she and Isaac registered for when they got engaged, to which she'd remained loyal when the rest of us turned to stemless or oversize, one shape for Chianti and another for cabernet.

A drink together and a little remembering. The conversation about nothing intimate, only that bit about Jamie's loyalty to the wineglasses, how she used to drink everything out of them. Orange juice in the morning. A Coke or water with lime, always without ice.

The two of you perhaps drinking cocktails from the wineglasses, because even a whole bottle of wine wouldn't have been enough. Cocktails and conversation about things that weren't Jamie. World events. Politics. Then a hint of Jamie creeping in. That night at dinner when Isaac had called Anna Page's latest date an "undiagnosed libertarian." How you all laughed at the phrase. It didn't matter what the guy's politics were. Had anyone ever seen him again?

A cocktail and a second one, and politics and that dinner memory rolling into Jamie hating ice in her drinks, Isaac laughing at the memory of how, if you put ice in her water, she would dump it out and start over. The two of you laughing.

A cocktail and a second one, then a third. You saying, "Wait a minute, why is not liking ice so funny? The water is filtered and ice isn't, so the ice ruins the taste."

Same genes, same taste buds. Same inadequate sphincter muscles, you might even have thought as you crossed your legs, laughing the way you do sometimes when grief and alcohol meet.

You can laugh together, or you can cry, and you've cried enough, haven't you?

Glasses empty again. Maybe refilled, or maybe not. Maybe in the laughter, you turn to each other, Isaac stifling his laugh in your hair so you won't wake Oliver. Your hair that smells like your sister's always did, that feels the same, too. Not thinking that consciously, but there it is.

Stifled laughter and closed eyes. A drunken kiss. Maybe a pause to consider before you kiss again, maybe not.

The kissing and the touching, hungry and

frantic, overrun by need. Isaac's hands on your breasts that are the one part of you that was ever different from your sister, that and your feet, which are not quite on solid ground anymore, and maybe you know that but probably you don't want to know it, probably you are letting the alcohol wash away what you ought to know.

The touching, hungry and frantic. Breasts that are not so different, that are still the same B-cup you always shared, the same scars. Hurried sex right there in the darkness of the porch in the middle of the night, up against the railing at the far corner, screened from the neighbors by the over-grown camellia. His boxers and khakis, your jeans and panties, all still wrapped around your grief.

33

"What a mercy that was not a pike!"
——from The Tale of Jeremy Fisher by Beatrix Potter

ANNA PAGE SLIPPED OUT OF HER BED IN HER private room at Ainsley's End sometime late that night and donned her rain jacket. Outside, she ran a finger through the calm lower pond of the fountain, the cherub still holding his platter. In the herb garden, she pinched some rosemary, which was damp from the misty air, and put it to her face. She would not have said she was looking for Graham. She would not have said she was looking for anything. She rarely admitted to looking, to wanting—not even when she was a kid dragging Jamie and Julie out into the night, the twins answering the pebbles plinked at their window. She'd never even admitted standing outside their bedroom, watching them share secrets together before they turned off the light and she tossed the stones.

She wandered along the bare paths of the rose garden, all cut back for the winter, and out to the kitchen garden, where a single pumpkin clung to a nearly dead vine. It was all so much less inviting than she'd expected that she turned back toward the towering house. She was heading down a lane of trees to a side entrance when she saw someone sitting under the cover of an arbor. He was completely alone, not even Napoleon with him. He had a sketch pad in his lap, a small reading light clipped to it illuminating the page. *I suppose it's what I do when I'm grieving, isn't it?*

She watched him, watched his head bent over the pad, his fingers moving as easily as hers did in the OR.

Ablution, is that the word? Catherine had been right about that, about what a sacred place the operating room became, if you let it.

Anna Page watched for a long time, thinking Graham might notice her, and thinking he might not. Thinking she rarely noticed anything extraneous in the OR. It was the one place in her life where she felt perfectly safe, despite everything that could go wrong. It was the one place she felt purified, and whole, and good.

She wondered sometimes if love was like that. Jamie used to say it was, and Anna Page used to believe her. Watching Jamie and Isaac together, especially with Oliver, it was easy to believe in love. Was that why she'd been so angry at Julie? So unforgiving of her, without questioning Isaac's role in the affair. Just like she'd always blamed her mother without ever questioning her father. But not just like it. Anna Page had slept with total strangers in the wake of Jamie's death, and found no more comfort than she imagined Julie and Isaac did. She supposed the truth was Julie and Isaac did find some comfort in each other that she never had found.

She circled around behind Graham, moving silently toward his unpartnered loneliness, thinking that it was only circumstance that had kept her from crossing the line Julie had crossed. She peeked through the slats of the arbor, peering into the splash of light. She stood there for the longest time, watching for what might take shape under his hand, on the clean white page.

34

What do Creeds matter, what possible
difference does it make to anyone today
whether the doctrine of the resurrection is
correct or incorrect, or the miracles, they
don't happen nowadays, but very queer things
do that concern us much more. Believe
there is a great power silently working
all things for the good, behave yourself
and never mind the rest.
——Beatrix Potter, in a September 30, 1884,
journal entry

I SAT ON THE DAMP PIER WITH THE MOSS
growing between the slats, holding tight to Anna
Page's phone and watching the sky and the water
move through the colors of morning, from solid
steel to a salmon edging the clouds and reflected
on the lake. The day was waking even more
quietly than it had faded that first night. No dip of
oars. No geese. No clap of cars over trestles on
the far shore. Only the beep of the phone interrupting the silence as I dialed home, starting the
conversation I had to have.

"Hope, God, I'm glad you called." It was late at
home, but Kevin didn't sound like I'd woken him.

"I need a way to reach you," he said. "Isn't there a way I can reach you?"

"I think—"

"Never mind. Don't think anything yet, Hope. Just listen."

"Did you sleep with a lot of women before we met, Kev?" Thinking about the tailgate party and the bike ride, the Potter quoting. How had he known to quote Potter, if not from Anna Page?

"Did I *what?* Hope, we both had lives before we met. We were thirty-three, for God's sake. You've always said that doesn't matter, that you don't *want* to know. And now you want to do this over the phone, six years into our relationship and thousands of miles apart?"

The first of the sun showed at the base of the lake, or so it seemed, with the light reflecting up this side of the water the way it always reflects from wherever you are. We'd both had lives before we met, except I hadn't. That's why I hadn't wanted to know who he'd slept with: because I hadn't wanted him to know that no man had ever wanted me.

"Listen," he said. "Please. Just listen. I want to apologize. I've been thinking about what you said, about my parents. You're right, Hope. You're right. I didn't know I wasn't telling them about you, but I . . . I guess I realized on some level that my parents might balk, that they might need to meet you at the same time they met with the fact that you're part Indian. Maybe that was wrong. Maybe I could have handled it better. But no one who meets you doesn't love you."

In the water under the pier, brown and yellow oak leaves floated in a lumpy mass with yellow and red maples, and something small and green that was more alive and yet uglier than the brownest, deadest leaf.

"God, I spent a lot of unnecessarily lonely school lunchtimes if—"

"Don't," he interrupted. "I'm sorry. I'm sorry. I didn't mean it that way. I mean, you know, you don't always celebrate the fact that you're mixed. Sometimes you hold it like a shield. The way you say it. 'My dad is from India and my mom is white. I grew up in California.'"

"Those are the facts, Kev. What am I supposed to say when someone asks me what I am? What I *am,* like I'm not as human as they are."

"The way you say it, Hope, it comes across with a gratuitous 'And fuck you for asking.'"

I fingered the rope around the base of the post, anchoring the tire bumper that hung halfway in the water. He hadn't wanted me to be saying "fuck you" to his parents. He'd stepped in and said it before I could, because they never would have forgiven me for offending them, or never forgotten it, while they would forgive their son anything.

"You don't have everyone who ever meets you trying to categorize you," I said.

"I'm expected. I'm obvious. People don't have to ask me anything to categorize me. I'm white male, common Irish northern Midwestern Catholic altar boy variety."

I dug with a nail at a strip of moss between the slats. "Except you're atheist now."

"People don't see that. It doesn't occur to anyone that I might be interesting. People *ask* you. People *notice* you."

"Is that why you married me, Kev? Because God knows everyone notices us."

"That's not why I married you. You know that. The question is, why did you marry me?"

In the silence, I studied the reflection of the boathouse in the morning lake.

"If you felt this way," Kevin said, "if you knew you felt this way before the wedding, why didn't you call it off?"

In the wavy water, a small yellow rectangle, a reflection of a sign on the boathouse that read "Private" that I hadn't noticed, although it had clearly been there for years.

"Okay, you don't want to say it, so I will," Kevin said. "Because it was too late. Because the invitations had already gone out. Because your parents would have been so disappointed."

I closed my eyes against the memory of those conversations with Mom, her refusal to listen when I tried to tell her it wasn't working out between Kevin and me. Would it have been easier to tell her before we'd married? Then what? The only other time I'd met a boy's parents—Rajiv's—they hadn't been any more pleased to see a girl who wasn't all Indian than Kevin's had been to see a girl they thought was.

"We can't help who our parents are," Kevin said. "We can't help that we love them—I can't and you can't and we shouldn't, even when we hate what they do. But we aren't them."

"You never even showed them a picture of me."

"Because on some level, I knew that if I did, they would set up against you without realizing they were. On some level, I knew that if they met you first, it would be easier. Not easy, but easier. My *parents* were prejudiced, Hope. Don't visit the sins of the father on the son."

"Sayeth my atheist husband."

An early-morning sailor passed midlake, the wind snapping the sail as he tacked, interrupting the silence. The waves picked up, making a small lapping sound against the wood posts and the boathouse and the tires. I hunched against the cold air, glad of my corduroy slacks and cranberry turtleneck, my bright blue cashmere sweater and purple vest that clashed dreadfully. The raincoat to cut the wind.

"You didn't say anything about all this before we married," Kevin said, "for the same reason I didn't let my parents know you were part Indian before they met you. It was one part wanting them

291

to be happy, and one part knowing that we love each other, that one way or another it would all work out. They're all gone now, Hope. How sad would they all be to imagine they were the cause of us breaking up? How sad would it be for us to break up because of the prejudices of people who are no longer alive to disapprove?"

35

[H]e is very nice with old people and anxious
to be friendly & useful. . . . He is 42 (I am 47)
very quiet—dreadfully shy, but I'm sure he
will be more comfortable married.
——**Beatrix Potter, writing about her fiancé,
William Heelis, in an October 9, 1913,
letter to Fanny Cooper**

JULIE WAS READING BY THE FIRE IN THE Ainsley's End library that morning, sitting in a chair beside Graham's mother's Indian-language books, when Anna Page interrupted her. Interrupted, that was the way Julie thought of it. The quiet of the house had been complete for an hour or more, not even a sign of Napoleon. It was the quiet of the library where she worked before the other staff members arrived—Julie's favorite part of the day, although she hadn't realized it until that morning. Just her and the shelves and shelves of books, the catalogs from publishers, the covers and brief descriptions and blurbs of works by the next Austen or Eliot, McDermott or McEwan or Morrison. Until Aunt Kath and Graham and I had left while Anna Page remained lollygagging in bed, Julie hadn't realized how much she'd been missing this solitude that put her life in order each morning, lingering in the world of words.

Lollygagging: an Aunt Kath expression.

"You're reading?" Anna Page said.

Julie held up the book to show the cover. "It's an advance reader copy your mom loaned me." She tapped the author's name on the cover: Robert Smythe. A collection of poems.

"But he drives boats," Anna Page said.

" 'A collection by' "—Julie read from the author bio on the back—" 'an Irish journalist who now lives in the English Lake District.' Not giving away much, our Robbie isn't."

Anna Page asked if it was any good.

"The poems tell stories," Julie answered, choosing her words carefully. "There's one called 'The Crier of Claife,' about walking the hills at night in search of a dead wife's bones. It will about convince you Robbie is the Crier."

Anna Page frowned, her big chin that was so like her mother's dipping in concentration, her short nails on her well-tended surgeon's hands running idly across the top of the wing chair she stood behind. "Graham is the Crier," she said. "He walks the hills at night with Napoleon, when he can't sleep." She smiled slightly. "But it's okay. He always takes his emergency kit."

Julie hesitated. She wanted to say it out loud, though, and she didn't think Anna Page would know what she was hearing. "There's a poem here about taking a boat across a lake in search of his dead love's first lover, a man she loved when they were in school together," she said. The last in the collection. " 'For Cornelia,' " she said.

Thinking maybe Graham and Robbie were both the Crier. Thinking she had a bit of Crier in her herself, and Anna Page did, too.

"Why would you want to meet a dead love's former lover?" Anna Page asked.

"He says something like . . ." Julie paused, gathering herself against the emotion evoked by the memory of the poem. "I'm paraphrasing, but the idea is 'He must be a good man, for the love she felt for him.' "

It was such an evocative story-poem, about a bighearted man whose soul is lost in a cavernous mansion of expectation he can't begin to furnish. After reading the poem, she'd wiped away the tears and closed her eyes, imagining Robbie and his wife sitting over a glass of ale at a pub, talking of the love she'd had when she was a young woman at Oxford, the man she might have married. She imagined Robbie not wanting to think of his wife ever having loved another man, but seeing the intertwined limbs and the sheets and the saying "I love you," or thinking it but unable to give the emotion voice. There was no sense of betrayal in the poems, though, no sense that the wife ever was unfaithful. Julie imagined Robbie, in the wake of Cornelia's death, going through her things and finding old letters from her school days. "Love, Graham." Had there been anyone left in the world who'd loved Cornelia but Robbie and this man Cornelia had loved first? She imagined Robbie coming to the Lakes on the excuse of a pilgrimage to touch the poets he so admired, and staying longer than he meant to, buying the boat business so that anyone going to Ainsley's End might come to him. He wouldn't have considered the possibility that Graham would rather drive around the long way than go out on the lake. How daft was that?

Daft. It was a Robbie word, there in his poems, which were lovely and funny and sad.

How many ways had Robbie looked to meet Graham in the months he must have lived here before he bought the boats? Months, at least, because he couldn't have written the Crier poem before he came, and here it was already typeset in a volume of poems about to be released. Months, or perhaps a series of trips over years before the old man with the ferry business died and Robbie traded journalism for this new way to earn a living, one that would allow him more time to write his poetry.

How often had he crossed Lake Windermere in the short time he'd owned the boats, hoping to meet Graham? How many hours had he spent floating on the water, looking up at the chimneys of Ainsley's End, imagining how different his own life would have been if his Cornelia had spent her life looking out the windows of the Prospect, rather than those of the little house in Ireland she'd shared with him?

"In another poem," Julie said to Anna Page, "he sits on a bar stool beside his wife's ex-lover, both of them drinking Hawkshead bitters. 'Hawkshead Bitter,' that's the title." Remembering her conversation in the boat with Robbie that night without Anna Page: *Our Lord Wyndham? But he isn't at all a creeper. . . . Surely he likes to have a pint at the local same as anyone. A Hawkshead Bitter, I'd think.* In the poem, the husband sits on the bar stool for hours, staring at the paint under the old lover's nails as he tries to come up with an opening line. Julie didn't tell Anna Page that, though. She said nothing about how the lover sets his money on the bar and leaves the husband sitting alone, with no words ever exchanged.

"He uses the night sky in the poem," she said to Anna Page. Andromeda, the daughter of that boastful but nonetheless beautiful Cassiopeia and her husband, Cepheus. The Alpha Centauries, two stars the human eye can't separate, with the red dwarf that can't be seen but is always with them. "It's heartbreaking, actually," she said.

She didn't offer the book up to Anna Page any more than she offered up the heartbreaking detail. And Anna Page didn't ask for it. She only asked where everyone else was, and Julie said her mother was out for the morning, probably until after lunch.

"She took off by herself?" Anna Page asked.

"She went with Graham," Julie said. "They took the car."

Anna Page frowned. "Hope, too?"

Julie laid a hand on the book's fragile pages as if to shield them from Anna Page. "Out for a walk. She asked me to tell you she has your phone."

"I guess that leaves you and me," Anna Page said.

Julie said she had work to do.

"You're reading a book," Anna Page said.

"It's one of the great perks of being a librarian," Julie said. "I can read whatever I want, whenever I want, and call it work."

Anna Page figured she may as well get some work done herself; surely the galleys for the *JAMA* piece would have arrived in her email. Graham had shown us his office earlier; he didn't have wireless, but we were welcome to make ourselves at home at his desk, where we'd find the Internet hookup. She took her laptop up to the office and plugged it in and booted up. While the computer made its way through the welcome, she took in the tidiness of the room: a stocky desk, much less graceful than the furniture elsewhere at Ainsley's End but clear and dust-free, scarred with rings and scratches so that any harm she might inadvertently do it wouldn't show; tidy files in wooden file cases (which, yes, she did open: tax returns for his business and for a charitable trust that had something to do with the Lakes). Try as she might, she could find nothing personal here, nothing intimate. There was not so much as a photograph, while the rest of the house was overrun with portraits.

She scrolled down through her emails, in search of the paper-clip icons indicating attachments, and found one from a dot-edu address that was familiar—perhaps a research assistant transmitting the *JAMA* galleys from her coauthor. When she opened it, a photo startled her. It was the transplant photo: the family of the dead teacher— Eliza James, her name had been—alongside the schmuck of a game designer who'd ruined his perfectly good heart with cocaine. They all stood together, the poor girl's mother and father, her two sisters, a brother in high school. How did you understand losing a much adored big sister when you were that young?

She wished her own sister would talk to her, or

just listen. She wished what her ma had said about her daddy were true: "His stroke wasn't your fault, Anna Page. Do you think after all the years I lived with your father that I wouldn't have seen the signs? Do you think your daddy could have had any signs of heart disease that Catherine wouldn't have seen?"

Catherine, her mother had said—the sound of her daddy's lover's name on her mother's lips almost as startling as the fact that her daddy had suffered a stroke.

The note that preceded the photo in the email left Anna Page angrier than she would have imagined: *I'm sending you this with gratitude for the second chance you've given me, Anna Page.*

It's Dr. Montgomery to you, she wanted to say.

She wondered if the twit was still doing drugs, or if needing a new heart had shocked some sense into him. She couldn't say why she was so intolerant of people who did drugs. It was an addiction like any other. Why did her daddy still smoke? There were always so many more people who needed hearts than there were hearts to give, though, that it seemed unforgiveable to squander one.

Please do allow me to keep this private, the email read. *It's not enough to repay the gift Eliza gave me, a heart I see now I haven't deserved but am so grateful to have.*

She scrolled down to the delete button. She

wouldn't waste her time with the rest of what he'd written. But she noticed a second attachment along with the photo: SJMN-HeartbeatFndtn.pdf. Heartbeat Foundation? She downloaded the pdf and opened it: a *San Jose Mercury News* piece about an anonymous gift to found a new charity to provide medical care for children with cancer, and schooling while they received treatment.

A hundred million dollars.

The article speculated about several people who might be behind the gift. Anna Page recognized some of the names but didn't know any of them.

She returned to the email and read:

> I would have liked the foundation to promote heart research and be named in honor of Eliza, but I couldn't figure out a way to do that which might not be traced back to me, and you and I both know I don't deserve the credit I would get if that were made public. With your permission, I'd like to appoint you to direct the foundation's board, and ask you to name whomever you would like to serve with you.
>
> If I predecease you, I would ask you to change the name to the Eliza James Heartbeat Foundation. The terms of the granting documents allow great latitude for what it can take on so long as it

involves medical research or the provision of medical services. Rest assured that I have already taken steps to employ top-notch administrators, so your responsibilities would be minimal in terms of time.

I will understand if you are uncomfortable taking this on, but please think about it. And please honor my request for anonymity.

She sat back in her chair and touched her hand to her chest, over her pulmonary artery, where she might so quickly bleed to death. His secret was safe with her. Who would she tell? Not Jamie anymore. Not Graham, whom she could see—now that he was giving his heart to her mother—had taken her own heart without her realizing it was gone.

36

From the Journals of Ally Tantry

28.7.2011, Moss Eccles Tarn, Near Sawrey. **We're sitting on the big slate boulders at the south end of the tarn, and is Bea ever in a petulant mood. She quite insists on being taken out on the water in a boat. But it was hard enough just to get her up here; Graham had** to bring us around in his car to Near Sawrey so we could walk the short way up. Also, it's quite chilly, even for this early in the morning. If we get wet, we'll certainly catch pneumonia.

On the walk up, Graham pointed out that my biological father——"our father," he calls him—— stayed with Graham's mother all those years after his sister died, before they had him.

——I thought you might like to know that your father was capable of great love, Allison, he explained. It's a strong love that can survive the loss of a child and the disapproval of both family and society. Not that our father should be forgiven for what he did to your mum. But it was his capacity to love that was to blame.

——It was his weakness that was to blame, I said. His inability to stand up to his family.

Graham didn't respond for such a long time that I began to regret my words. What good was there in depriving him of the fiction that his parents had shared some great love he himself might still hope to find?

——Yes, he said finally, but that takes more courage than most of us have. You're extraordinary for having done it. You do see that, don't you, Allison? I think our father would have admired you more than you can imagine.

I swallowed back a bitterness I thought I'd finally left behind, thinking what an irony that was: the father who abandoned me would have admired me for something that had caused the woman he'd abandoned to cut me off. And yet it was comforting, the idea that my biological father would have been proud of me when my mother was not.

At the tarn, Graham collected his paints from the boot (I love that word, "boot"; so much rounder and softer than "trunk") and suggested he paint while I write.

——I'm not writing anything today, I replied. I don't have the energy.

Graham gave me the funniest look.

——Aren't you? he asked.

He seemed quite certain that I was going to write, as did Bea. Those two both think they know so much more about me than they do.

——I cannot rest, Bea said. I must draw, no matter how poor the result, and when I have a bad time come over me, it is a stronger desire than ever.

——Is Graham having a bad time, Bea? I asked her.

——I must write, no matter how poor the result, Bea amended.

I've stayed on the rock outcropping, journal in hand to appease them, while Graham walked around the tarn to paint the scene looking back toward us. I'd feel self-conscious, but if any living thing shows up in the painting, Bea and I will be rabbits or field mice or perhaps frogs. We told him we felt like frogs today, but the truth is, our legs are quite running on empty. It's been such a tough year, losing Jim and Jamie both. We might not have come up to the tarn today, but it's Bea's 145th birthday, and this does seem the only proper place to spend this day, at this tarn where she and Mr.

Heelis spent so many evenings. She's decided we'll all go out in her boat, and I haven't the heart to remind her it hasn't been kept at the tarn for years. Graham brings a raft up for us sometimes, but I didn't have the energy to carry the oars today.

——Yes, that will do, Bea says to me.

——What will do for what, Bea?

——A story about the two of us, she says. Rather than about me or about you.

She begins unlacing her shoes.

I pull my jacket more tightly around me and hunch up over my journal, staring out at the water, stealing a glance at Bea. She can't actually mean to take her shoes off, not my proper Bea, not in this chill. Perhaps she's loosening them to ease the circulation. I might loosen mine as well.

——I could write a story about you and Hope, I say, thinking part of me would like to shed my own shoes, to strip my feet to the skin and press my soles flat against the cool slate.

Bea finishes loosening one shoe and begins on the other, with the first, as I suspected, stolidly on her proper feet. I suppress the laughter that threatens: she is so funny about being proper. Across the tarn, Graham is lost in his painting, yet I'm left with the sense that he and Bea are exchanging a knowing glance.

——Allison, Allison, Bea says, you may fool yourself, but do you really think you can fool me?

She finishes the laces on the second shoe——all those eyelets——and stretches her legs out on the hard slate boulders, arranging her skirt around them. She doesn't seem the least bit cold.

——You've been writing about Hope since before she was born, she says. Since Hope was only a dream you didn't know you could make real. She needs you to write for her now. Something that will help her understand all of the things you've already written.

She bends her knee and begins tugging at the heel of her shoe with her hand, which I see is old and gnarled. How have I not noticed that before?

——You can title it "Searching for Allison Tantry," she says.

I watch as she pulls off one shoe and then the other.

——If I wrote that story, I say, I would have to title it "Searching for Beatrix Potter."

——That's already written, for the most part, isn't it? And why in the world drag me into it?

I look across the water to Graham as I consider the question. Why do I drag Bea along on this journey?

——Because it's in coming to find you that I've found whatever it is I've found here, I suppose, I say.

What have I found here?

——Besides, Bea, you're quite charming, you know. And Hope always has adored you.

She begins to roll down her stockings. I watch the pale, veined leg emerging from underneath. I'm not sure I can say any more why I came here at first. To try to understand my mother? That's where this started, in some sense, with that first day trip to Manchester while Jim was in his London meetings. I've returned again and again, looking for some suggestion that Mother's disowning me wasn't disowning me, but rather some part of her bitter past she'd been unable to accept. An understanding that has come to me only with the wisdom of old age. Surely a mother can forgive a child anything, yet how hard it must have been for her to look in my face every day of her new life, to see the echo of the man who fathered me and abandoned her.

But I've kept returning to England. I found that explanation some time ago, and yet I've kept returning, having found something else here as well, I suppose. Graham, of course. But something more that has little to do with him. Something that is here in the journals, in my conversations with Bea. Something I can't quite articulate.

——Well, Bea, I say. I suppose the truth of it is that I, like Hope, have always adored you.

She pauses in the stocking removal.

——Have you, now?

——I have.

——You aren't just saying that to make an old lady feel better at the end of her life?

I scoot down to sit at her feet and take up where she left off removing the stockings.

——Bea, I hate to tell you this, I say, but you're not an old lady. You died sixty-seven years ago.

She watches me remove first one stocking, then the other. She wriggles her pale, fat toes.

——But of course, she says, I'm not the old lady I'm speaking of, am I?

I feel the press of stone against the bare soles of my feet, surprisingly cold. My hiking boots, sitting beside me now, have nearly as many eyelets as Bea's old-fashioned shoes.

——You aren't even speaking, I tell her. I'm the one who's been doing all the speaking on this journey of ours.

——You are taking some of my lines word for word, she says. From my private letters, no less.

She smiles knowingly.

——That I am, Bea, I admit. That I am.

I resist pointing out that her private letters are now public, that even her coded journals have been deciphered. I stand, the stone warming underfoot, thinking she must have wanted them to be public. She was famous long before she died. If she hadn't wanted her personal thoughts made public, she could have destroyed them or arranged for them to be.

I make a mental note to have the Wednesday Sisters swear again that they'll burn my journals the minute I die.

——I'd like to have Hope come here with me sometime, Bea, I say.

——I'm sure she would come if you asked her to, she says.

She stands and takes my hand in hers.

——Careful on this slate, it's slippery, she says.

——The water is going to be freezing, I say.

——Getting in will not be half as horrid as getting back out, she says.

307

At the water's edge, we look across to Graham, bracing ourselves. His gaze remains fixed on his brush and his palette, his canvas.

——I would ask Hope to come, Bea, I say, but she and Kevin are having such a hard time finding space for each other that I hesitate to separate them for even a few days. Someday I'll share all this with her, though.

——Yes, Bea says. Someday you will.

37

The visitors are perfect terrors . . . and they
are least in the way on the fells—if they would
shut gates when they come down again . . .
I have seen a pretty good [automatic gate]
in Wales, worked with a log, but it won't stay
open for a cart unfortunately.
——Beatrix Potter, in an August 27, 1913,
letter to Hardwicke Drummond Rawnsley

I LEFT A NOTE IN MOM'S COTTAGE SAYING I was walking up to Beatrix Potter's tarn so if the others came looking for me they wouldn't worry, and I set off over the hill. It was almost crisp, but not quite that cold, and by the time I reached the look-back over the lake, patches of blue had opened up the wide swaths of cloud. Smoke rose from the Ainsley's End chimney, from the fireplace in the library where I'd found Julie reading Robbie's poetry earlier, before I'd called Kevin. I stuck my hands in the raincoat pockets for warmth as I caught my breath, and found a handful of my mother's ashes there. "Heavens to Betsy, Mom," I whispered to the morning quiet, "did I forget to put you away the last time I wore this coat?"

I was perspiring from the hike—happy not to have lost my way—when I arrived at the tarn's edge. I'd met no one on the path from Ainsley's End, but hikers coming up from the Near Sawrey direction carried picnic baskets and blankets, walking sticks, cameras. From the outcropping of boulders at the south end, the hard sunlight sharpened the gentle summits across the tarn, the shadows deepening the valleys, the water in the foreground reflecting everything so that the mountains stretched from reflected peak to real, with not a cloud in sight.

"I wore the raincoat for you, Mom," I whispered as I fingered the ashes, recalling how often she'd made me schlep an unneeded raincoat on overcast mornings that would turn into perfect days. "But don't think I'm any happier about it than I was in high school."

What would I do about the things of her life here: the cottage and the bed, the love seat, the box of coal fire tools? "You'll have the desk, of course," Graham had said, meaning the bookcase with its hidden desk. It had been his father's, he'd told me. My biological grandfather's. Graham had made a gift of it to Mom.

I said aloud, "And the pictures, too."

The only responses to my words were the wing-flutter of a bird taking flight at the tarn's edge, the gentle splash of a duck, the crunch of footsteps on the dirt path behind me.

I turned to see Aunt Kath making her careful way across the bank of boulders. "Lordy, someone has stolen your puppy, haven't they, Miss Asha Tantry?" she said. When she reached me, she rested a hand on my head for a minute, as if I were still a child. "Even coming the short way, this hike will put me in my . . ."

Put me in my grave, she'd been about to say, one of her favorite expressions. Put me in my little puzzle box, after the bone fragments that are all that's left of me have been ground by machine into dust that everyone calls ash.

Aunt Kath and Graham had gone to Hawkshead for breakfast, then come around to Near Sawrey and walked up from there. "He's brought his paints," she said. He was across the tarn, setting up an easel. *And the pictures, too.*

She didn't think he'd seen me yet. She'd noticed me herself only when she'd looked out across the tarn, and even then she wasn't sure. "I don't know why you girls insist on hiding your pretty faces under those ball caps your Aunt Linda favors when you might wear proper ladies' hats," she said as she settled on the hard granite beside me, touching the brim of a University of Michigan ball cap that had been my father's, that shaded me from the glare of the sun. "This tarn would make a lovely book jacket, wouldn't it? Perhaps with a small wooden boat. An empty boat with just an open journal in it. We could Photoshop that in."

A rowboat like Beatrix Potter and her husband used to take out in the evenings, when he was done with his legal work for the day and she'd written herself out, or finished her farm work, or put away her paints.

"Why did Mom spend the last days of her life here writing a biography about a dead woman, Aunt Kath?" I asked.

The up-tip of her not insubstantial chin almost left me regretting the question, but there was understanding in her plain brown eyes. "Your mama wasn't fixing to die, Hope, so it's a bit unfair to tag her with ignoring you and Sammy on her deathbed."

I stretched my legs out on the cold stone and tilted my face to the sunshine, letting it slip under my hat.

"Would it raise your biscuits to know it wasn't a biography she was working on?" Aunt Kath asked. "If it was something more personal?"

I glanced behind me as though the answer might be found in the lone cow grazing the emerald grass in the valley, which was sectioned with long stretches of stone wall as if anything at all in life might be parceled and contained.

Aunt Kath tossed a pebble into the water, her throw surprisingly easy. The tiny stone landed with a cheerful plonk, stirring up circles of ripples that grew and grew.

"She meant to collect material for a Beatrix Potter biography here, but she found something else," she said.

We looked across the tarn to where Graham stood before an easel, what must be a paintbrush poised in his hand, although it was hard to tell from where we sat.

"Graham is part of it," Aunt Kath said, "but not the hind roast, or more than but a slice of the meat."

I tossed a pebble beyond the ripples echoing out from the stone Aunt Kath had thrown. We watched as the wake of mine washed over the fading edges of hers.

"Your mama . . . She gave me a pretty fine draft, Hope—to get my thoughts on it, that's what she said—a few days before she died. She didn't know she was dying, although your mama, if our seats were changed and she were sitting here telling this to Anna Page, she might say it was preordained."

"A sign," I said, feeling a smile edge onto my face.

"She could be two sandwiches shy of a picnic sometimes, your mama could. She could give your Ama a run for her money when it came to that mystical crap."

"Mystical crap?" I said.

"Heavens to Betsy, did I say that?" Aunt Kath said in mock horror, and we both laughed a little. "You laugh exactly like your mama did," she said.

She looked out over the water, where I imagined my mother with her imaginary Beatrix Potter companion, perhaps rowing together. "The manuscript, it's a lovely piece of business," she said. "I'm sorry I hadn't looked at it before she passed, that she isn't here for me to tell her so. 'Searching for Beatrix Potter.' Your mama's journey here, with Beatrix Potter at her side, the two of them laughing together about how odd and inflexible their own mamas were." She tossed another pebble, and I followed suit, the stones plinking closer together this time, the wakes lapping into each other. Across the tarn, a bird called out a hopeful caw. Graham looked up to see it, and kept looking.

"It's a memoir of sorts, I suppose, but maybe that's my needing a place to put it on bookstore shelves," Aunt Kath said. "It's really just your mama trying to get comfortable with who she is."

"But she was just Mom."

Aunt Kath smiled a little. "We're all difficult in

our own ways, honey. Don't imagine any of us isn't. And don't imagine becoming a mama yourself would make life any easier to understand."

Graham offered a tentative wave. Aunt Kath didn't notice, but I offered a small return wave. He kept looking, trying to make out who I was.

"The little books for Sam and me," I said, "do you think Mom would like them to be published?"

Kath's big eyes and her big chin and her gray hair so familiar. I'd known her all my life.

"Writing those books wasn't like that for your mama," she said. "Having you, Hope, that was her dream."

"But she was always telling me I could do anything, like I *had* to, when she didn't do anything herself. Career-wise, I mean."

"Your mama and I, we weren't raised with those expectations, honey."

"But you became a swanky editor."

She frowned at my bright yellow and gray plastic raincoat. It didn't add to the red-turtleneck-blue-sweater-purple-vest look, her expression said. She reached over to me and zipped the jacket up a few more inches, never mind that I was nearly forty years old.

"I needed a job," she said, "and then I was fair to middling at what I did for a lot of reasons, but most of all because I'd failed so miserably at my marriage and I was sorely in need of a success. One door closes but another one opens. The good

Lord watches over fools who can't care for themselves."

She looked across the water to Graham. She smiled and waved enthusiastically, and he waved back, although his puzzled expression suggested that he hadn't determined who I might be.

"How it would have mortified me when I was young to imagine that I would need to support myself," she said. "It's funny, isn't it? So often it's the things that mortify us in our youth that become indispensable."

The things that mortify us in our youth. *Yes, but what* are *you?*

As we set off around the water's edge toward Graham, I pulled off my cap, ran a hand through my hair, and surreptitiously unzipped my jacket the bit that Aunt Kath had zipped it up. Graham, recognizing me, waved brightly, and stood watching us before returning to his painting. Aunt Kath smiled slightly, at him or me or both of us. She put a hand at the back of my neck, fingering my hair where it rested against the plastic of my raincoat hood. "All of you Wednesday Daughters have great big ol' hearts," she said. "Even my Anna Page. Maybe the five of us Wednesday Sisters can take some solace in that, never mind that we do get so many things as wrong as wrong can be."

I glanced at Aunt Kath's lined face, her silver hair. "I think Mom meant for you and Graham to meet," I said, the words coming as if in a whisper over my shoulder, Mom and Beatrix Potter urging me on. "Maybe she wanted her ashes brought here so you two could meet."

"Bless his lecture-prone little heart," Aunt Kath said. "If your mama had him in mind for me, she was perfectly able to make some wacky request to drag me here. And she'd have missed the mark by a generation, if that was the mischief she meant to make." She sighed. "Of course, when it comes to men, my oldest daughter doesn't have the sense God gave a goose."

As though on cue, one of the geese feeding on the tarn honked at another, a short squabble ensuing. Graham looked up and smiled.

"What's that thing Anna Page likes to say? 'A heart at rest is death'?" she asked, something in her tone leaving me with the idea that she wanted me to share whatever Anna Page had told me about Uncle Lee. But Anna Page had told me nothing; if she was burdened by worries about her father, she wasn't laying them on my shoulders while my pockets were filled with Mom.

" 'A heart at rest is death,' " I said. " 'To save it, we have to take it there and bring it back.' "

The first time I'd heard Anna Page say that, she had been trying to convince me to go to medical school. But my father had wanted me to become a lawyer, like him, or I'd thought he did, and I'd wanted to be like him even more than I'd wanted to be like Anna Page. I'd loved to write stories, but I'd assumed about Mom the way people assume about Kevin. I'd categorized and dismissed: unpublished failure. I decided I would be like my successful lawyer dad.

"Fortunately for Anna Page, she has you for a fusionist," Aunt Kath said, "keeping her alive while her own heart is repaired."

"She doesn't, though," I said. "Anna Page doesn't let me anywhere near her heart."

Aunt Kath pulled a dying leaf off a tree as we passed it, and rolled it between her fingers. "My Anna Page is too busy being mad at her daddy and me to allow that there might be something worth loving anywhere in this whole world," she said, "but she fell in love with you the day your mama and daddy brought you home from the hospital, when even Mr. Pajamas made you look like a puny runt."

She cocked her head and studied me. "Lordy, she was matchmaking even then, wasn't she? We tried to talk her into choosing something smaller than Mr. Pajamas, but a body never could find any peace until you went along with that girl. Yes, I do believe she fell in love with you the moment she saw you in that Polaroid photo, with your baby face turned toward the bear she'd picked out for you."

"She loved Jamie, too," I said.

"Lordy, she did," Aunt Kath said. "Lordy, she surely did."

We walked quietly, watching the two bickering geese settle again into feeding on the underwater grasses.

"I didn't want you to come up here," I confessed, "but Kevin told me I had to let you because Uncle Lee had a stroke and you needed to tell Anna Page."

She looked past the reflected-water mountains to the real ones, perhaps considering the unkind words I ought not to have said. "Lee acts like he thinks the sun comes up to hear him crow, but he doesn't believe that," she said. "Perhaps you had to have known him as a boy to see that, but he never has. And no one ought to be left old and sick and alone." She looked down the water's edge to Graham, his canvas much bigger than the illustrations in the Labradoodle book. "Anna Page is such a fine, responsible woman," she said. "She deserves—" She stopped speaking so abruptly that it made me look more closely at the weariness in her lined face. I tried to connect the dots between what she'd said about Uncle Lee and Anna Page, but they made no picture.

"I suppose the truth is, I love Lee, Ally," Aunt Kath said.

Ally. I blinked against the sound of my mother's name instead of my own, but I didn't correct her.

"Lordy, how I cried when he told me we were going to Stanford for his medical school. I couldn't imagine raising my babies all that long

318

way from home for even those few years. But I've had a good life. I suppose I've enjoyed my career more than I would have enjoyed any life I might have had if I'd married a better man than Lee. It's allowed me to define my own sense of who I am, rather than have it folded and put away for me."

Clouds edged over the mountain behind Graham and reflected in the water, storms gathering from nowhere to drench us again before scurrying off to find other victims out for sunny-day walks.

"And Lee was a good father. When I'd start thinking that raising children was like being pecked to death by chickens, he would get away from the hospital long enough to scoop them up and cover them with love. I'm not excusing him. But there's a lot of goodness in Lee."

"A good father," I repeated, the conversation dots connecting from Lee to what Anna Page did and didn't deserve. If Aunt Kath didn't take care of Lee, the burden would fall to Anna Page and her brother and sister—that had been what she'd almost said earlier. Taking care of Lee would fall to Anna Page alone, really, because her sister, at forty-five, probably never would move from a world that revolved around her into one where others had needs, and her brother was a man who left all the taking care of to his wife.

Someone would have to carry Lee through his dying, and Aunt Kath didn't want that someone to be Anna Page.

Aunt Kath would have told me, if she'd said anything, that taking Lee back was a last act of selfishness, a way she could, by preserving her children's happiness, preserve her own. She didn't say anything, though. I suppose she didn't want any truth she might have admitted there at Beatrix Potter's tarn to travel from my lips to her daughter's still-fragile heart. I suppose she must have figured her own heart was tough enough to carry it alone, or to carry it long enough to deliver to the feet of the Wednesday Sisters, who had always accepted her choices the way that, I can see now, Anna Page and Julie and I accepted one another's, even when we didn't agree with them.

38

Mr. Heelis & I fished (at least I rowed!) till darkness. . . . It was lovely on the tarn, not a breath of wind and no midges.
——Beatrix Potter, in a June 17, 1924, letter to Louie Choice

ACROSS THE TARN WHERE GRAHAM WAS painting, the view was different than it had been from the rocky outcropping: not toward the hardwater reflection of mountain and sky and the bleak gray of the growing cloud bank, but to the long stretch of green valley, the ancient-walled geometry, the winding dirt path to Near Sawrey. That was what Graham was painting, this softer view, but with a boat on the tarn that wasn't there in reality, a blow-up raft that looked surprisingly inviting in watercolor yellow. It was what Mom and Graham used to paddle around in, a white-water raft complete with D-rings and grab lines (which you didn't need on this tarn, but it was what Graham had). "Can you imagine portaging anything heavier all this way, even motoring around and hiking up the shorter track?" he said.

Without our noticing, Aunt Kath had slipped closer to the tarn's edge, leaving us to ourselves. Watching her, I realized she hadn't said why my mother had wanted me to bring her ashes here, although I felt certain she knew.

"It's a bit rough coming up here without your mum, isn't it?" Graham said. "I had such a sense of . . . belonging when I was here with her. Belonging, yes, I suppose that is the word." He touched a brush to the empty boat on his easel, painting three quick bolsters into the boat's center. I put on my Michigan hat that had been Dad's, threading my hair through the hole at the back.

"How can you be sure you and Mom are related?" I asked, an easier question with him turned from me, not looking into my doubt.

He put down the brush and selected a thinner one. He added grab lines in the center of the boat like the ones on the outside. "Love isn't blood-limited, Asha," he said. "By the time we might have thought, say, to have a DNA test? It no longer mattered."

I ran my fingers through the grainy ash of my mother in my pocket. "She wanted her ashes brought here to you."

He turned from the painting, his long lashes behind the wire-rims blinking, my mother's long lashes. "Asha, Asha," he said, the way my mother would when I was upset. Not Hope but Asha. Not once but twice.

He set down his paints and took my hands in his. "There isn't a person in this world your mum loved more than you and your brother. She never questioned that she belonged with you. I think perhaps she was . . . I think asking you to bring her ashes here was a gift to me." He took off his glasses and wiped his eyes with his hands, leaving a streak of the yellow of the boat across his cheek. "Because I needed something of her more than you or your brother did. Because you had each other. Or perhaps this was her way of bringing you to me, now that she's gone." He wiped his eyes again, leaving a second, fainter yellow streak. "She told me once, when we were working together on the mutt book—"

The mutt book—a phrase that had to be Mom's.

"I'm sure you grew up hearing this, but I didn't," Graham said, "and it meant a lot to me.

She told me I wasn't two halves of anything. She told me I was a whole something new."

Mom's voice in the words.

"She told me that, too, all the time when I was growing up," I said. "I don't know if I ever believed it."

"You should," he said. "You should."

"Or even knew what it meant," I said.

Graham chose another brush and began adding something in the water beside the boat. A water lily, I thought at first, but then it took shape, improbably, as a candle floating in the water.

"Do you think this is where Mom wanted me to leave her?" I asked him, and I turned to Aunt Kath, rejoining us, to include her in the question. "Here at this tarn?" I scooped the ash of my mother from my pocket and held it in my fist, lest it blow away. "I've been carrying her around with me, little bits of her, hoping she would somehow tell me when I'd found the right place." I looked out across the tarn again, thinking if I spread her ashes here, I would do it from this side, facing the peaceful valley rather than the more dramatic mountain view I preferred. "I feel like wherever I choose, I ought to make it some big ceremony," I said, "but I can't imagine how to do that, either."

"Your mama didn't stand on ceremony," Aunt Kath said. "I can't see her resting in peace in a marble orchard. Surely she'd come back to haunt us all if we did anything fancy."

A light breeze kicked up then, and I imagined the ghost of Mom sitting at the sprawl of our dining room table, leaving little ghost bits of herself everywhere.

The clouds, having broken past the barrier of the mountains, were rolling quickly overhead. Lightning flashed behind us, an echo of gentle thunder lasting far longer than the quick pop of light.

"It's a sign!" Aunt Kath said. "Your mama telling you to pour on the grits while the griddle is hot. You Wednesday Children think all of life has to be lined up perfectly before it can be lived, but the Lord's good truth is that it doesn't ever line up the way you want it to. You just have to trust it to line up the way it ought, and plunge on ahead."

Aunt Kath touched my hair where it poked out of my father's Michigan cap, a tender caress that I'd taken for granted my whole life.

"Sam thinks she belongs at home, near us," I said. I didn't have to tell her that he'd declined to make this trip with me, that he'd tried to persuade me not to come.

Graham set down his brush. In the painting, candles floated on the water, circling out from the boat like the first ripples from a tossed pebble. The sky over the field beyond the tarn, where we'd seen the sliver of crescent moon that first morning here, was free of clouds despite the heavy gray overhead.

"It's Diwali," I said, realizing it only as I said it. "No-moon day. The festival of lights. Ama always sent us candy and saris. In India, you light lamps."

"To mark the end of the harvest season," Graham said. "To pray for a good harvest in the year to come. My ama sent candy, too, but sorry, no saris for me!"

I remembered standing in Mom's bathroom one Diwali, torn between wanting to climb into the tub with her and not wanting to take off my new sari. It was evening, and she had the candles lit, celebrating Diwali in the tub although Diwali was my father's holiday, Christmas hers. "You don't have to choose, Hope, you can put the sari back on after the bath," Mom had assured me. Yes, instead of my pajamas. She didn't think the sari would be all that comfortable to sleep in, but I could give it a try if I liked.

"Mr. Pajamas needs a sari," I'd informed Mom as she tucked me in that night. "And Mr. Jackson."

She'd kissed me and suggested I take that up with Aunt Frankie. I don't remember if I ever did.

39

Cecily Parsley lived in a pen,
And brewed good ale for gentlemen.
——from Cecily Parsley's Nursery Rhymes
by Beatrix Potter

JULIE READ THROUGH TO THE LAST POEM IN
Robbie's book, and sat in the Ainsley's End
library for a long time before heading out to the
wonderful little phone nook off the entry hall, and
finding the number for Robbie's boat taxi service,
calling him and saying she needed a ride across
the lake.

"Do you, now?" he asked. "And where will you
be going?"

"I thought we might go to Hawkshead," she
said. "I thought I might buy you a bitter."

He laughed his easy laugh and said, "You can't
get to Hawkshead from Ainsley's End on a boat,
but I do expect you know that."

She allowed that she did.

She could hear the smile in his voice as he
answered, "And the best place to have a bitter
wouldn't be Hawkshead; that would be too easy,
and neither of us likes the easy way, do we? The
best place to have a bitter would be at the Drunken

Duck. They make a fine one at Barnegates Brewery, beside it. That idn't on the water any more than Hawkshead is, but I could fetch you in the banger, if that would do."

A bitter, it turns out, is a gorgeous pale beer. "Hoppy and bitter. Perfect after a day out on the fells," Robbie said after their first sips, to which Julie said perhaps that was the problem, she hadn't had her daily hike yet. But the Drunken Duck was lovely, from its very name on. The legend, which Robbie was ripe to share—Julie wondered if perhaps it would show up in a poem someday—had it that centuries ago a barrel slipped its hoops, draining beer to the floor and into the ducks' customary feeding ditch, where-upon the birds made good use of it, to the bad effect of regaining consciousness already plucked and oven-bound. "But the landlady, a kinder sort than likely exists in the realm of restaurant owners who gather dead birds off the road," he said, "had mercy, and even knitted the poor defeathered birds waistcoats of Hawkshead yarn to wear until their feathers grew back."

Julie laughed.

"Now you'll be wanting your legends believable, I'm sure," Robbie said.

The bar was all clean leather and soft lights, wide-planked oak floor and beamed ceilings, an open fire, a helpful barman who told Julie, when asked, that the bar top was made of Brathay Black slate from a quarry on Duck Hill. He suggested she might prefer a Cat Nap to the Tag Lag. It was fruitier, with citrusy zest.

She took a first sip from the new mug, looking over the top and into Robbie's patient gaze. "They don't serve Hawkshead Bitter here," she said. "In your poem . . ."

"Ah," Robbie said. "Is that what this is about? The ladies will wet the tea leaves for a poet, won't they. So much more romantic than a river rat."

Julie, ignoring him, said "Hawkshead Bitter" was a lovely poem. She'd thought it must be set at his favorite drinking hole.

He ran a weathered hand over the black slate bar. "Perhaps a hawk's head is a better metaphor than a tag lag or a catnap. Perhaps this *is* my favorite drinking hole. Or perhaps I thought this place would most impress a lass who prefers a biro to an oar."

"I did read your poems," she admitted. "Aunt Kath, after she met you, called someone at the office and had them messenger out an advance copy of your book. She said it hasn't come out yet, that it releases next month." She looked away, to the water. " 'For Cornelia.' That one breaks your heart."

"It's a long time ago now," Robbie said. "Coming here, this was the last thing I had to do."

"To meet Graham."

He looked into the pale circle of ale in his glass,

the bitter. "Is anything in life that simple, d' you suppose?"

Julie guessed if it were, we would have no need of literature, but she kept the thought to herself.

"I'd not be the first poet to come to the Lake District for inspiration," he said. "But it's true that the hills here are steeped with Cornelia. He's carried her around here as I've carried her around at home. And I've had no one to share the love of her with before."

"But you haven't ever told him."

He held her gaze, considering. "It's a way of sharing, idn' it? Being with a body even if they don't know all that you know."

"Or writing it into a poem," Julie said. When he didn't answer, she said, "He'll know when he reads the poems."

"He'll have the silver tray and the china but not the poetry books," he answered. "He's a good sort, but he's not a poetry-reading sort."

She supposed he was right. The books Graham had shown her that first day at Ainsley's End, when he'd been so determined to show her his library, had been his grandfather's and his father's but not his own.

"He would read a poem written about himself," she said.

"And how will he know of it? His Mrs. Anders will not read poetry, either."

"Why don't you want him to know?" When

again he didn't answer, she said, "I feel understood. When I read your poems, I feel understood. Even though they aren't about me at all."

Robbie nodded, and she could see that he was gathering his emotions, uncomfortable somehow with what she'd said.

"Thank you," he said finally.

She realized then what a compliment she'd paid him, that this was what the best poetry was about: uncovering hearts.

"It's a funny thing," he said. "You pour a cup of your grief out into a line of poetry, or twelve lines, or two hundred, and this thing you can't swallow yourself becomes a thing others want to drink."

In his words, in the phrasing, she remembered talking with her mother over the strawberry waffles before her mother went in for the surgery she couldn't promise them she would survive. *Always, always, you make me the happiest mommy in the world.*

Julie adjusted the position of the beer mug, the saltshaker, the cup of nuts, aligning them straight and tidy, as if they were library books. "Maybe you'll write a poem about me someday?" she said—ironically, and not.

Robbie watched the movement of her fingers until she, self-conscious, brought them back to rest on the cold mug.

"But they'll all be about me, won't they," he said. "My poems, they're about the falls, and they're about the stars that aren't there anymore, they're about Cornelia and Erin, about Graham, even. But in the end, they are all about me." His blue eyes dark with the black of the Brathay slate. "I can see a lot, Julie, but I can't see everything, and it's not the same as seeing it yourself, is it? That's the thing. To see it yourself. That's the only way back from loss."

He touched her elbow like he had that night in the boat, as if all her grief might be there, or it might connect directly to her heart.

"How can you stand it?" she asked. "How can you stand to write about the love Cornelia had before she loved you, the love that she still felt? That's what your poems suggest."

He tilted his mug so that the circle of ale became an oval, like the old lover in "Hawkshead Bitter" does. "Love isn't a tap you turn on and off with a handle, a temperature you can mix," he said. "It's a crashing force that washes you down rocky cliffs and into gentle eddies. It meanders so that sometimes you seem to go in the wrong direction, but all in all, it takes you toward an open sea. If the riverbed ever dries to muck, there is something wicked wrong, but the wicked wrong is at the source." He traced a finger around the rim of the mug, like the husband in his poem does after his wife's lover sets his money on the black slate bar and disappears out the door. "We all have scars," he said. "We all do things we regret. Mortallers, even. Capital S sins. Not a one of us will get into any heaven run by a wrathful god. The thing is to understand that we're human. Not to imagine how we might have done better, but to accept that we are who we are, that we do the things we do, and if we had a chance to do them again, we'd sure enough make the same choices, because we can't see around the bend. And what good would a life be if we could? What good would a life be without the gifts, or even without the regrets?"

He ran a finger from her elbow to her palm, ran it over the silver rings on her fingers. "Maybe you'll write a poem yourself someday," he said.

She studied his weathered face in the reflection of the bar mirror but didn't answer.

"If I tell him," he said, "I lose the last possibility."

"The last possibility of finding someone who shared the love of Cornelia?" she said, remembering the line in the poem. And when he didn't answer, "Or maybe you find it."

His touch lingered on her one empty finger, where only the indent of her wedding band remained. "I already have, haven't I, in your reaction to the poems."

All the emotion that had welled in his face when she'd said the poem made her feel understood—he'd have heard this from an editor, but maybe not face-to-face. And it's a different thing to be able to see, to be able to touch.

"Maybe Graham, not being a poet, needs it even more than you do," she said. " 'It's a way of sharing, idn' it? Being with a body even if they don't know all that you know.' But that eases only your grief. It doesn't help him at all."

Robbie traced his finger up to her fingertip, then took up his beer mug, turned it a half turn so the handle was at his right hand, then turned it back. "Ah, you'll be the bard, then, Julie Mason. You'll be taking all the literary prizes I'm hoping to find draped all over myself."

40

From the Journals of Ally Tantry, the Final Entry

The Groom's Cottage, Ainsley's End. Bea and I spent another morning at the Armitt Library going over her manuscripts, she again suggesting what I wanted to see were the mushroom drawings. "Fungi," she insists. Afterward, Graham joined us to stretch our legs with another hike up to Stock Ghyll Force. I do think I've come to like that hike at least as much as the trip over the hill to Moss Eccles Tarn, although I don't think I'll ever tell Graham that. The tarn is his favorite place, and he likes that we share the love of it. But Hope would love Stock Ghyll Force, the drama of the ninety-foot waterfall. I feel her beside me whenever I'm there.

——But of course the best part of the Stock Ghyll loop is the latter part of the longer hike, Bea says, as it circles up toward Troutbeck Park.

Troutbeck Park is her favorite of her farms. But she was too exhausted to tackle that seven-mile hike today.

——I was tired, Allison? she says.

I drew a bath when we got home, and was letting it cool when Bea said maybe she would have a go of it.

——A bath? I said.

——You're not the only one whose poor old bones ache after a day on the trails, Bea said.

——My bones don't ache, I protested.

——No, of course not, Allison. I forget. That's my purpose here, to take on the pains you're reticent to admit. Well, perhaps you could be persuaded to turn your back while I undress?

I gathered the candle from the cabinet in the bathroom, and several more from the kitchen, and I lit them all over the room for her; there is nothing much nicer than a bath by candlelight. Now I've stretched out on my bed with my journal, waiting for the water to cool, while Bea is submerged to her chin the way Hope always loved to be.

——Didn't you ever want to be a mother? I ask.

Perhaps I'm still in search of that fresh angle that Kath wants for the biography. Or perhaps in understanding Bea, I mean to understand Hope's reluctance to have a family.

——I never have cared tuppence for the modern

child, Bea answers. They are pampered and spoilt with too many toys and books.

——Too many books, Bea?

——Too many books.

——You don't mean that.

——I had Water Lily, of course, she says.

——Oh no you don't, Bea. We are not going back to the sheep.

Bea takes a loofah I've set on the marble table by the tub and submerges it, lifts it up, and squeezes, letting the water trickle down slowly, like Hope used to do with washcloths in the tub with me.

——I suppose I'm simply tired, Bea says.

——Or saying dramatic things just to be dramatic?

——I'm a tired, old, nearly blind lady who can no longer paint, she says. I suppose the thing about no longer being able to do a thing is that you have to decide it's no longer worth doing, so the loss doesn't break your heart.

——Oh, Bea, I say.

She stares into the small flame burning on the table beside the tub.

——Those years of Mr. Harold Warne nearly ruining the business with his forgery spoilt the writing for me.

——But you told me the other day that you cannot rest, Bea. That you must draw, no matter how poor the result, and when you have a bad time come over you, it is a stronger desire than ever.

——Did I? Well, perhaps you're right. Perhaps I'll write again. Perhaps I'll find a new publisher who will appreciate rather than expect. Or perhaps we could do a book together. Your friend Kath might publish us.

——But you're dead, Bea, I remind her. I fear it might be tough to market anything we purported to write together, since you died the year I was born.

——I see, she says. Yes, there is that impediment, isn't there?

In the silence, I pick up the photo of Hope and Sammy on my nightstand, Hope with that empty lunch box she was so intent on taking to kindergarten, as if Anna Page herself were sequestered inside her gently used gift.

——You know what I'll miss most, Bea, when I'm gone? I ask.

——What will you miss most, dear Allison?

——The baths I used to take with Hope when she was a child.

——But those are a thing of the past already, dear. Your daughter is all grown up. You don't want to be like my mother, pushing her around in a perambulator——

——Until she gets out and says she would rather walk, I finish.

——I've told you that before, then.

——I believe you've told me just about everything at this point, Bea.

I stare into the flame of the candle on my bedside table, smaller and gentler than the aggressive heat of the coal fire.

——I wish she would have a child, I say.

——Water Lily?

336

——Hope, Bea. She's all twisted up about how she'll be a mother and still have her career, and what her children will be like, and whether Kevin ... Kevin can seem so certain about things that he leaves Hope doubting herself.

——Men often seem certain when women doubt, don't they? Bea says.

She runs a hand through the bubbles.

——Love is only the starting point, of course, she says. It's the kindnesses that make the difference in a marriage, the everyday kindnesses that make the long days of a relationship work.

——So Hope keeps putting it off and putting it off.

——Perhaps she doesn't want children, Allison.

——But Kevin does.

——Does he, Allison? Or is it someone else in your daughter's life who wants children for her?

I touch a finger to the candle on my bedside table, the melted wax clinging to my finger smoothing the crevices of my unique fingerprint. Hope and Sammy have been the joy of my life. I can't imagine their lives would be complete without that joy.

——My mother couldn't imagine I could be happy marrying a man who wasn't "a gentleman," Bea says. Your mother couldn't imagine you happily married to an Indian man. Hope is making her own choices. You ought to be proud of her.

She squeezes the loofah again, the dripping water reminding me of the stream that flowed from the feet of Hope's poor Mr. Jackson after his bath.

——That isn't your fault, Allison, Bea says.

——About Mr. Jackson?

——That your parents weren't proud of you.

——If I'd managed to say it better, to make them understand——

——You can't make people listen, Allison. You can only say a thing as well as you can and hope they will hear. And I do think marrying the man you love is about as nice a way of putting a thing to say as there is, don't you?

I suppose she's right. I suppose I know that.

——But of course you do, she says. You and I are one and the same, aren't we?

The coal fire is settling, finally, into a warm glow behind the tub. Funny that I'd never made a coal fire before I moved here. Heavens to Betsy, did my first effort smoke! I had to open the windows and the door. I do believe that's why Graham rushes down to start the fire for me when I first arrive. He's afraid I'll burn the cottage down.

——Hope will like Graham when she meets him, I say. They'll have that in common. The tortured identity.

——Unlike you. You've never felt tortured about your own identity.

(Offered with a wry smile. Well, I deserve that, having poked her about being dramatic and ignored her pleas for me to write about her infernal sheep.)

——I liked what Graham said when we were hiking today, I say. When we were talking about being biracial.

"The fact that another person suffers more than we do doesn't make our own suffering less."

——"The fact of another's suffering doesn't lessen our own," Bea says, setting me straight about Graham's exact phrase the way Hope always has set me straight about my Beatrix Potter quotes.

——He's Hope's and Sammy's Uncle Graham, although I don't suppose they'll ever call him that, I say.

——Their Uncle Graham, Bea repeats.

She runs a hand through the water, and a hint of vanilla mingles with the warmth of the coal fire.

——There aren't any of us Potters left, she says wistfully. My brother, Bertram, didn't have children, either.

I move to the end of the bed and reach across to cup a handful of water——still hot. My hand comes up bubble-covered and red from the heat.

——They aren't a thing of the past, Bea, I say.

——What aren't, Allison?

——The baths with Hope when she was a girl. They're there in her face every time I look at it. I know she's struggling, but I also know she'll sort it out, because I see that in her eyes. Her eyes are shaded where they used to be bold, but all the little-girl cockiness, all the before-the-world-got-to-her confidence, that's still there.

Bea sinks lower in the bubbles, dipping her nose into the vanilla smell that always makes me think of Hope, and she closes her eyes. We're both so tired.

——Careful, there. I can't have you drowning on my watch, I say.

——You forget, she says, I'm already dead.

I scoop up a handful of bubbles and set them on her pale white knee, the way I used to set them on Hope's tiny little perpetually skinned ones, remembering how often I used to misquote Bea's books to Hope just to see the pride in her face as she set me right.

——Those baths with Hope are with me every time I sink into this bathtub, I say. Every time I open that funny blue door into this cottage. I think it's why I love this place so much: because the tub is here in the center of everything, forever reminding me of Hope.

——Giving you Hope even when she isn't with you? Bea says.

I laugh, thinking of Jim as I again test the water, which is slightly cooler. Jim always did love a good pun, or even a bad one.

——Do you think Hope will ever come here, Bea, after I'm gone?

I'd like her to. I like to imagine that even after I'm gone, Hope will come here to write, like I have. I like to imagine she'll fill this tub with bubbles, and her daughter will come looking for her like Hope used to come looking for me, and she'll pull her knees up in the water and make room for her daughter to join her.

——Her daughter, should she choose to have children, Bea says, won't have far to come looking.

She smiles up at me, a small bubble beard on her chin.

——Did Hope really have a Mr. Jackson doll when she was a child? she asks.

——Two of them, I assure her. Mr. Jackson the First never did recover from that bath.

——I do love the irony of a toad never recovering from a dip in the water, Bea says.

——A toad who "lived in a drain below the hedge, in a very dirty wet ditch," I say. A line Hope was forever correcting me on. Do I have it right even now?

——Perhaps that was the problem, Bea says. Perhaps it wasn't the water so much as the clean soapy bubble bath that did Mr. Jackson in!

I laugh again, the way I used to laugh with Hope and Sammy when we read Bea's books. I love her gentle sense of humor.

——All right, old girl, I say, it's my turn for the tub.

She asks me to hand her a towel and turn my back, and I indulge her in this.

——I'm not really dead, you know, Allison, she says to my turned back.

——Aren't you, now? I say with amusement.

I turn again to the slipper tub and the coal fire, the candle burning on the table beside the bottle of vanilla bubble bath, saying she may be right, I suppose she'll never be dead as long as children read.

I'm surprised to see not Bea but Hope standing there, a little toddler Hope holding a soggy Mr. Jackson. She giggles and leans over to blow out the candle, like she always did at the end of our baths. I blink, and she is gone as surely as Bea is, really, and I'm left alone with only the candle beside the tub burning gently as the coal bricks in the grate grow riddled and craggy, but remain warm.

41

Dear Mr. Warne, . . . I wonder if you will care for either of these. . . . I'm afraid you don't like frogs but it would make pretty pictures with water-forget-me-nots, lilies etc.
——Beatrix Potter, transmitting the draft text of **The Tale of Mr. Jeremy Fisher**, in a February 2, 1905, letter to Norman Warne

RAIN POUNDED ON THE COTTAGE ROOF AND the slate patio and the windows, on the lake you could barely see through the storm. I set a fire and took the last match from the tin box, and lit it, and tossed it right onto a fire starter. "Here we are, Mom," I said as the flame sprang up. "You and me and the rain." I turned on the tub water, and when it began running warm, I wedged the rubber stopper on its metal chain into the drain, and I tipped the bottle of bubble bath into the stream of water, watching the blue mingling with the clear and the bubbles foaming. While the tub filled, I sat on the love seat with Mom's puzzle box, tracing a finger from the inset wood of the baby's halo over the edge, to the first hidden panel. The mother didn't have a halo, I realized as I slid the first panel down; only the child had a halo. I was still thinking about that as I took a handful of what was left of my mother, and climbed into the tub.

At Ainsley's End that afternoon, I called Kevin from the telephone in the alcove off the front entry.

"Hope," he said gently when I remained silent after his hello, trying not to cry. "Hey," he said. "Hey, it's going to be okay."

I wanted to climb into his voice and settle there, the way I used to climb into my parents' laps.

"You've let her go, then?" he murmured.

I nodded, gathering myself.

"You're nodding that way you do when you don't trust yourself to speak, aren't you?" he said softly.

"A little," I managed, feeling a hint of a smile even through the sadness. "I let a little of her go."

"I can't bear not being there to help you through this," he said. "I could be on a flight in three hours. I could be there by morning your time. Let me help you through this, Hope, please?"

The wind outside gushed, rattling the windows.

"It's raining," I said.

"I don't mind a little rain."

"I had to shed my rain gear in the entryway outside the door," I said.

"I don't mind a lot of rain."

In the silence that followed, I listened to the world outside. Perhaps the rain had stopped. Perhaps it was only the wind I was hearing. Things were so changeable here.

"She used to let me climb in the bath with her," I said. "Mom did."

"She loved that," he said.

"She has a slipper tub in the middle of her cottage here, not in the bathroom but between the fireplace and the bed."

Had a slipper tub. I supposed it had become my slipper tub.

"Does she?" he said gently. "By the fireplace, where she would have been nice and warm."

"I took a bath with her," I confessed.

I knew from his long silence that he was imagining it: my too thin nakedness sinking into the water, the bubbly wetness mingling with the ash in my hand, the awful paste I hadn't anticipated. I'd skimmed her along the water's surface, rubbing what was left of Mom together with the fresh vanilla bubbles. I'd smoothed it all over me, on my face and on my shoulders, on my breasts like the breasts she used to cover with a washcloth, on my knees where she'd piled up bubbles whenever I climbed into the bath with her.

"I'm glad," Kevin said. "She would have liked that. Mom would have liked that."

In his words, I heard Mom's voice the day we married, Mom in the snow-softened spring day looking up at Kevin, who had volunteered to her that he would take great care of me. She put both hands on his tuxedoed shoulders, gently laughing as she reached up. "Heavens to Betsy, don't let her catch you at it!" The words said to Kevin but directed at me. "You'd best let her think she's doing all the caretaking, Kevin, perhaps with a little help from Anna Page."

She'd turned to me and said, "He's not like Mr. Jackson, Hope. Aunt Frankie can't make you a replacement Kevin if you drown this one. If his feet are muddy now and then, just accept a little mud into your pantry. You'd grow bored with a man whose feet are always clean."

"Kev," I said, "can I ask you something?" In the long moment I took to gather my courage, I lost it. "The thing about teaching me how to save the sponge," I said, thinking of the last stupid argument we'd had, about how to wash a pan, "was that a joke?"

He laughed a little, then said apparently it hadn't been, he wasn't always as funny as he meant to be.

"Jules and Ape both laughed," I said.

"Alas, not my intended audience."

"What a drip I am sometimes," I admitted.

"Pun intended?" He laughed again. "Get it? You were washing a pan, right?"

"I'm sorry," I said. "It's just been so much, with Jamie and Dad and now Mom."

"I know," he said. "It's okay. I know. And don't worry. The how-to-wash-a-pan lessons can wait."

And so it was very late that night—when he called me from the airport in New York to tell me he'd gotten the overnight flight to Manchester—before I asked how he'd known the Beatrix Potter quote. "That first day at the register," I said. "Anna Page told you to say that, didn't she?"

"When we bought your bike?"

"She slept with her sister's fiancé."

"God, that guy was such a jerk," he said. "Lacy is lucky Anna Page saved her from him."

"But did you?"

"Did I . . . ?"

There was such a long stretch of painful quiet over the phone that I was sure he had.

"You don't imagine I've ever cheated on you, Hope."

"But before."

"Before we met? Because I knew the Potter quote?" He sighed. "Anna Page told me if I found myself wanting to win your heart, I should take you to buy something and quote the line to you."

"She told you to buy me a bicycle?"

"I think she had in mind a ticket to the football game."

"You never read *Ginger and Pickles* to your fifth-graders? You just remembered the line Anna Page fed you from before we met?"

"I had her write it on my arm at the tailgate party."

In the long silence, I heard a pan being set on the stove in the Ainsley's End kitchen, Aunt Kath fixing midnight cocoa.

"Did she show you a photo of me?" I asked. Like she'd shown Isaac the photo of Jamie, except that it had been Julie.

Kevin laughed his easy General Opie laugh. "Hope, if Anna Page had shown me a photo of you, I'd have memorized the whole of *Ginger and Pickles* before the tailgate party. I'd have made sure I could quote every line of it."

I ran a finger along the looped cord, the old-fashioned Ainsley's End phone. Did the rest of it matter? I'd always known Kevin had slept with other women before he met me. Did it matter who they were?

"I was attracted to Anna Page," he admitted. "She was attracted to me. I sometimes wonder if that isn't why she started talking to me about you almost from the moment we met. Because I'm basically a decent guy."

Upstairs, a door squeaked on its hinges.

"Anna Page sleeps with absolute jerks she can abandon, Hope, before they abandon her. Guys like Isaac and me, she gives us away to her friends so we're out of bounds. So she won't sleep with us. So we can't cause her the hurt that she doesn't seem to realize we never would."

I heard, in his words, the truth of them. Or the almost truth. Anna Page wouldn't have slept with Kevin. She would hurt someone like her father, as he would hurt her even if he didn't realize he did. But she wouldn't hurt people who loved like her mother loves. She would put them in the hands of someone who would love them the way they deserved to be loved, a love she believed herself incapable of.

42

I am sorry to tell you I have jibbed at the pigeons. I have never been good at birds; and whatever you say—I cannot see them in clothes.
——Beatrix Potter, in a March 4, 1921, letter to her then publisher, Fruing Warne

MAYBE IT WAS THE CAFFEINE IN THE HOT chocolate her mother brought her just after midnight, Anna Page thought as she slipped from her bed at Ainsley's End for the second night in a row, or maybe it was the fact that Kevin was arriving the next morning that unsettled her. Outside, it wasn't raining, but she raised her hood against the cold. She circled around through the herb garden, stopping to smell the rosemary, looking without meaning to be caught looking. She wandered along the bare paths by the roses and circled around to the arbor. Graham was in the same spot he'd been the night before, alone on the bench with only his sketch pad and the reading lamp for company. She watched him as she had the prior night, his head bent over the pad, his fingers moving easily over the page.

Was it five minutes? Fifteen? Fifty? Did she move? Did she make a sound? He saw her this time, and he called to her. She supposed she'd meant him to. She supposed when she'd come upon him the night before, some part of her had wanted him to see her, to invite her into his world.

She exhaled against the sense of something fluttering quietly in the darkness, a bat, perhaps.

"Don't worry," she said to Graham. "I have an emergency kit with me."

Had she heard him laugh before, really? His mirth as soothing as "Moonlight Sonata," the music she plays as she closes patients in the OR, and at home at night, alone.

"You're safe here," he said. "I could have heard your call for help."

"Could you?" She looked to the house with its square center tower, its slate roofs, the dark windows. The whole world was unlit by the thin sliver of moon that had left her feeling so vulnerable and exposed, somehow, when she'd seen it that first day in the clear blue sky. "I'd think those stone walls would keep out every sound."

"Perhaps that's why I'm out here. To hear you."

She pulled off her hood and ran her hand through her wild hair. "I'm not in need of help."

"How bloody wrong of me, then," he said, a teasing lift in his voice. "I had you pegged as the type who might use some help but would never call for it."

He moved the box of charcoal pencils beside him and scooted over on the bench—dry under the protection of the arbor—accidentally kicking over an empty wineglass at his feet. It cracked but didn't shatter. He set it aside and lifted the bottle from the ground: the English wine he'd served that first night, uncorked but still full. He offered to fetch new glasses.

She took the bottle from him and put it to her lips, took a sip. "Ma used to say I'd be drinking bourbon right out of the bottle before I was eighteen, but I don't imagine even she foresaw me drinking swanky British wine that way."

He laughed again.

She held the bottle out to him. "I'm good at sharing, if not at asking for help."

He didn't ask what she was doing out so late, and she didn't, either. He only accepted the bottle from her, took a sip himself, and set it on the bench.

He'd been sketching: trees in the foreground, the fortress of the house beyond them, what looked like a little birdie apartment house tucked up under the highest peak of roof. She looked from the page to the real house. The same little aviary was built up against the stone of a tower wall, above a single window high up in the stone.

Was the world ever this dark at home?

"Allison always thought this would be a splendid setting for a book," he said. "Perhaps about the birds."

"Some furry animal would live at the bottom of the tower," Anna Page said, "where the little door would be even smaller." She looked at Graham's drawing. "Like in your sketch."

The door in the tower opened out into the geometrically rigid herb garden, which in the story would play some role she couldn't imagine, being a heart surgeon without an ounce of creativity, she always says—although she's plenty creative at making up wild stories about her own life, hiding the truth behind theatrics that are exaggerations when they aren't completely untrue.

She started to say how glad she was that he and her mother were getting along, but the thought got all twisted up with the night and the scent of rosemary on her skin, the taste of the wine, so that the words came out as a question she hadn't imagined asking: "Did it bother you that your dad was a bigamist?"

He sketched a small beak poking out of one of the round holes.

"One doesn't know when one is a child," he said finally. "One doesn't accept the truth about one's parents until there is no choice."

She took a sip from the bottle, recognizing the truth of this as he said it: all those Sunday morning breakfasts with her father. Church. How ironic that the only thing they'd ever done together as a family was go to the church that represented the sacredness of the vows her father flouted every day.

Graham sketched for another minute, and she sat silently beside him, imagining a bird landing at one of the circle-doors and disappearing into the aviary.

"I blamed my mother," she said finally.

He tilted his head slightly. She braced herself for a defense of her mother that she didn't want, didn't need.

"One does, doesn't one?" he said. "Fathers are so . . ."

His pencil remained still between his fingers, which were long and large, not graceful, not at all like she would have imagined an artist's hands.

"I didn't know my father was with another woman," she said. "I thought he didn't want to be with Ma. I thought Ma drove him away."

Graham set the charcoal on the pad and tilted the wine bottle to his lips, then offered it to Anna

Page. "Of course, my mother *was* the other woman," he said.

"But she was your father's first wife."

"Yes, well . . . it wasn't seen that way here."

She supposed it wouldn't have been, if everyone saw the neighborhood prince married to a fair young maiden before learning of the other wife.

"We didn't know you were a half," Anna Page said. "That's not my term. It's the way Hope talks about herself when she isn't . . . liking herself, I guess."

"How does such a lovely person not like herself?"

"I don't know," Anna Page said. "You tell me."

She tilted her head at him, and smiled slightly, and took another sip of the wine, wondering how she ever could have blamed her mother for her father's philandering. She never did blame her father. She never did blame the other Kath. She'd thought that if her mother were a better woman, the kind of woman she would be herself, her father wouldn't have left. Even after she knew who the other Kath was, what Catherine's relationship to her father was, Anna Page always imagined herself as the woman a man would leave others for, not the one who was left.

"It didn't bother me that my father had other women," she said. Women, she said, although as far as she knew, it had only ever been Catherine. "It bothered me that my mother put up with it."

This wasn't true, exactly, but she didn't know how to phrase the truth, or perhaps how to face it. It bothered her that love was never quite complete anywhere she turned. It bothered her that this was true in her own life, that she didn't love the way you were supposed to love, the way her mother did love her father: completely, with reckless disregard for herself. It bothered her that if you gave yourself over to love, you ended up hurt, and that if you didn't, you ended up hurt. It bothered her that a heart was such a fragile, vulnerable thing, that it would beat on for others long after it was taken from where it belonged.

"Do you think you could ever give your heart away?" she asked Graham.

He closed his sketch pad and folded his hands over it so that the little light illuminated his charcoal-smudged fingers.

"It's what I do," she said. "I take hearts from bodies that have no more use for them, and I cut open chests and chop out useless hearts and put in new ones. Not new ones. Used ones. But I don't know if I could do that myself. I'm not sure I could give away my own heart to save someone else."

She had wept so over that photograph of the transplant and the family the first time she'd seen it. She didn't know why. She doesn't weep in the operating room; that wouldn't do. She doesn't weep when she's talking with patients, or with donor families, or with other doctors or nurses or lecture rooms full of students, or with her parents and her friends. She doesn't weep in front of her mother or the other Kath, and she certainly doesn't weep in front of her father. She'd never told my mother about the weeping, not after weeping with her after that first loss. She'd never told Jamie. And they'd abandoned her to her secret, neither leaving behind a heart to share with someone else.

"It's the generosity people show in the face of tragedy, it makes me weep sometimes," she said to Graham, whom she hardly knew. "People who've lost everything. What they are still willing to give."

He wiped a tear from her cheek, one that had been pooling in her eyes since that night in the forest, when she'd suggested he might like her mom. She hesitated, but she pulled the silver box from her coat pocket and handed it to Graham. "I'm sorry," she said.

Graham eyed the box, confused, before taking it from her palm.

"I took it that first afternoon, when we had tea in the Prospect," she said. "I saw it, and I was afraid Hope would see it and know it was from her mother." Though it wasn't that, was it? Thinking about how Hope would feel had come later, to justify the taking. If that had been all there was to it, she'd have given it back at that first dinner in the Ainsley's End dining room, when she'd learned who Graham was.

"Do you know how to open it?" Anna Page asked. "I can't figure it out."

Although she had already, the night she'd taken it. What was inside was too intimate to admit having seen without having been invited to.

He handed the box back to Anna Page and trained the reading light on it, indicating where to start. "It's a very simple puzzle. Most are."

She worked the panels at his instruction.

"And now you slip the lid aside," he said.

"Is it empty?" she asked, beginning to doubt: he would let her see the strands of hair inside, but could she bear to see them again? "I saw the box and I . . ." She began to reverse the steps she'd just taken. She didn't want to know what explanation he might give.

Graham kissed her, then, his lips soft and full on hers, his mouth warm and oaky with the taste of the wine that was the English wine and not the American one. His sketch pad slipped from his lap and fell to the dirt, sprawling open to a sketch caught in the small pool of the reading light: a woman with wild dark hair. The page bowed under the weight of the cardboard backing but didn't crease as the charcoal pencil rolled to a rest against Anna Page's gray hiking boot. She closed her eyes to it and to everything as Graham wound his large, unexpected hands into her hair and pulled her closer, again kissing her. She touched her fingers gently to his chest, as if to string a line of dental floss, to make the cut with the scalpel straight. What her bare skin met, though, was the strong beat of his heart and, beside it, the beat of her own in the moonless night.

43

[Pigling Robinson] had crossed five big fields, and ever so many stiles; stiles with steps; ladder stiles; stiles of wooden posts; some of them were very awkward with a heavy basket. . . . Robinson sat down to rest beside a hedge in a sheltered sunny spot. Yellow pussy willow catkins were in flower above his head; there were primroses in hundreds on the bank, and a warm smell of moss and grass and streaming moist red earth. . . . The walk had made him so hungry he would have liked to eat an egg as well as the jam sandwiches; but he had been too well brought up.
——from **The Tale of Little Pig Robinson**
by Beatrix Potter

KEVIN EMERGED FROM CUSTOMS THE NEXT morning with tired eyes, a red stubble of beard on his chin, and a single small bag hiked over his shoulder. I watched him for a minute, thinking of the reassuring sound of his voice: Not horror that I had taken a handful of the pulverized bone that had been my mother into the bathtub and smeared it all over myself. Understanding. *She would have liked that.* And there had been nothing to do then but pull the rubber stopper and let that bit of her disappear down the drain.

His gaze found me, and his face lit in a wide grin. He waved and I waved back, and he circled around the exit rail, dropped his bag, scooped me up in his arms.

"I'm sorry I let you come without me," he said, his breath warm in my hair.

"I'm sorry I insisted," I said.

"I'm sorry I let you insist."

We spent the whole afternoon together, just the two of us. We walked down to the cottage and collected Mom's bicycle, and Kevin rode me on the handlebars up the path to Wray Castle. We circled the empty beast of a place, riding down to the front gate and back up to the broken clock tower, glad to have no reminder of the passing time. We rode on to the Wray Castle boathouse, where a young boy and his dog eyed us suspiciously even after I'd hopped down from the handlebars and muttered the obligatory "Hiya." Kevin put the bike on the kickstand and stooped to rub the dog's ears.

"What's this fella's name?" he asked the boy, and before the public launch arrived some twenty minutes later, we knew everything there was to know about a lizard the boy had caught that morning but not yet named. When I proposed the name Judy—having read in Mom's journal that Beatrix Potter had a pet lizard of that name—Kevin and the boy looked at me like I was loony. They settled on Wormtongue, with a long and pedantic explanation for my sake about wizards and devious servants and how easy the Rohirrim people were to manipulate. *"Lord of the Rings,"* Kevin explained.

Kevin and I crossed the water to Ambleside on the public launch. We left Mom's bike outside an old cemetery and wandered the winding streets. Plenty of inviting restaurants beckoned on the walk, but it was such a soft evening that we hated to leave it. We wandered inside only when we came upon a charming bookstore at the top of the town. There, we read each other passages from the little Warne editions of Beatrix Potter's books.

Outside again with a copy of *The Tale of Ginger and Pickles* tucked into Kevin's jacket pocket for our nephew, we wandered across the street to Bridge House, a tiny, charming stone place built on a stone arch over the river. We settled on the wall downstream from it, watching the water run underneath the house.

"Could you imagine living in such a small place?" I asked.

Kevin replied, "Couldn't you?"

44

A gentleman had a favourite cat whom he taught
to sit at the dinner-table where it behaved very
well. He was in the habit of putting any scraps he
left on to the cat's plate. One day puss did not
take his place punctually, but presently appeared
with two mice, one of which it placed on its
master's plate, the other on its own.
——Beatrix Potter, in a January 27, 1884, journal entry

"I THOUGHT I MIGHT OPEN A NICE BOTTLE OF
wine and watch the sunset in the Prospect, and I
wondered if you might join me," Graham said to
Anna Page. "As an enticement, I will tell you
there is plenty more silver that you might pinch."

Anna Page laughed easily and said there was a
small silver-handled knife she had her eye on.
The blade as sharp as a scalpel, she thought as
they settled on a settee before one of the
windows, with a view to the sloping grade of
forest to the west.

He poured two glasses from the bottle and set it
at his feet as he had the night before, even though
there was a table that would have served the
purpose well. She liked somehow that he left the
table clear, nothing before them but smooth wood

and clear glass and the softening colors of the cloudy sky.

They clinked glasses and he said, "To . . ." But then didn't finish the thought.

"To this lovely view," she said. "To you, for putting Ma up. For putting us all up."

He put an arm around her and said, "To you, Anna Page. More lovely than the sky."

"And growing as gray," Anna Page said—stupidly, she thought. She was usually so good with men. She could get them to say whatever she wanted them to say. And he was, Graham was saying all the right things, the things she wanted him to say. Why was that making her so uncomfortable?

He tipped her head down, observing her hair at the part line, where the grays were creeping in. "I prefer the gray," he said.

She looked down to the hiking shoes on her feet, the ones he'd brought that first morning. The shoes were broken in, more comfortable. *I'm a fair guess at clothing sizes, but feet don't always match the rest,* he'd said that first morning, before he'd even said his name.

He kissed her then. Kissed her as he had the night before, this time without the cover of the dark night and the outdoors.

She touched a hand to his hair, healthy and thick but graying. She imagined the feel of it on her breasts, on her belly. She imagined running her fingers through it as he kissed the parts of her that she loved to have kissed.

She might seduce him now, she thought. She might have it over with and move on.

She sat beside him, watching the colors edge the clouds, listening to the quiet of the evening coming up: the crackle of the fire in the room's large fireplace warming their backs, the lap of the lake, the flutter of a bird disappearing from sight in the direction of the aviary high above the tiny door to the herb garden, which was tinier in his sketch.

"I'm not very good in relationships," she said.

"I haven't been with a woman since Cornelia," he said.

Cornelia. She'd heard that name recently. Where had it been?

Cornelia was a girl he'd loved at Oxford, he said, when he was too young to appreciate how rare a Cornelia was, or too wrapped up in his own problems to see that she was the solution, or part of it. As he told her about his old love, she remembered something Julie had said about a poem she'd been reading in the Ainsley's End library, something Anna Page had only half heard, because what did she care about poetry? A poem about a man taking a boat across a lake in search of his dead love's first lover, whom she'd known in school.

She remembered the first boy she'd slept with,

when she was barely in high school, only fourteen. She'd imagined she loved him, but after she'd slept with him, she hadn't liked even the sound of his name.

"I've been with men, but I've never had a Cornelia," she said. "Why didn't you ever go to Ireland to find her?"

At the horizon, clouds threatened the pink-orange sunset. Somewhere beyond the ridge, tiny drops began to plink into Moss Eccles Tarn, circles overlapping into ripples that, slowly and surely, would send the smooth water's surface into something wilder, scarier, and more interesting.

"I did once," he said. "I took the Lancaster ferry across, in a storm so fierce that we turned back even before reaching the Isle of Man. She was already in love by then, with a man more deserving of her, a journalist who wrote about the things she cared for. Irish, like her."

45

The shop was crammed with customers,
and there were crowds of mice upon
the biscuit canisters.
Sally Henny-penny gets rather flustered
when she tries to count out change,
and she insists on being paid cash;
but she is quite harmless.
And she has laid in a remarkable
assortment of bargains.
There is something to please everybody.
——from **The Tale of Ginger and Pickles**
by Beatrix Potter

ON THE WAY BACK DOWNHILL FROM BRIDGE
House, Kevin and I passed the specialty grocer
with the round woman at the register. A few
minutes and a few not-farthings later, we were
sitting on a bench at the harbor with a bag of
takeaway, the bicycle on its kickstand beside us,
the last of the boats tucking their white sails into
blue canvas as the sun set beyond the water and
the pier and Mom's cottage, the high chimneys of
Ainsley's End, the long stretch of woods. Kevin
handed me a cup of warm mulled wine, then set
his on the pavement beside our bench and

removed from the bag a banana toffee pudding and a piece of something called Cumberland Rum Nicky, a sort of dried fruit and nut pie with heavy rum. At the water's edge, a child chased ducks and geese, white gulls, a single white swan.

"I can see how your mother would have written in this part of the world," Kevin said. He set his hand over mine on the bench. "Couldn't you imagine writing a novel here?"

"It isn't that much money, what I inherit," I said.

"It's never been about the money, Hope."

"What would we—"

"Your dad would have hated to think his expectations keep you from doing what you want to do."

I watched the bird-chaser. He would never catch a thing. Although perhaps I was wrong about that. Wormtongue's owner had caught a lizard, and they were quick.

"Dad loved to talk about the law with me," I said.

He took a bite of the pie and handed it to me. "I think we'll call this one 'dinner.'"

"As opposed to the creamy banana thing?"

"The 'fruit salad,' you mean?"

We savored the flavor of rum and nuts and spices and watched the boy. He was about Oliver's age, and he wore the same saggy blue jeans. His hair was the same brilliant blond as Oliver's, the color Jamie's had been when she was a girl, and Julie's.

"It's not enough to pay off the mortgage," I said, "much less buy the house with the double tub."

"We don't need the tub, Hope. Anyway, we've got a fabulous slipper tub right next to a fireplace, in viewing distance of the bed."

The boy sprinted off after another bird. It was hard to imagine harm coming to him here, or to anyone else.

"A tub that would need to double as a desk," I said, thinking *double as a crib* but unwilling to say that, unwilling to go into Mr. McGregor's garden.

Kevin scooped a bite of the banana pudding. "All serious writers need their potassium," he said as he fed it to me. "Remember that first day we rode through the Rodin sculpture garden?" he said. "I had this idea you were imagining yourself sitting there beside me, pen in hand."

"In the rain?"

He laughed. "I don't mind a little rain. Do you?"

I looked out over the water, remembering the passage from my mother's journal, her sitting at the lake trying to talk Beatrix Potter into removing her stockings. The last passage, my mother turning to Bea in the tub and finding me standing there. I hadn't decoded much of her journals—it was a time-consuming process, and emotionally draining—but when I couldn't sleep the night before, I'd done that last page, then slept with my hands wrapped around the journal as I had the first night at the cottage, as I used to sleep with Mr. Pajamas and, later, Mr. Jackson, too.

Kevin spooned a bite of the banana dessert and fed it to me, sweet and creamy-smooth, comforting and comfortable, and we watched the boy skimming the water's edge but not getting wet.

" 'A person can't live on seed wigs and sponge cake and butter buns,' " I said.

"Can't we?" he said.

The boy giggled and set off after another bird, refusing to give up.

"Maybe a sabbatical?" Kevin said. "Three months next summer. If we're not happy here, we go back. Nothing lost."

A bird fluttered easily away from the boy and landed just out of reach. A woman sitting not far away—the boy's mother; she looked so much like him—smiled.

"What would I write, Kev?" I asked.

"Oh, Hope," he said, his voice softening. He dipped the plastic spoon in the banana pudding and fed me another bite before taking one himself. "Writing isn't like that," he said. "You don't have to know."

"Unlike religion," I said.

He watched the boy. "Einstein believed in God," he said finally. "Kepler. Gregor Mendel. Newton. Planck. I expect the list of scientists who believe in a god of some sort is far longer than the list of those who don't." He shrugged. "If I had to plan out what I'm writing before I start, I never would start. You sit down and put a word on the page, and then another. Like everything else in life, you can always change them."

"Until they're published."

Kevin said I was one of the few people he knew who would be editing her work even after it was published. "It's what will make you so great at it," he said.

I felt the small thrill of his confidence in me, the same way I had felt on that first bike ride, while everyone else was at the football game. I hadn't worried then that I might fall off the handlebars. I hadn't worried that it was his bicycle, that he was steering, that I was precariously perched, with no control over where we went or how fast, whether we skirted the rough spots or bumped straight through.

"What if I can't?" I said.

Kevin set down the takeaway and placed a hand on my hip, like in the Rodin sculpture before we first kissed. I wondered if he could see all the ways I was not like my mother and never would be.

"What if I can't write?" I said, not ready to hear his answer to any of the other what-ifs.

He took my face in his hands and kissed me and smiled. "Asha my love," he said, "wouldn't the bigger failure be to let your pride get in the way of your dreams?"

The mother called to the bird-chaser in some language I didn't recognize. He called back and ran to her almost as fast as he had run after the birds, and she knelt down to his level to wipe his nose with a tissue. She slipped his bird-empty hand in hers, and they headed toward the hut that sold tickets for the public launch. Their pale hair and pale, intertwined hands disappeared behind the ticket booth, then appeared on the other side of the hut before disappearing into a building that was an inn, and probably had been for centuries.

"Kev," I whispered, "I don't know if I could bear to have people assume I'm my children's nanny."

He wrapped me in his arms, and he kissed the top of my head, and he kissed it again. "I know," he said. "I know."

We sat watching the light fade over the boat masts and the water and the far shore, the broken Wray Castle clock, the chimneys at Ainsley's End. Somewhere in the distance, a bell rang the hour, gentle and warm. And when it was dark and our cups of warm wine were empty, we collected the bike and walked it together to catch the last launch back across to Wray Castle. And if anyone saw the Crier of Claife that night, it was probably our single bike light shining on the path, helping us find our way home in the lightest sprinkling of new rain.

46

Thank God I have the seeing eye.
—**Beatrix Potter, in a February 15, 1937, letter to Caroline Clark**

THE CLOUDS HAD STACKED RATHER THAN scattered the next morning—did it ever dry out here?—by the time Robbie came to fetch us in his launch for the hike up to Stock Ghyll Force. Heavy drops began to fall as we arrived at the bank building that marked the hike's start. We talked about turning back, but Aunt Kath had to leave the next day for meetings in New York, and I found I wanted her to be with me for this after all; I found myself sorry that I hadn't asked all the Wednesday Sisters to come.

Kevin said to Napoleon, who'd taken a liking to him, as children and dogs always did, "What's the worst that will happen to us, Mr. Bonaparte? We'll get a bit damp, right?"

"Quite drenched, probably," Graham said.

"Washed away in a flood," Robbie suggested, with a smile at Julie that left me wondering if the Ambleside library might need a very competent if somewhat stylish American librarian.

"Lordy," Aunt Kath said, "the animals will be

starting to pair up, won't they?" Meaning the rain, I think, although she might have been referring to Anna Page and Graham, who walked alongside each other, Napoleon herding them together each time they wandered apart.

"That makes Hope and Anna Page all the more determined to push on," Kevin said. "Neither of them can turn away from a challenge."

I longed to slip my hand in his, to have our fingers intertwining, but I didn't want to drop Mom's puzzle box. As though reading my mind, Graham asked if he might take a turn carrying Mom. "I expect she's heavier than she looks," he said.

Anna Page pulled up her hood, tucking all that wild hair away, and responded in a mimic of my mother, "Heavens to Betsy, Graham, are you saying I've gotten fat?" We all laughed together as we set off up the road, glad of the chance to let some steam out of the emotion pot.

"This park was created as a Victorian pleasure garden," Graham said as we turned toward a woods, its entrance marked by an old-fashioned metal turnstile and a newer wooden gate. "Bathing was permitted in the 1880s between six and nine in the morning, and again after seven-thirty in the evening, and towels were provided. It used to cost a penny to get through the stile into the park. Now, of course, it's free."

"You're sure this doesn't go back to your

ancestors, the ancient Romans?" Anna Page said in a teasing voice.

"I don't—Oh, I see, you're laughing at me!" He laughed at himself. "I do go on, don't I? Allison used to tell me that. It comes of living too long alone."

He pushed through the wet turnstile, with my mother tucked under the protection of his mackintosh. Napoleon, left on the other side with the rest of us, stood alert.

"What do you keep inside the puzzle box Mom gave you, Graham?" I asked.

Anna Page turned away, touching a hand to Napoleon's noble head as Graham looked back at us through the turnstile's metal bars.

"A lock of hair your mother gave me," he said, "in case I wanted to do DNA testing."

Anything precious. Anything you wanted to keep just for yourself.

He went to the wooden gate and lifted the latch to let Napoleon in. The rest of us circled one at a time through the turnstile, although it would have been easier to follow the dog through the open gate.

Robbie fell in beside Graham on the path, saying, "I've a message for you."

They walked along together in silence before Graham said, "I hope you were good to her."

"So you've known, then."

"Not at first. Even when I heard your name the

other day, I thought, no. Even when you knew all the poetry. You were a journalist."

Robbie nodded. "It's the pleasure of being a boatman, idn' it? Nobody notices you. Nobody stops long enough to judge."

"I suppose it's a sad thing that I hate the water," Graham said.

"She never stopped loving you, you know," Robbie said. "She would want you to know that. She'd be glad of the things you're doing here, glad of all this beauty and wildness that you've made it your work to save."

"My work?" Graham said.

"Ah, but isn't it? Though surely our Cornelia would be taking the credit, saying she turned you to your calling."

Graham laughed. It was okay for a British gentleman to laugh, if not loudly, if not in improper circumstances. And it was easier to laugh than to cry.

We hiked uphill alongside an enthusiastic waterway—more than a stream but not quite a river, the rain splashing up in little drops as the water rushed downhill. The path was largely slate, wet from the rain and slippery, so it was with relief that we stopped again and again at the lookouts. "This is beautiful, this is gorgeous," we kept saying, thinking one run of water or another might be the much advertised waterfall to which the signs pointed us.

"That'd be the weir, wouldn't it?" Robbie said at one point.

As the rest of us set off together, Julie and Robbie stayed back.

"You'll be leaving soon, with the others, then?" he asked her.

Julie closed her eyes, listening to the wide rush of water falling from the solid rock ledge to the more turbulent streambed, the way she used to listen for the plink of Anna Page's stones on the bedroom window. She was always the one to whisper that Anna Page was waiting for them. She wondered sometimes if she might ignore the sound of pebble on glass, but the truth was she never wanted to. The truth was she liked to be included in the midnight wanderings. She liked that Jamie wouldn't go without her, wouldn't leave her behind.

In the closed-eyed darkness, two birds chirped at each other somewhere up in the trees. Robbie's feet shifted on the leafy-wet ground. The water crashed relentlessly over the weir, leaving her wondering if it would ever run dry, or change course.

"I had a twin sister," she said to Robbie. "A twin born in a different year. She was the Aphrodite. Not for Halloween but for everything else."

She opened her eyes, inhaling the smells that seemed sharpened by the moment without sight: the fresh water and the fallen leaves, the wood bark.

Robbie rolled his lips together, leaving them glossy, his face soft and warm, unwavering. "Was she?" He smiled slightly, listening.

Julie looked down at the sheet of water changing levels in its busy rush, in search of the right words, the poem she ought to write. Jamie would have turned fifty this December thirty-first, she imagined saying. She died a year ago this week.

Jamie had a son, she imagined saying. Oliver. He's only six.

Oliver's dad, she imagined saying. He's the "involved."

That cluster of stars, three together, the red dwarf in need of a binary system to hold him in place—none would be visible tonight.

It was a way of sharing, she supposed, being near Oliver even if she couldn't be with him, spending late nights with Isaac even if he never said her name. But that only eased her own grief, and maybe Isaac's. It would never comfort Oliver. It would never bring anything but hurt for Oliver.

Robbie touched the edge of her hair underneath her hood, his finger lingering there before trailing down her arm to her elbow, circling the bone under the plastic of her jacket with his finger. "I've a crown and a cushion of foam for you, Julie," he said, "should you ever care for it."

She wanted to reach up and touch the roughness of his pockmarked cheek, but she didn't.

Cornelia, she imagined him thinking. *Her name was Cornelia.*

"Jamie," she said. "Her name was Jamie, but I liked to call her James."

Lightning flashed overhead, but if there was thunder to accompany it, I didn't hear it over the sound of the rain and the falls as Kevin and I followed the others uphill.

"That woman who read our horoscopes was right, you know," Kevin said. "About us belonging together."

On the far bank of the river, a waterwheel turned with the force of the moving stream.

"It's sort of hard to imagine having kids," I said, "but being here somehow makes it hard to imagine not having them. I . . . Right now I wish I could have had a child who walked here with Mom, you know?"

He put his wet-jacketed arm around my wet-jacketed waist. "We don't have to decide that right now," he said. "We don't ever have to decide about kids. We can let the decision make itself. And I don't expect you to do everything, or even most things, if we do have kids. I can be the parent people mistake for the nanny."

In the waterlogged silence, I tried to imagine Kevin's and my children, perhaps a daughter with Mom's big eyes and her taste for bohemian clothing.

"And they'll know Mom through us," he said. "If we decide to have children, Hope, they'll know Mom through us. We'll make sure they do."

Stock Ghyll Force was unmistakable when we first caught a glimpse of it, around a bend and through the trees: water rushing in dramatic falls through a gorge, two higher streams pooling together before falling into two lower streams that pooled again, pausing before continuing their downhill flight. The rain was letting up. We stood for a long time silently watching, the way you do with things that are too striking to capture in words. Only Napoleon remained moving, seeming to want to interpose himself between all of us and the ledge, to keep us safe.

"There's a large rock outcropping across the force," Graham said. "I thought that might do. Room for us all."

We crossed on the wooden bridge over the falls and climbed carefully onto the outcropping. Kevin held Mom's puzzle box for me while Graham held an umbrella over us, and I traced my finger from the baby's halo around the edge, to the flower and the panel that was the first step to opening it. Slide, push, adjust until the mother and baby moved aside.

"I believe the rain has stopped finally," Graham said, setting down the umbrella.

"Or paused," Anna Page agreed.

She was the first to reach into the box and take a small bit of Mom. But she didn't keep it for herself. She took Graham's hand, and placed the ash in his open palm, and closed his fist over it.

A heart, when she brings it back out of surgery, Anna Page will tell you, doesn't start beating again all at once. It stirs, and it stops, and it stirs again. Sometimes it has to be shocked into action, but it's best to let it start on its own if you can.

She took a bit more ash for herself, slipped the fingers of her empty hand through his, and stood beside him. Napoleon nosed his big head in between them but didn't push them apart.

Julie stepped up to the box, followed by Robbie and Aunt Kath, and Kevin. I took some, too. Not all of her. I would take the rest of her home to Palo Alto for Sammy. The Wednesday Sisters had already arranged for a bench to be put in Eleanor Pardee Park in her honor, not far from where they'd felled all those lovely sycamore trees. When no one was looking, we would sprinkle the rest of Mom around the new tree at the far end of the bench, where she once brought iced tea and said hello to the women who, with her, had become the Wednesday Sisters, mothers of the Wednesday Daughters, and lifelong friends. Sammy could sit there and watch his children play where we used to play. Kevin and I could, too, perhaps. If I closed my eyes, I could imagine a watercolor Labradoodle playing riot grrrl music in the mansion that once stood there, before Sammy and I were born.

Kevin set Mom's puzzle box on a flat spot on the rocks behind us, underneath the tilted umbrella and on a handkerchief Graham extracted from his pocket, so the wood wouldn't get too wet. We all stood as close to the edge of the slippery rocks as we thought safe.

I just about lost one of my shoes among the cabbages, Hope, I remembered Mom saying. *I was sure the water might reach up and sweep me away.*

Ally, I thought. *Her name was Ally Tantry. But I called her Mom.*

I opened my fist and held my palm up to the wind, which lifted the bit of crushed bone and carried it over the water before setting it gently down in a sprinkle of soft gray that was gone as soon as the water took it in. Even Napoleon watched for a long, quiet moment, as if he understood.

The others let their handfuls go just as a big gust of wind came up, not blowing the ashes back at us so much as washing us all with the mingle of ash and spray from the force.

"Heavens to Betsy!" Anna Page said, and we laughed as we wiped the spray from our faces.

Kevin collected the puzzle box from the ground and came up behind me, and put it in my hands. He wrapped his arms around my waist, as if to warm me, and set his chin on my head. We stood like that, in the mist of the parallel falls rushing toward the same pool. "No more twist," he said.

Anna Page linked fingers with Aunt Kath, leaving me thinking how often I'd seen her fingers intertwined with my mother's, and how Anna Page's hand had seemed to belong in Mom's more than my own had. Her nails that had always been dirty—she'd been such a wild young girl—were clean and tended, like her father's would stay even without his hours in the operating room. But her hands were a younger version of her mother's hands, strong and sure.

My fingers on my mother's box, my mother's fingers in my father's skin. There was twist, still. This personal secret box would soon be empty, but Mom's stories, her Beatrix Potter book, her journals never would.

A bit of the spray had moistened the ashes inside the box despite our efforts, a little of Mom's English Lake District catching a ride home with her. I began working through the steps that would close her safely away. When the wooden edges were smooth, the entry hidden, Anna Page asked, "How do you know how to open it?"

I put the box in her hands and placed her index finger on the baby's head. "You trace from the baby's halo to the third flower here," I said, showing her. "Then you slide the flower down. See?"

In the gesture, I remembered my mother's soft voice saying that some things in life, you just have to know. Someone tells you and you remember it, and you tell it to someone else. Sometimes you tell it directly, and sometimes you tell it through stories. It's one of the ways we show our love.

Author's Note

MY INFATUATION WITH BEATRIX POTTER began not long after my son Chris was born, when we received as a gift twenty-three enticing hardcover books—each no bigger than an adult reader's hand—lined up in their own portable shelf. Bea's watercolors on those pages are exquisite, but for me, a word person, their greatest charm lies in the simple words strung together to bring funny characters and fantastic worlds alive. As in the best of children's fiction, Bea's gentle humor is as appealing to adult readers as it is to younger folk.

Most of Bea's characters were as new to me as they were to my son: Jeremy Fisher with his mackintosh all in tatters; poor Tom Kitten, who narrowly escapes being the main ingredient of a "kitten dumpling roly-poly pudding"; Mrs. Tittlemouse and her friend Mr. Jackson, who never wipes his feet. Chris (now an economist) learned the meaning of credit from Ginger and Pickles, whose mouse and rabbit customers "come again and again, and buy quantities" despite their fear of the dog and cat store owners—and never do pay their bills. I can't see those books without Chris and Nick's little fingers wrapped around their bedtime choices, giggling in anticipation as Jemima Puddle-Duck collects sage and onions for "the sandy whiskered gentleman" fox whose idea of having her for dinner is quite different from her own, and hearing their delighted laughter as Jeremy emerges from a trout's mouth without his galoshes, exclaiming, "What a mercy that was not a pike!"

So it's telling, I'm sure, that the first thing Mac and I did when facing the empty nest left by our sons heading for college was to fly away to the quiet side of Lake Windermere, in the English Lake District Beatrix Potter called home. From our little cottage there, we could hike to Bea's Hill Top Farm, now preserved as a museum, as is the seventeenth-century building that was her husband's office. At the Armitt Museum in Ambleside, you can see more of Bea's mushroom drawings than you could possibly desire. You can walk the fells she adored, where she grazed her prize-winning sheep.

It does bring a person alive, to walk with your own true love up the path she walked with her late-life husband, to sit beside Moss Eccles Tarn, where they fished and rowed sometimes until it was quite dark. To chat with a child on the grounds of Wray Castle, where Bea roamed the summer of her own childhood when she first began to paint. To see the cement patches in her baseboards where the rats had to be "stopped out." To study the markings on the paintings she sent off to her publisher, all that careful attention she paid to details like the precise size of the illustrations, the exact color of a puddle duck's coat. To cross the lake at Ferry Nab, where she crossed to visit her difficult mother. To see the coded pages of her journals, unguarded observations not meant for anyone's eyes but her own.

Bea wrote more than 200,000 coded journal words—the length of two copies of *The Wednesday Daughters* and then some. She wrote extensive letters to friends and family. She wrote picture-letters to children that folded up to make their own envelopes, often responding to children's letters in her characters' voices and signing their names.

The Bea I hope comes alive even in death on the pages of this novel would not have been possible without the work of Judy Taylor, who collected Bea's letters in *Beatrix Potter's Letters* and *Letters to Children from Beatrix Potter*, and Leslie Linder, who decoded Bea's journal, published as *The Journal of Beatrix Potter*. I came to these books through Taylor's *Beatrix Potter: Artist, Storyteller, and Countrywoman* and Linda Lear's *Beatrix Potter: A Life in Nature*. Reading these, rereading Bea's amazing little books, and visiting her world were among the greatest delights in writing this novel. When I first conceived *The Wednesday Daughters*, I hadn't imagined Bea would be a character on its pages, but as I came to know her, I couldn't resist.

Beatrix Potter with Spot
(compliments of the Beatrix Potter Society)

Acknowledgments

A MILLION THANKS TO . . .

Mac Clayton, charming Lake District cottage dweller, intrepid fell hiker, ferry rider, and closed-eyed winding-single-track-road passenger. If I'd known how great you'd look in a raincoat these twenty-five years later, I wouldn't have been so coy about those first five asks.

Chris and Nick, for so many things. Perhaps the loveliest part of writing this book was having the echo of your childhood laughter over Mr. Jackson and Mrs. Tittlemouse, Ginger and Pickles, Jemima, and Mr. Jeremy Fisher to keep me company even as you were off learning from other books. No mom is prouder.

Cord, Yvonne, Tim, and Emma, who lead by example.

Reader extraordinaire and first-paragraph coach Brenda Rickman Vantrease; I'm so glad we share this journey.

My sister-in-law, Ginny Waite, and my mom—with extra thanks for reading; Dad and Pat for their truly amazing support; Father Pat for the doll that morphed into Ally's puzzle box lid, and for instilling in me a curiosity about the world beyond the borders of my home; and the whole Waite-Clayton gang for showing up and sharing, and everything else.

The Wednesday Gang at Random House/ Ballantine: Libby McGuire, Jennifer Hershey, and Kim Hovey (with particular thanks to Kim for fitting a manuscript read into her hectic summer and, well, for being Kim); Caitlin Alexander, who helped me get it started; Kara Cesare, whose enthusiasm in taking it on midstream has been a godsend; and Lisa Barnes (with thanks to Miles for sharing his mom). Robbin Schiff (for the *stunning* cover), Diane Hobbing (for the gorgeous interior), Gina Centrello, Jane Von Mehren, Susan Corcoran, Theresa Zoro, Sonya Safro, Beth Pearson, Annette Szlachta-McGinn, Sarah Murphy, Hannah Elnan, Quinne Rogers, Ashley Woodfolk, Rachel Wagner, and so many others. The abundant friendship and support you've shown me are indispensible to the quality of my writing, the extent of my audience, and my sanity.

Marly, my happily-ever-after agent, and Michael.

The Wednesday Sisters book club, the WOMBA gang and the Division house one, and my poker pals, all of whom enrich my life even as the latter empty my pocketbook. Also the dear friends who keep me in good wine and good cheer but elude easy categorization: John Willison for the "undiagnosed libertarian" comment and Eric Hahn for inspiring it, and Elaine Hahn and Debby Meredith. And Ellen Michelson, for sharing her extraordinary collection of Beatrix Potter books with me.

Cally Affleck, for the groom's cottage accommodations and for so warmly opening Belle Grange to my curious eye (and our dirty laundry!); Lucy Nicholson of Lucy's of Ambleside (next time, we're coming for the cookery school as well as the restaurant); the staff at Bodysgallen Hall in Wales for making our stay in the cottage with the blue door so luxurious; and the folks at One Three Nine in Bath, England, for the utterly charming two days in the top room with the slipper tub at the end of the bed.

Everyone at the Palo Alto libraries, who do so much for me, including pulling from the shelves so many Beatrix Potter sources (some of which are listed separately in my Author's Note), as well as *Healing Hearts* by Kathy Magliato, upon which I relied in making Anna Page a heart surgeon, and *Mixed: Portraits of Multiracial Kids* by Kip Fulbeck. Also Julie DuVall and the other librarians on LibraryThing, welcome sources of library-patron-based humor and online friendship.

So many booksellers who have provided such fabulous support for my writing that I couldn't possibly list them all even if I knew them, but especially Margie Scott Tucker, Nancy Salmon, and fellow literary refugee Linda McLaughlin Figel, and . . .

The many *Wednesday Sisters* readers who

suggested this sequel of sorts that I never meant to write. It was such a warm pleasure to rejoin these old friends and their now-grown daughters, and I would never have thought to do it if not for you. I hope the daughters find as comfortable a place in your affections as their mothers did, and as you have found in mine.

About the Author

MEG WAITE CLAYTON IS THE NATIONALLY bestselling author of *The Wednesday Daughters*, *The Four Ms. Bradwells*, *The Wednesday Sisters*, and *The Language of Light*. Her essays and stories have appeared in the *Los Angeles Times*, *Forbes*, *Runner's World*, and *Writer's Digest* and on public radio. A graduate of the University of Michigan Law School, Clayton lives with her family in Palo Alto, California.

Center Point Large Print
600 Brooks Road / PO Box 1
Thorndike ME 04986-0001 USA

(207) 568-3717

US & Canada:
1 800 929-9108
www.centerpointlargeprint.com